I brought a pad of graph paper and a pen outside and sat. I knew writing it all down it would help clarify my thoughts.

I started with Krystal Sand Krueger. She wanted her food truck to be a success. If I had to stay closed, or if I got a reputation for serving unsafe food, that would only help her business. I added Orland Krueger. He owned the food supply business, and I now knew he also had years of experience identifying mushrooms. He would be the most direct link to the box that delivered the bad ones. He could have slid them in to help his wife, with or without her knowledge.

I couldn't omit Francis Sand, one of the former owners of the business. He would want to help his daughter, and he also held a grudge against my aunt. Hattie Sand was more of a long shot, but she was also a former owner. She might have a weird notion that my selling antique cookware threatened their antique store. Either one of the Sands would know how to interrupt the delivery company's supply chain.

And then there was Jan Krueger O'Neill. She hadn't seemed happy about Abe and me marrying—and she knew about mushrooms, too. Orland was her brother. He could have told her about his new enterprise, given her a tour. She could have figured out how to include the toxic fungi in my order . . .

Books by Maddie Day

Country Store Mysteries
FLIPPED FOR MURDER
GRILLED FOR MURDER
WHEN THE GRITS HIT THE FAN
BISCUITS AND SLASHED BROWNS
DEATH OVER EASY
STRANGLED EGGS AND HAM
NACHO AVERAGE MURDER
CANDY SLAIN MURDER
NO GRATER CRIME
CHRISTMAS COCOA MURDER
(with Carlene O'Connor and Alex Erickson)

Cozy Capers Book Group Mysteries
MURDER ON CAPE COD
MURDER AT THE TAFFY SHOP

And writing as Edith Maxwell

A TINE TO LIVE, A TINE TO DIE
'TIL DIRT DO US PART
FARMED AND DANGEROUS
MURDER MOST FOWL
MULCH ADO ABOUT MURDER

Published by Kensington Publishing Corp.

No Grater Crime

A Country Store Mystery

MADDIE DAY

KENSINGTON
PUBLISHING CORP.

www.kensingtonbooks.com

KENSINGTON BOOKS are published by

Kensington Publishing Corp.
119 West 40th Street
New York, NY 10018

All Kensington titles, imprints, and distributed lines are available at special quantity discounts for bulk purchases for sales promotion, premiums, fund-raising, educational, or institutional use.

Special book excerpts or customized printings can also be created to fit specific needs. For details, write or phone the office of the Kensington Sales Manager: Attn.: Sales Department. Kensington Publishing Corp., 119 West 40th Street, New York, NY 10018. Phone: 1-800-221-2647.

The K logo is a trademark of Kensington Publishing Corp.

First Printing: September 2021
ISBN-13: 978-1-4967-2319-2
ISBN-10: 1-4967-2319-8

ISBN-13: 978-1-4967-2320-8 (ebook)
ISBN-10: 1-4967-2320-1 (ebook)

10 9 8 7 6 5 4 3 2

Printed in the United States of America

For all the cozy book bloggers, including Mark Baker, Lori Caswell, Kim Davis, Lorie Lewis Ham, Lesa Holstine, Kathleen Kaminski, Lisa A. Kelley, Dru Ann Love, and Missi Stockwell Martin. Thanks for spreading the word about our genre!

ACKNOWLEDGMENTS

The origins of the real Story Inn in Story, Indiana, are closely linked with the origins of this series. I loved taking Robbie to visit Story, as I did when I was writing *Flipped for Murder*, the first Country Store mystery. My fictional wedding organizer at the inn is completely imagined, however. I also have fond memories of being a Morris dancers' groupie on a May Day many decades ago in Bloomington, Indiana, attending their rowdy Dance-up-the-Sun festivities.

Many thanks to my sister, Janet Maxwell, for an eagle-eyed read of the manuscript. I thought I'd sent her the best book I could write, and she improved it. Sherry Harris's comments then made it even better, for which I am grateful. Sherry suggested inviting you all to the wedding, so I did. It takes a village, people!

I borrowed the wedding colors scheme from my son and daughter-in-law's wedding three years ago. I suspect the design was more the wonderful Alison Russell's doing than my Allan's—I hope I did it justice, dear Alison! I stole a few other details from their lovely ceremony, too.

I availed myself of my great friend Leslie Budewitz's excellent *Books, Crooks, and Counselors: How to Write Accurately about Criminal Law and Courtroom Procedure* for the definition of negligent homicide and a couple of other legal matters. She also writes compelling mysteries you'll want to read.

Thank you to Hallie Ephron—friend, mentor, and master of writing suspense—for the reminder to put a light bulb in the glass of milk, as Hitchcock did in *Suspicion*. That is, to make the ordinary creepy. I did my best.

Thanks to yet another author friend Annette Dashofy for the phrase "on the right side of the grass," said often by her Midwestern father. And gratitude to author Ann Cleeves for letting me discover Buck's grandmother's origins. I binge-read the entire Shetland series while I was writing this book. Cleeves, whom I was delighted to spend time with at the 2019 New England Crime Bake, writes darker than I do, and more brilliantly. I aspire to those heights.

I nipped the name, interior, and chefs of my favorite local Massachusetts bistro, Phat Cats, for the Bloomington restaurant where someone died. No one has ever been poisoned at the real Phat Cats Bistro! They had to close for a few months during the pandemic last year, and I'm so happy they're up and running again. If you're ever near Amesbury, be sure to eat there, and say hi to chefs Christina and Paul for me.

I used several mushroom research sources, including *The Book of Poisons: a Guide to Writers* by Serita Stevens and Anne Bannon. Thanks, too, to Ann of Ann's Ginger House. I took her highly educational medicinal mushroom walk in New Hampshire while I was working on this book and learned so much—including about *Amanita pantherina*—after I picked her brain about the opposite of medicinal fungi: the deadly ones.

Gratitude, always, to my agent, John Talbot. To my editor, John Scognamiglio, and the rest of the talented crew at Kensington, including publicist Larissa Ackerman and talented cover artist Ben Perini. To my Wicked Authors blogmates—you're the best. And love, always, to my sons, my daughter-in-law, my sisters, and my beau. Your support means the world.

Rather unbelievably, this is the ninth full-length Country Store Mystery. I am so very grateful to all of you readers who love these stories. Thank you for your reviews, for telling your friends, for giving the books as gifts and asking your libraries to acquire them. I'm immensely happy I can bring you reading joy.

CHAPTER 1

"Watch out, Robbie." Aunt Adele grabbed my elbow. "Here comes trouble."

I scanned the row of white and green tents covering booths stretching out in front of us at the huge outdoor Scottsburg Antique Fair. I spied caned rocking chairs and gleaming bureaus. Rusty washboards, tin toys, and vintage red-handled beaters. Old tools and lovingly embroidered linens. Vendors smiled and chatted on this bright morning on the last Saturday in April, and shoppers browsed for special finds. The mood was upbeat, with everyone seemingly happy at the warming trend and the first outdoor fair of the season. Trouble didn't seem to be part of the equation.

"What do you mean?" I asked Adele.

She pointed. "See that couple?"

A few booths down from us, a lean, gray-haired man

with a trim beard and a petite woman wearing a wide-brimmed straw bent over a table arrayed with silverware sets. They picked through the pieces, setting some aside.

"Yes," I said. "And? Do you know them?"

"Let's just say Francis there won't be happy to see me." She raised a single eyebrow. "Old story."

"Do you want to turn around?" I wasn't surprised my aunt recognized folks here. She, a former mayor and fire chief, and a lifelong schmoozer extraordinaire, knew people wherever she went.

"Nah. They're busy. I didn't do nothing wrong, any-hoo." She tucked my arm through hers and steered me to the opposite line of booths. She walked with a brisk stride instead of a shopping stroll.

I pulled a wheeled shopping cart in my other hand. We passed a booth full of antique kitchen implements across from where the couple stood. I slowed, disengaging my arm, at a table piled with metal graters. Box graters, cylindrical ones, flat graters with all sizes of holes, rotational graters with a hand crank. They all looked to be in pretty good condition, too, particularly one box grater with a light green Bakelite handle and intricate metal stamping. Adele moved on.

"Where are these from?" I asked the vendor, an aproned young man with multiple piercings and an engaging smile. I picked up the green-handled one to inspect it. The bottom had a small blue stick-on label with $2 written on it.

"My grandma's barn in a itty-bitty town south of Louisville," he said, pronouncing it *LOW-uh-vul*, swallowing the last two syllables as everybody around here did on both sides of the border with Kentucky. "She collected stuff like this, but she died last year. Pa thought we should make a few bucks off the stash." He shrugged.

Graters and all kinds of other cooking tools were my primary reason for being here, that and a fun outing with Adele. I was running low on vintage cookware to sell in Pans 'N Pancakes, my country store in South Lick, Indiana, eighty miles north of this scenic town on the Ohio River. I made most of my money off the breakfast and lunch restaurant in the store, but many people were drawn first to my shelves of cooking tools and baking pans. Adele and I had driven down yesterday and stayed at a cute B&B. We wanted to get an early start this morning before the wares were picked over. Plus, the fair was enormous and would take all day to explore.

"Adele," I called to her. "I'm stopping here."

She turned around at the same time the gray-haired man did. He stared at her. Was that steam coming out of his ears? The woman with him turned, too. He took a step toward my aunt. His wife grabbed his arm. He shook her off. Adele moseyed back to me.

"Hey, there, Francis, Hattie." She waved at the couple. "Come on the heck over and meet my niece."

The wife—Hattie—followed her husband across the busy aisle. At five foot three, nobody would call me tall, but I had at least two inches on Hattie.

"Adele Jordan, of all people," Francis said. He smiled, but it was grim. Over his shirt he wore a tan vest with a bunch of pockets like a birder or a fisherman.

"Hello, Adele." Petite Hattie did not smile, but her expression was friendly. Even though she had to be in her early seventies like my aunt, the skin on her face didn't show age spots or sun damage and was nearly free of lines. Due to a hat-wearing habit? Probably, at least in part.

"Haven't seen y'all in a year of Sundays," Adele said. "What's it been, a couple few decades?"

"Twenty-three years," Francis said. "And fifteen days." His slate-colored ski-lift eyebrows met in the middle. His beard didn't quite conceal a receding chin and an overbite.

What? Whatever was going on here wasn't pleasant. I glanced at Adele, who nodded slowly at him. We should get this little chat over with and move on. I could return to the cookware booth later.

I smiled at the couple but didn't extend my hand. We'd all gotten out of the habit during the pandemic, and nobody much had resumed it. "I'm Robbie Jordan, Adele's niece."

"That's my girl." Adele beamed.

Right. Girl of almost thirty, but I didn't mind.

"Nice to meet you, Robbie." Hattie also kept her hand to herself.

Her husband didn't speak, and his gaze on Adele didn't waver.

"Robbie's got herself the cutest country store in South Lick, and she sells vintage kitchen whatnot," Adele went on. "You should oughta stop by one day soon. You can eat breakfast and lunch at Pans 'N Pancakes, too. Why, her cooking is to die for." She turned to me. "Francis and Hattie live over in Gnaw Bone. They run a wholesale food business, last I heard."

Gnaw Bone was the small unincorporated town a few miles east of Nashville, the county seat for scenic, hilly Brown County, where South Lick was also situated.

"We're not in the food business any longer." Francis folded his arms over his chest.

"Yes, we retired from that," Hattie said. "As it happens, we're opening an antique store in South Lick soon. High-end items. It's been our dream for years."

"Well, isn't that nice, now," Adele said. "Where at in South Lick?"

"Twenty Main Street." Hattie lifted her chin a smidge.

I stared at the woman. So that was what was going on with the two-story limestone house directly across the road from my store. It had been bustling with carpenters and electricians lately. I hadn't gotten around to asking who was renovating the nineteenth-century building. I liked the sound of "high-end." That meant they wouldn't be in competition for the contents of my retail shelves.

Adele blinked, then gave her head a little shake and restored her smile. "Then you know exactly where Robbie's place is." Adele squeezed my hand. "Isn't that nice, hon? They'll bring in more customers for your restaurant."

"We'll see about that." Francis unplastered his gaze from Adele and laid his arm across his wife's shoulders. "Dear, we wanted to look at the vendor in row fifty-two, didn't we?"

CHAPTER 2

An hour later, Adele and I browsed tables full of flowered tablecloths, neatly pressed cloth napkins, lacy dresser runners, and high-thread-count bed linens. The Wyandotte Fire Department manned the booth, quite literally. Not a single female firefighter was among the men in their navy blue WFD polo shirts, cargo pants, and combat boots. Young and old, they seemed to be enjoying talking about household goods with the mostly female shoppers.

"Ya gotta love a man in uniform," Adele murmured.

True, but I had a man waiting for me back in South Lick. I wasn't in the market for another one. I picked out a half-dozen pretty cotton tablecloths for the small table in my apartment kitchen. Or maybe I would set up a display in the store with a tablecloth and some of the vintage cookware items.

Adele held up a pair of pillowcases embroidered with tiny flowers. "For your trousseau, hon." She had a wicked twinkle in her eyes.

"Is the little lady getting married?" An older fireman gave me a grandfatherly smile.

I blushed as I glanced at the ring my now-fiancé Abe had given me in December. After his teenage son Sean told me he approved, I'd said yes to Abe's proposal. The modest round diamond on a simple gold band sparkled in the most magical of ways. We'd settled on Memorial Day weekend for our wedding, so I had only a month to wait. We planned to hold the festivities out at Adele's farm with a pig roast and a barn dance, but we still had a lot of details to finalize.

"Fred, seriously?" A fresh-faced firefighter who looked younger than my twenty-nine shook his head at the older man. "You can't be calling women 'little lady.' It's not respectful." To me, he added. "Sorry, miss."

I laughed. "Thank you. It's fine. I'm not very tall, after all. And yes, sir, I am getting married, but not with a trousseau, exactly." I elbowed Adele.

"Hey." She elbowed me back. "Who doesn't need a couple few new pillow slips out of fine cotton with pretty flowers sewed on them?"

I paid Fred for the tablecloths—and the pillowcases.

As we strolled on, I said, "Adele, please tell me what that was all about, with Francis and his wife." I'd asked right after the Sands had hurried off down the row, but she shook her head and pretended to be interested in a stash of vintage knitting books.

"It's an old story. Nothing to worry your head about."

"I'm not worried, but I'm curious."

"I wonder when they're gonna take and open their antique store."

Way to evade the question. "Last I saw, the renovations were winding down. It could be soon."

"Danna and Turner minding the store today?" she asked, referring to my two younger employees, Danna Beedle and Turner Rao.

"Yes. They could do it with their eyes closed, nearly. Danna pulled her boyfriend in today to bus and wash dishes."

"Isaac's good people," Adele said.

I was about to agree about the burly welder when someone behind me called my name. I twisted around.

"Lou!" I smiled at my cycling buddy.

She hurried toward us with a slender man following behind. Lou and I exchanged hugs. The guy, a couple of inches taller than Lou's five foot nine, was barely more than a boy. He looked familiar, but I couldn't place him.

"You know Adele," I said to Lou.

Adele held out her arms. "'Course we do." They hugged and she stepped back. My aunt had conformed with social distancing while it was required, but she was the first to kick it to the curb once the pandemic's danger had clearly passed.

"And this must be . . ." Adele's voice trailed off as she glanced from Lou to the dude and back. "Your brother?"

Brother? I thought Lou's only sibling was a younger sister. I hadn't met Leah, but I'd heard stories about her from my friend and had seen her picture. I'd also heard about their father, who was such a devotee of old-fashioned records that he wanted all his children to have the initials *LP*. A brother had never been part of the stories. Or in the pictures.

"Yes," Lou said. "This is Len. Len, my good friend Robbie and her aunt, Adele Jordan."

He nodded at Adele. "Pleased to meet you, ma'am." His voice was reedy, and his eyes matched Lou's pale green ones. His close-cropped dark hair did, too, including a new-looking beard that hadn't filled in completely.

"Lou's been holding out on me," I said. "I'm delighted to meet you, Len. You guys here shopping?"

"We're having a little sibling time," Lou said. "Our grandma lives in Fredonia not too far from here. We spent last night with her and thought we'd check out the scene at the fair for the morning."

"I scored some awesome used books." Len fingered the straps on a backpack that looked heavy.

"Cool," I said. "You both want to walk around with us? We could grab some lunch together after a while."

"Thank you, but I have to get back." Len's smile was tentative.

Lou opened her mouth, then shut it and swallowed. "He has basketball practice this afternoon."

"Let's grab a bike ride soon," I said to Lou. "Maybe tomorrow afternoon?"

Lou made a thumb-and-pinky phone gesture at her ear. "I'll call you."

"All righty, then," Adele said. "Nice meeting you, young man. You all have a nice day, now."

He acknowledged her with a nod, then turned away.

Lou gave me an inscrutable look before hurrying after her sibling.

"Ooh, would you take a gander at that there ice cream freezer?" Adele crossed the aisle to a booth on the opposite side.

I watched Lou and her brother stroll off with similar easy, athletic gaits. Something was up, but I wasn't sure what.

CHAPTER 3

"Lordy, don't my pins ache," Adele said from the passenger seat.

I steered her small truck homeward at six o'clock. We'd stopped at a fried catfish place she knew in Scottsburg for a bite of dinner after antiquing all day. I'd thirstily eyed her beer but opted for a sweet iced tea. I could wait until we arrived back in South Lick to indulge. My stomach was full of the best fried catfish sandwich I'd ever eaten, and the bed of the truck was packed with our haul. I'd purchased bags and boxes of kitchen implements, including the collection of assorted graters I'd been eying when we encountered the Sands. For her part, Adele found an attachment she'd been wanting for her antique tractor. She also picked up a beautifully carved pair of carders for the wool she sheared off her two-dozen sheep.

We passed a sign for Marino Caves, a place Abe liked to go spelunking with his son, Sean. Abe always invited me to go along. I always declined. I knew my fear of small, enclosed spaces was irrational. So far, I hadn't figured out a way to overcome it. Ever since I'd read an article last year about a student trapped in a cave for sixty hours, I'd been afraid for Abe and Sean, too.

I shook off the thought. It was time for my aunt to finally answer my questions. After Francis and Hattie Sand had hurried away from us, Adele had evaded talking about whatever grudge he held against her.

"Adele, we still have an hour and a half's drive ahead of us." I glanced over at her. She might fall asleep if I didn't get her talking.

"Lemme guess. You want to talk about Len Perlman."

What? "Uh, not really."

"You realize he used to be Lou's sister."

I blinked at the road. Instead of heading east and then north on the Interstate, we'd opted for the smaller state route. We had two and a half hours until sunset, and Route 135 was a lot prettier. The road beelined straight up to Nashville but was only one lane in either direction. I didn't want to turn and stare at my aunt to absorb this news and risk crossing the center line.

"Her sister? Oh. He's a transgender man." How had my seventy-something aunt seen that, and I hadn't?

"Whatever you call it. Yes, that's what I'm saying."

I fell silent. Leah was now Len. It made sense. I knew he looked familiar. He was clearly Lou's sibling. I hadn't missed hearing about a third sibling. But why hadn't Lou told me? Because she'd been busy finishing her doctorate, maybe. And we hadn't been riding much together this spring, between her schedule and mine. Or maybe Leah—that is, Len—hadn't wanted Lou to share his news.

Basketball. Len had wanted to get back to basketball practice. Now I remembered Leah had been a high school star, with her height and a physique, like Lou's, that lent itself to sports. They must also share a drive to push themselves. I pushed myself when I biked the hills of Brown County, but that was about it.

"Good for him," I said at last. I was distracted by the pretty sight of redbuds and the graceful layered branches of dogwoods blooming in a patch of woods. The landscape opened up to newly plowed fields on either side, one with straight rows of something green sprouting. In general, southern Indiana was hillier than the flat northern parts, but farmers grabbed level ground wherever they found it. I grabbed hold of the conversation again. "The transition couldn't have been easy."

"I don't expect it was." Her voice grew lazy, along with her eyelids.

"What the—?" I yelled at a big box truck barreling straight for me as it passed three slower vehicles. I leaned on the horn and cursed him with my most colorful selection of words.

"Hey, now, girl." Adele sat up straight. "Mind your tongue. You're like to make a sailor blush."

I let out a noisy breath after the truck crossed back into its own lane at the last possible minute. "Sorry, Adele. I don't know where people think they need to get to in such a freaking hurry on a Saturday evening."

"As Samuel says, they're all children of God." A Cheshire cat smile crept across her weathered face, possibly at the thought of getting home to her octogenarian lover, Samuel MacDonald.

"Of course." I swallowed and steered back to the subject of my curiosity. "Adele, please tell me what history you have with Francis Sand. If those people are my new neighbors, I should know what I'm dealing with."

It was her turn to refrain from speaking. After a minute, I nudged her leg. "Come on. Out with it."

"It was like this." She twisted in her seat to face me. "It happened back when I was South Lick's fire chief. Francis was divorced from his wife. Him and her had a son, Teddy, who was a girly sort of boy. Kids bullied him without mercy."

"That's so sad. Did the son live with his mom or with Francis?"

"With his mother. By then Hattie was Francis's common-law wife."

I rolled my eyes at the term but kept quiet. Adele was one of the most accepting, nonjudgmental people I knew, and it was simply a phrase she'd grown up with.

"The ex told anybody within earshot she didn't want her boy living under the same roof as no harlot," Adele continued.

I shook my head and kept on driving.

"The mayor at the time was worth less than a two-legged fox guarding a coop full of hens, and his useless brother was chief of police. Old Francis asked for my help to protect his boy."

"What could you do?" I whisked my left hand up to protect my eyes from a late-day ray of sun reflecting off a metal barn roof.

"In the end, not much. I met with the lad, asked him to shadow me at the fire station. I thought maybe having an honest occupation would help, and he could work out with the crew. Get strong enough to defend himself. But

Ted was a high school senior by then. He'd gotten in with a crowd of outcasts who found weed to smoke and liquor to steal. He didn't last long at the station."

"What happened to him?"

"The bullying only escalated. The night before graduation, he was driving too fast and wrapped his car around a tree. He didn't survive the crash."

My breath rushed in. "No." I exhaled the syllable.

"His daddy has blamed me ever since for not trying harder to straighten him out."

CHAPTER 4

I lay on the floor the next morning at six, thinking about my car conversation with Adele instead of doing my sit-ups. I'd told her it wasn't her fault she wasn't able to help Francis's son, and that it was unfair of him to blame her. She'd said she was all done talking about it.

Last night Adele had helped me unload and then had driven herself home. I'd fed Birdy and let him into the store, poured a glass of Four Roses bourbon, and done breakfast prep, as I did most evenings. I assembled the dry ingredients for pancake batter. I cut butter into the biscuit mix and kneaded it. I chopped peppers and onions for omelets and melons for fruit dishes. I readied the big pot of water to be heated for oatmeal. Danna had left a note that she was doing spring scones for a Sunday breakfast special.

After prep was done, I'd set to work washing, pricing, and displaying the new cookware. I hadn't expected to hear from Abe. He and Sean had gone to a Pacers game in Indianapolis and wouldn't be back until late.

Birdy pounced on my stomach, interrupting my reverie. I giggled and pushed him off. "Kitty, I don't need your help." My little black-and-white cat, always looking sharp in his tuxedo, thought anyone lying on the floor was a bed. He jumped back on. I finished my hundred crunches, which had followed a hundred lunges, and stayed lying on the mat I'd unfurled in my living room. I'd be on my feet in the restaurant for the next eight hours. I could take a few more minutes to rest now, although the lure of brewed coffee was strong. I always started a pot before doing my brief morning fitness routine. The commute to work wasn't a problem, since I lived in an apartment attached to the back of my country store.

For now, that is. Abe and I had agreed to combine households into his place after we married. He lived in a three-bedroom Craftsman-style bungalow, a classic architecture in this part of the state. My one-bedroom apartment had been perfect for the few years since I renovated the building and opened the store and restaurant, but it would be way too crowded for two of us and didn't include space for Sean for the times he stayed with Abe. His house was only a mile away. It wouldn't take me long to bike over here in the mornings or to drive in the winter.

When I pushed up to sit cross-legged, Birdy finally made his exit, but stayed at my side. I was going to miss this space that was mine and mine alone. I would bring to Abe's the pieces of furniture my late mother had crafted. "And you, Birdman." I stroked Birdy's long, silky fur. He purred as I gazed around the apartment. I'd thought about renting it out, but I wasn't sure I wanted a stranger living so close to my restaurant. I already had B&B customers coming and going in the three rooms upstairs, although I didn't have any right now. I'd decided to leave the apartment with basic furnishings and available for guests or whatever need might arise.

My phone rang in the bedroom where I'd left it charging overnight. "Excuse me, kitty." I pushed up to standing and hurried in.

"Good morning, my wife-to-be."

I could hear the smile in Abe's voice.

"Good morning to you, husband-to-be." I smiled, too. "How was the game?" I wandered into the kitchen and poured a mug of coffee.

"Fun and more important, it gave us some father-son time. Being nearly sixteen means he's a lot busier than he was even at thirteen."

"And basketball is his sport." The boy was getting taller and taller. At six feet he already towered over Abe. Sean's mom was as tall as Abe's five feet nine and Abe had told me her brother was over six feet.

"Right. I don't think my boy has dreams of playing professional ball, but he sure loves watching it. How was your antiquing?"

"Adele and I came home with quite a haul. And I learned a couple things. You know that old house across the road from here? The one they've been fixing up?"

"Sure."

"It belongs to a couple named Francis and Hattie Sand. They're going to open an antique shop in it. Adele knows them."

"Is there anyone she doesn't know?" He laughed.

"Yes. But . . ." I let my voice trail off as I thought

about the man's reaction to Adele yesterday, and the backstory she'd filled in on our drive home.

"But?"

"Francis was furious when he saw Adele. She told me later that he blames his son's death on her, even though it's been twentysomething years."

Abe didn't speak for a moment. "Was his name Teddy?"

"Yes. Did you know him?"

"Sort of. I've told you I was in Four-H when I was young. Teddy was, too. He was four or five years older than me, but I remember him from when I joined. He adored animals. I always thought he'd end up being a veterinarian or something."

"Adele said he was bullied really badly in high school," I said.

"I'll say. Schools weren't as on top of bullying as they are now. He got called a fairy and a faggot. And worse, much worse."

"The poor kid."

"But I can't believe Sand would blame Adele for his death," Abe continued. "I remember my parents saying she had kind of taken Teddy under her wing at the South Lick Fire Department, even though by then Teddy's dad lived over in Gnaw Bone."

I glanced at the antique clock my mom had made a tall case for out of glowing maple. "Shoot, it's almost seven. Abe, darling, I have to run. Danna will be in the restaurant any minute now, and I haven't even showered."

"Gotcha. Dinner tonight here?"

"I'd love to."

CHAPTER 5

By eight-thirty Pans 'N Pancakes was hopping faster than I could flip hotcakes. Unlike Tuesday through Saturday, when I unlocked the door at seven, we didn't open until eight on Sundays. Today the early-breakfast crowd had all showed up at once. Danna delivered plates as quickly as I could fill them.

"The lemon-rosemary scones are a big hit," I told her.

"Thank goodness I made plenty of scone dough yesterday," she said. "I had Isaac zesting lemons for hours. We could have served them with a glaze, but I knew that would take way too much time."

"Smart move." I pointed to three plates waiting under the warming lights. "Here's the kitchen sink, that's the hope with fruit, and this one is the flopped two, floated." Translated? An omelet with everything, a dish of oatmeal with fruit, and two fried eggs over easy with gravy. It always made me smile to use diner lingo with Danna. She had picked it up in a previous job and taught Turner and me the colorful shortcuts. We also had a mushroom omelet for a special.

The timer dinged for the big pan of biscuits in the oven. A man in a churchgoing suit held his mug in the air and pointed to it in the universal "I need more coffee" gesture. A party of six wearing athletic gear pushed in through the door, leaving the bell jangling. Turner would be here at nine, but we could sure use an extra pair of hands if he showed up early.

"Good morning. Please have a seat in the waiting area or feel free to browse the store," I called out to the new-comers. "We'll seat you as soon as we can." I'd positioned a bench and an easy chair near the door for customers waiting for a table.

Danna hurried back and grabbed the pot of just-brewed coffee. I rescued the biscuits, started a new pot of java, poured out six disks of pancake batter, and slid four nicely browned links to the edge of the grill.

A minute later Danna returned an empty coffeepot. "What is *up* today? This is crazytown."

"I know. Turner will be here soon."

"Looks like you scored big-time with cookware yes-terday." She gestured toward the retail area with her head, her reddish-blond dreadlocks today covered by a rainbow-streaked baggy beret.

All I could do was nod. The cowbell on the door jan-gled again. I groaned to myself and turned the pancakes before looking over. My frown turned to a smile.

"Looks like you can use some help." My friend Phil, who baked the desserts for our lunch service, flashed his megawatt smile, arms loaded with a wide covered box.

Full of desserts, no doubt. He set it on the counter and grabbed one of our blue store aprons. He'd also designed the store logo, a grinning pancake holding a skillet, which adorned the aprons and the sign outside.

"We sure can," I said. "You are sent from heaven, Phil. Can you bus tables and pour coffee?"

"You know it." He'd formerly worn his hair in a trim Obama cut, but recently he'd let it grow out into an Afro. When he turned the brim of his IU ball cap to the back it floated above the frizz. He tied the apron and soaped up his hands at the sink.

"Thanks," I said. "Turner will be in soon, but right now it's a madhouse."

"It's spring, Robbie." He gestured toward the windows. "Everybody's delirious now the weather has warmed up. They can get outside again, and they want to fuel up before they do."

I stopped groaning every time the bell jangled. With Phil's help, we fed and cooked and cleaned, making customers happy right along with my bank account. I just hoped Turner hadn't come to harm.

"What's going on across the street?" Phil asked after he deposited a load of dirty dishes in the sink.

"I don't know." I folded over a veggie-and-cheese omelet and loaded it onto a plate with three crisp rashers of bacon. "What do you mean?"

"A big van is in front and dudes are moving pieces of furniture in. Plus an old guy and a lady are up on ladders with a wooden sign and a drill."

"Can you take over cooking? I'll go take a look."

After he nodded, I hurried to the door and stepped onto my store's wide covered porch. A new sign with a vintage design was now mounted above the front door of the house across the road. Large gold-painted letters read *Antiques*, with smaller ones underneath spelling out *Sand's Timeless Home Furnishings*. If it had been Francis and Hattie putting up the sign, they were gone now, although the ladders remained on either side of the door. A ramp ran from the van to the walkway that led up to the house. I stood next to one of the wooden rocking chairs on my porch and watched a burly man carry a bureau by himself, while another toted two end tables. Judging from the wind and clouds, they'd better hurry before the rain started.

I'd never paid much attention to the old house, which was the only structure in a stretch of woods here at the edge of town. Its creamy yellow limestone bricks were more common in institutional buildings like banks and the older halls at Indiana University than in houses. Maybe this structure had been built by a wealthy merchant in the 1800s. Adele would know its history. The building had been unoccupied when I bought my store and had only started showing signs of life after the renovations started this winter. Hattie had said the store was opening tomorrow. It looked like they were on schedule.

Francis and a woman almost his height with light hair sticking out from under a Cincinnati Reds cap came out of the house. I raised my hand to wave, but he didn't see me. A touring minibus pulled up in front of me. I held open the door to the store for nearly two-dozen seniors.

"Welcome," I said. "I'm Robbie Jordan, proprietor. Where are you all from?"

"Equality." The lady who spoke had a cloud of white hair. She blinked at me with a blue-eyed, innocent expression.

Right. Me, too, but I wasn't asking about her moral stance. I must have looked confused, because the man with her chuckled.

"Equality, Illinois." He rolled his eyes. "She loves to pull that on strangers. Our town isn't too far from the Kentucky border down beyond Evansville."

"That's a pretty area. It's where that wilderness area called Garden of the Gods is, right?" I smiled. "I visited the region a couple years ago." Equality must be a tiny town. Despite the remarkable name, I didn't remember it.

"Sure is, hon, in Shawnee National Forest."

"Well, you must be hungry right about now," I said.

"That's true, but we didn't drive all that way today," the woman chimed in. "We spent the night in Bloomington."

I stepped back so they could enter. "It might take us a little while to seat you all, but you're welcome to browse the cookware shelves."

"That's one reason we came," another woman told me. "We've heard about your vintage kitchen stuff, and your breakfasts, too."

I smiled, happy to have achieved cross-border fame of a sort.

"Is that antique store open today?" She pointed across the street.

"I don't believe so. It's new."

"I'll have to come back then."

I stole one more glance at the Sands' establishment. Maybe tomorrow I'd bake them something and take it over on a courtesy visit. Right now? I had twenty hungry tourists to fit in somewhere.

CHAPTER 6

"We're already almost out of mushrooms," Danna muttered at nine-fifteen. "Everybody wants the omelet special." She'd minced fresh thyme and rosemary to sprinkle on the mushrooms and had grated Gruyére for the cheese.

"I know," I said in an equally grumbling tone. "And we're almost out of potatoes. The stupid supplier never brought the rest of the order."

"That's bad. We should stock some frozen hash browns as an emergency backup."

"We might run out of mustard at lunch if the truck doesn't show up."

"Ugh." Danna glanced around. "Where's Turner?"

"He's late." I pulled out my cell, but he hadn't texted or called. "Not a good morning for being tardy."

Every table was already full. People wanted coffee re-fills, but the pot was still dripping. I hadn't taken orders for two tables. And five hungry-looking—and wet—diners waited. It looked like the spring rainstorm had started.

"These are ready for Adele, Samuel, and Buck." Danna gestured to the waiting plates. "The pancakes and sausage are for the single guy next to them."

"Got it." I loaded up my arms, and first delivered the pancakes to the hunched-over senior citizen, whose skin had a yellowish tint. The man, who always prayed over his meal, dined here a few times a year. I hadn't been suc-cessful in getting him to call me Robbie, and right now I couldn't remember his name. "Enjoy your breakfast, sir."

"Thank you, Miss Jordan." He closed his eyes, his lips moving silently, and folded his hands.

I turned to the adjacent four-top. "The double-everything with everything for Lieutenant Buck Bird, oatmeal and fruit for Samuel, and the mushroom omelet special for Adele. Yes?"

"You got mine right." Buck and his legendary appetite looked eagerly at the plate of the omelet special next to bacon and buttered wheat toast, with a side of biscuits and meat gravy and another of pancakes.

"Mushroom?" Adele asked. "I can't eat 'em no more. They don't agree with my system. I'm sorry, Robbie, hon. I ordered the special without looking at the dang board."

"I'd trade, my dear," Samuel said. "But my doctor ad-vised me to avoid eggs and cheese, as you know."

"I'm sorry, Adele." I reached for her plate. "I'll take it back. Do you want a veggie-and-ham omelet, instead?"

The man at the next table piped up. "I have not yet

touched my pancakes. Would you like to trade, ma'am?" he asked Adele. "I'm rather partial to mushrooms and didn't realize they were on the menu."

"That's kindly of you, sir." Adele beamed. "I'll take you up on the offer."

Samuel twisted in his chair. "I thought I recognized that voice. Good morning, Mr. Ward."

"Good morning, Mr. MacDonald," the man said. "I hope you are well."

"I am keeping well, thanks to the good Lord." Samuel smiled. "And yourself?"

"As well as can be expected."

"I appreciate you helping out my sweetie, here," Samuel said. "Mr. Ward and I attend the same worship services," he added to Adele. Samuel was a devout Christian. Adele not so much, but he didn't have a problem with her not going to church. Likewise, she'd never griped about his devotion to his Friday men's prayer breakfast, his Sunday worship, and other church activities. I even occasionally hosted a Bible-and-brew event on a Friday evening for him, which was usually surprisingly well attended. I served the beers and appetizers, but it was BYOBible.

I swapped out their breakfasts and thanked the man. "Enjoy your omelet, sir."

Danna dinged the ready bell as Turner pushed through the door. He pushed back the hood of a dripping rain jacket and hurried toward the kitchen area. I met him at the grill.

"I'm sorry, Robbie. A tree blew over onto our driveway and it took me a while to move it." He glanced around the restaurant. "Looks nuts in here. Where do you want me?"

"That's what they all say, dude." Danna grinned even as she worked high-speed magic at the flattop grill with a turner in each hand.

"No worries." I was just glad he was here. I picked up the ready plates. "Coffee, busing, orders. You know."

"I do, boss." Turner shed his coat, aproned up, scrubbed his hands, and grabbed the now-full coffeepot.

For my part, I delivered food and kept an eye on the flow. During a pause, I called the wholesaler again. And again left a message on voice mail. *Jeez*. Where were they? Was I going to have to make an IGA grocery run and buy them out of potatoes and mustard? I wasn't sure I had an alternative to this supplier, and I'd been happy with their online ordering software.

I seated a couple I hadn't seen before. They looked to be in their forties and had an easy way about them. "Welcome to Pans 'N Pancakes. I'm Robbie Jordan, proprietor."

The round-cheeked woman, barely five feet tall and with a big smile, thanked me. "I'm Chris and this is Paul. We own a dinner restaurant in Bloomington and have been hearing about your country store."

The man—Paul—spoke up. "You have an excellent reputation."

"Thank you. I'm glad to meet you both. What's your restaurant?"

"Phat Cats Bistro, spelled *p-h-a-t*," Chris said. "We also do catering. It's such a nice morning, we decided to finally get over here."

"I'll have to eat at your place soon." The ready bell rang. "Our specials are on the board up there. I'll give you a minute to decide what you'd like to order, all right?"

"Thank you," Chris said. "I also want to check out your cookware after we eat."

"Please do." I hurried back to the cooking area.

"That's it on the mushrooms," Danna announced.

"I'll erase the special." I'd have to order double the amount next time.

It looked like Adele and company were finishing up, so I fished their checks out of my apron pocket and went over to them. "What's up for the rest of the day?" I asked the trio.

"We have a couple few errands to run, and then we plan to finish that jigsaw puzzle back at the house," Adele said.

Samuel laughed, patting Adele's hand. "You mean, I will finish it and you'll fix to bake something."

"Might could happen." Adele nodded.

Samuel handed me two twenties. "Cover Mr. Ward's, too, will you please?" He tilted his head toward the next table.

I returned one bill to Samuel. The man who had accepted the omelet had left a few minutes ago. "I told him it was on the house."

Samuel shoved the twenty back at me. "Then put this in the tip jar. I insist."

"Thank you." I knew better than to argue with him.

Phil sauntered up wearing a big smile. "Good morning, Grandpop, Adele, Buck."

I'd relieved him after Turner arrived and thanked him.

"Hello, Philostrate." Samuel held out his arms for an embrace from his grandson.

Phil hugged him, then looked at me. "By the way Robbie, that box? I brought trial cupcakes."

"Wedding trial?" Adele asked.

Phil nodded. "They're not for a court trial, that's for sure."

"Thanks." Abe and I had asked Phil to make our wedding cake, but we hadn't settled on a flavor. "What do we have?"

"Lemon, carrot, and chocolate," Phil said. "You can serve them for the lunch dessert, but taste them, too. See which you like the best and let me know."

"You got it." I loaded my arms with dishes from the table. I'd save aside one of each flavor for Abe to taste in case he couldn't get in for lunch.

Adele rose and bussed me on the cheek. "We'll talk soon, hon. Mind if I grab a couple cupcakes for the road?"

"Not at all," I said. "Take one of each and give me a call later about which you like."

They bustled off to the kitchen area, accompanied by Phil.

Buck pushed up to his feet. Way up. The guy was more than a foot taller than me, and his lanky frame made him look even taller. He swayed a bit, grabbing the table.

"Buck, are you all right?" I peered at his face, which looked paler than usual. I'd never known him to be sick. He wasn't even fifty and was in good shape.

"Sure. I'll be fine. Just a touch of indigestion." He clapped his uniform hat on his head and smiled, albeit wanly. "Entirely possible I'll be back for lunch. Y'all have a good day, now."

CHAPTER 7

"Mom, you wouldn't even believe how busy we've been," Danna said to her mother—Corrine Beedle, the mayor of South Lick—at noon. "We usually have a lull around eleven. Not today."

Corrine had come straight to the kitchen area after she entered. Danna had taken over the grill and Turner was busing and setting up. Even with three of us, we were running a bit ragged, since Phil had taken off at around ten when Adele and Samuel had.

I surveyed the tables. "But there's an empty table in the corner. You'd better grab it while you can," I told Corrine. "I'll be by to take your order in a flash."

"Thanks, hon." Corrine's red sweater matched her nails and her four-inch heels, even though today, being Sunday, she'd paired them with pressed jeans instead of a pencil skirt. Our mayor never did anything halfway. She handed me a bottle in a paper sack. "Got me some guests coming. Can you take and open that for me after they arrive?"

I peeked inside to see a champagne-style cork. Because I didn't hold a liquor license, Indiana law allowed BYOB, as long as I opened and served it.

"What's the occasion?" I craned my neck to gaze up at Corrine. With the heels, she stood over six feet tall. Danna had gotten her mom's height, and then some. She didn't need heels to slide over into the six-foot range.

"Folks are opening a new store across the road," Corrine explained. "The Sands. You know 'em?"

"I met them yesterday." I probably should have gone across in the last month to introduce myself and see what was going on. But they hadn't stopped by here on a courtesy visit, either. Because of the grudge Francis held against Adele, I expected. It was good Adele hadn't stayed for lunch today.

"I try to celebrate any new business that opens here in our lovely town. We'll need four glasses, if you please." Corrine beamed and made her way across the restaurant.

Four? The Sands must have a business associate.

The mayor stopped and greeted everyone she knew, plus a good smattering of strangers. By the time Corrine was seated, Francis and Hattie had come through the door. I made my way over to greet them.

"I'm so glad you both could stop by," I said. "It looks like you're getting all your antiques moved in." It also looked like the rain hadn't lasted long. None of the recent newcomers had been in rain gear or sported wet hair.

"Working on it," Francis said in a terse tone. His gaze roved over the tables, finally alighting on Corrine's. "We're dining with the mayor."

"She mentioned that," I said. "I'll be over shortly to take your orders."

"I'm going to check out the competition." Hattie pointed at my retail area. Without her hat, her short, curly purple hair made quite the statement. She had an enormous quilted bag slung over her shoulder.

"Competition?" I cocked my head. "Won't your store sell primarily furniture?"

She patted her hair in a preening move. "We're setting it up like a home. The kitchen is fully stocked with cooking implements from the past. Additional items are for sale in the barn behind." She turned, sauntering toward my shelves full of cooking implements from the past.

She could be all the smug she wanted. I made a lot more money on my restaurant than I did on the cookware. I sold it mainly to draw in customers, but also because the store had come with a cool collection of pans, tools, and implements. I loved the homey feel of seeing cake pans and beaters, pie tins and graters, tongs and cookie cans, all from many decades ago.

I carried the bubbly to Corrine's table, along with four stemmed glasses. "Sorry I don't have actual flutes." I set down the glasses.

"We have a nice selection for sale," Francis said. "Come by tomorrow and I'll give you a special tour."

"I might, thanks," I said. "We're closed on Mondays."

"It'll be our first day open to the public, but we're doing the grand opening and ribbon cutting on Saturday."

"Yours truly is cutting the ribbon, too." Corrine winked at me.

"Shall I pour now, or wait for Hattie and the other party?" I held up the bottle.

"The other party might be late," Francis said.

"Y'all can leave it for me to pour, hon," Corrine said.

"Madam Mayor, I'd love to, but you know I can't." I had no idea who the state used to enforce their liquor laws. Any one of the diners around me could be here to check on my practices. I had no intention of violating the regulations.

"Go ahead and pour, then," Corrine said. "Here comes Hattie now."

"Congratulations on your opening." I tilted each glass and poured carefully. "I'll give you all a minute to look at the menu. Specials are on the board there." I cleared out before they began toasting. I didn't need to hear Hattie to start gloating about how much better her cookware collection was.

I puttered among the tables, delivering a ticket, stuffing cash into my apron pocket, asking diners if there was something more they wanted. Buck hadn't come back for lunch. I hoped he was enjoying a well-earned afternoon off at home with his wife. On weekdays—or when a murder investigation was underway—he was a regular in here for both breakfast and lunch. He not only had a hollow leg and could put away huge amounts of food, he was also an inordinately generous tipper.

Danna hit the ready bell. I waited as she filled plates with a hamburger, a turkey burger, and a grilled cheese with tomato, all with sides of coleslaw and chips, plus two small plates of dessert. She'd told me that yesterday Phil had delivered a big load of peanut-butter-chocolate-chip cookies along with his usual brownies.

"Danna, I had an excellent fried catfish sandwich for dinner yesterday. We have catfish fillets in the freezer. Tomorrow I'm going to see if I can re-create it in the oven. If it works, we can offer it as a special next week."

"Good idea. I love me some catfish, and it would be a lot easier to oven fry a bunch at a time."

"That's what I thought, too."

"That new store isn't going to hurt our cookware business, is it?" she asked.

"I don't think so. Hattie Sand might have a different idea, but I don't really care."

"I love her hair." Danna gestured with her chin toward Hattie. "I'm surprised Adele hasn't thrown some turquoise or red on her own hair."

I laughed. "I'm not sure that's Adele's style." The doorbell jangled, admitting Adele and Samuel, back for lunch, apparently. "But you can ask her yourself."

I loaded my arms with the plates and made my way across the restaurant, setting them down for a party of three. "Enjoy your lunch, now."

"Thank you kindly, miss," the ruddy-faced man said. "We love coming here for lunch on our Sunday drive. We take Mother out for a change of scenery every week." He smiled at the little lady now hunched over her grilled cheese.

"I'm pleased to hear it." I wove through to Corrine's table. "What can I get you all to eat today?" I pulled out my order pad.

Hattie craned her neck to see the Specials board. "I'll have a bowl of the mulligatawny soup, please."

"It's one of our most popular specials. I think you'll like it." Abe had made a big pot of the curry-flavored chicken soup for the store a year or two ago. People liked it so much we'd put it into our regular specials rotation.

"I'll take the grilled cheese on whole grain," Francis replied. "And a bowl of fruit."

"Gimme a hamburg with the works, Robbie hon," Corrine said. "And both a brownie and a cookie bar. My sweet tooth is on overdrive today." She gazed past me. "Well, looky who's here."

Adele materialized at my side, with Samuel behind her.

Uh-oh. I hoped we wouldn't have any more barely restrained fireworks from Francis like I'd witnessed yesterday.

"Howdy there, Francis, Hattie," Adele went on. "Come to taste my niece's cooking, have you?"

"Well, now, of course they have, Adele," Corrine said. "We're celebrating their new antique business opening up." She lifted her glass.

Hattie raised hers, but Francis stared at his hands, which were clasped in a death grip on the table.

"Let me introduce my dearly beloved, Samuel MacDonald," Adele said. "Samuel, this here's Francis and Hattie Sand. You know Corrine."

"I am pleased to meet you both." Samuel nodded his grizzled head.

"Likewise." Hattie frowned at Francis.

He didn't budge. The tension could have been played like a banjo string, it was that taut.

"All righty, then." Corrine sipped from her glass.

Samuel took Adele's elbow. "Adele, my dear, let's let them enjoy their libation."

"There's a two-top near the grill." I ushered the couple away. We'd avoided a blowup. For today, anyway.

CHAPTER 8

Adele and Samuel paid me for their meal at a little before twelve-thirty. "You should oughta come out to
the farm tomorrow, Robbie," my aunt said. "We got our-
selves a couple few more details to hammer out about
your big day."

She hadn't interacted with Francis again, for which I
was grateful.

I smiled. "I'll do that. I have some ideas for centerpieces."

"Bring the man for dinner if you want."

"I'll ask him tonight, thanks."

Corrine and the Sands had nearly finished their lunch
ten minutes later when a tall man joined them. The business associate? I thought I might have seen the dude
around town, but I didn't know his name, and I didn't

think he'd eaten here before. I delivered the hot-off-the-grill plates I held to a waiting couple and made my way to Corrine's table.

I smiled at the newcomer. "Welcome to Pans 'N Pancakes. Would you like to order lunch?"

Hattie introduced me to the man. "This is our son-in-law, Orland Krueger."

"Ma'am." He acknowledged the introduction with a nod. "I'd like the Grated Everything as a sandwich, please." He carried a bit of weight on his big frame and looked around forty, with dark eyes and heavy black eyebrows on a jutting brow that gave him a menacing look. Not smiling amplified it.

"Certainly. On white or wheat?"

"White."

"And would you like it with ham, or the vegetarian version?" I asked.

He gave me an are-you-kidding-me look. "With ham, of course."

"Can you pour him the last of the bubbly, Robbie?" Corrine asked. "He's the one what took over Francis and Hattie's food business."

Orland covered the empty glass with a massive hand. "No, thank you."

"All righty, then," Corrine said. "Why don't you go ahead and top the rest of us up, then."

I emptied the bottle and carried it back to the kitchen. Turner was on the grill, while Danna rinsed dishes and loaded them into the dishwasher.

"Do either of you know that man?" I gestured with my head toward Corrine's table. "His name is Orland Krueger."

"Nope," Danna said.

"I don't think I've met him." Turner scooted two grilled hot dogs into toasted buns and laid them on a plate. "But a woman named Krueger was also a student in my culinary class on sauces. It's not a common name around here."

"He looks kind of ominous, doesn't he?" Danna said.

"A little." And he was tall enough for Buck to have called him a cobweb rig if he'd seen him, a phrase that had made me laugh out loud the first time he'd used it to describe a tall person. "Anyway, he wants a GE on white bread, Turner, with ham."

The special was a grilled fritter of grated potato, onion, carrot, ham, and cheese, with an egg and a bit of flour to bind it, plus a touch of curry powder to jazz it up. Turner—whose father was from India—had proposed it for an easy special today along with the soup, and it doubled as a vegetarian meal if the diner ordered it without ham. We didn't go overboard with vegetarian dishes, but I liked to make them available when I could.

"Coming right up." Turner scooped out two disks of the mixture, added the ham, and threw two thick slices of white in the toaster.

I headed over to straighten the cookware shelves. When people shopped, they sometimes picked up an item and set it down backward or in another area. I liked to keep the cake pans together. Likewise for beaters and graters, pie tins and cookie cans, choppers and pastry cutters. Each had its own section. I picked up a red-handled rotary beater nestled in a hexagonal Swans Down cake pan and returned it to the beater area. A vintage Maxwell House coffee can lay on its side next to the mixing bowls.

A curved chopper sat forlorn in . . . *what?* I stared. Where were the new graters I'd bought at the fair? I scanned the shelves. Not a grater to be seen, especially not the pretty one with the stampings and the green handle.

We couldn't have sold them all. I would have noticed. In fact, I didn't think we'd made any cookware sales today. I hurried over to Turner.

"Did you sell any graters today?"

"Not a one." He loaded Orland's GE patties onto the toasted bread and added two pickle spears and a dish of coleslaw to the plate.

Danna came back from busing a table and set down a load of dirty dishes.

"Danna, did you sell any cookware today?" I asked.

"Negative. Why?"

"Neither did I. The new graters are all missing. I can't believe it." I set my fists on my hips. "Someone must have stolen them."

"Uh, sorry, but that guy's lunch is ready," Turner said. "And he was acting impatient."

Danna took a look at me. "I'll take it."

She'd seen how upset I was. Nobody had ever stolen from me before. Sure, South Lick had experienced a few murders in the last couple of years. But never petty larceny, at least not on my property.

I watched Danna take Orland his plate. He didn't even acknowledge her. She waited, arms folded, until he looked up and said something. Good for her. We didn't get too many rude folks in here, and we three had all fallen into the habit of gently encouraging common civility from our customers.

Hattie looked my way but quickly focused on the others at her table again. I spied her patchwork quilted bag hanging off the back of her chair. It was bigger than a reusable grocery bag. Had it looked so full when she and Francis came in earlier? She wouldn't have hot-fingered my graters. Would she?

CHAPTER 9

When Abe came in, I smiled and pointed to an open two-top for him. Buck drifted back in at about one-thirty with his cousin Wanda. He still didn't look a hundred percent but sank into a chair at his favorite two-top at the back. Wanda, in her brown and tan county sheriff's uniform, sat across from him.

I carried over the coffeepot. "Hey, Wanda. Haven't seen you in a while."

"Yep. Had a special detail up to Fort Wayne. Got back last week. How're things?"

"Not bad. You?" I poured coffee for her.

Buck held his hand over his mug with one hand. He held his phone with the other and stared at it.

"Huh," he said to the phone. He looked up at the Specials board. "Robbie. I'll take a double burger, please, and a chocolate milk."

"I like the sound of that grated thingy," Wanda said. "But hold the bread. And can I have me a green salad with?"

I blinked. This was a change for her. I'd never known her to skimp on food, but the customer is always right. "You bet. Coming right up. Buck, have you recovered from this morning?" I asked.

"Pretty much." He focused on the phone again.

"I'll go put those orders in." When I'd opened Pans 'N Pancakes, Wanda had also worked for the South Lick PD. Sometime later, she'd moved over to a job with the county in their detective branch and had then struck up a romance with the state homicide detective. I wasn't sure if that was ongoing and decided not to ask. "Good to see you, Wanda."

"Likewise," she said.

Abe sat eating at a two-top near the kitchen. Between Turner on the grill and Danna holding down the front of the house, things seemed under control. I gave Turner the orders for Buck and Wanda's orders, then touched Abe's shoulder. "Phil brought us wedding cupcakes to trial. Ready?"

He swallowed his last bite of grated stuff sandwich. "Absolutely."

"Be right back." I fixed a plate with three cupcakes cut into halves and sat across from him.

"That sandwich was pretty amazing, by the way," he said. "But the mixture isn't deep-fried, right? I saw Turner pull a pan of it out of the oven."

"Right. I hate deep-frying. That's why I didn't replace that old fryer when it stopped working." I'd served French fries during my first year. People loved them and other occasional deep-fried specials. But it was hot and messy, and I'd had to figure out where to dispose of the used oil. People grumbled for a couple of weeks after I stopped having fries on the menu, and then they accepted a bag of chips with their delicious lunch. "Anyway, I'm glad you liked it."

He bit into the carrot cupcake first, swiping a smear of cream cheese frosting off his upper lip. "Mmm," he murmured, nodding approval.

I savored my half. The contrast between the carroty, cinnamon-flavored cake and the tangy, creamy frosting was perfect. I glanced over at Buck, who frowned at his phone. He looked up, met my gaze, then returned to the device. Something must be happening in the local crime world.

"That one was good." Abe picked up a lemon cupcake half. "Agree?"

"You bet." I popped a bite of the next one into my mouth. The tart lemon popped in exactly the right amount. The icing was lighter than light, as was the crumb of the cake. "Good, no? It's angelic."

"If you like your angels tart." Abe grinned. "Which I do."

I nudged his foot with mine under the table as I picked up the chocolate half. It had a lighter-colored frosting, which Phil had said was mocha flavored. Abe licked the frosting, nodded, and popped half of his half into his mouth. Before I could do the same, Buck wove his way between the tables straight for me.

Uh-oh. Something bad was up.

"Robbie, I think we have a problem." Buck pulled up a chair from an empty table and straddled it next to us. He kept his voice low enough so only Abe and I could hear him. He did not smile.

Abe swallowed. He reached for my hand.

"*We*, like you and me?" I asked.

"Hear me out, now." Buck folded his hands, but not in prayer. "We got word in of a cluster of folks reporting ill at the Nashville urgent care center."

"I'm sorry to hear that." So was the pit of my stomach, waiting for the other shoe to drop.

"They all had breakfast here this morning."

Exactly what I was afraid of. Chefs, restaurant owners—we wanted to nourish our diners and make them happy with delicious foods. Not make them sick. Plus, food poisoning could mean financial ruin for any food establishment.

"Do you mean these people got food poisoning from eating Robbie's food?" Abe asked.

"We don't rightly know for sure yet." Buck rubbed the top of his head as he often did when he was thinking, making his sandy hair stick up all which way. "Doc who took and called it in said a South Lick country store meal this morning was the only commonality."

"Lots of people ate breakfast here, Buck," I said. "They can't all be sick."

"Seems it was only the ones ordering up your mushroom omelet who took ill."

Mushrooms. The box the wholesaler had sent contained several varieties labeled *Gourmet Mushrooms*. What if one was poisonous? But how could that happen? I looked at Abe. He knew all about mushrooms. Abe picked up on my glance and raised his eyebrows. He didn't need ESP to know my brain was working overtime.

"I got those mushrooms from the food wholesaler," I said. "They were delivered yesterday." I thought some more. "But you ate the special this morning," I protested to Buck.

"I did. It was one of your tastier omelets. But I admit to feeling poorly after I did." Buck nodded. "Not so much as to drive over to the clinic, but I was not myself for an hour or three. Thing is, I got me a steel digestive system. Hardly nothing bothers it."

"Did you eat the mushrooms, Robbie?" Abe's brow furrowed.

I thought back. "No. Danna, Turner," I began. "Did either of you taste the mushrooms this morning?"

"Not me," Danna said as she loaded her arms with plates ready to go out. "Remember how busy we were? Plus it was a popular omelet, and we ran out by eight-thirty."

"I got here just after that," Turner said. "So I didn't eat the special, either, or taste the shrooms. Why?" His voice went up. "Was something wrong with them?"

"Tell you in a minute." I lowered my voice again as Danna headed out with her plates. "Buck, the people who felt sick. How are they doing?"

"Seems most of them are going to be all right. One old geezer got took to the hospital over to Bloomington."

The IU Health Bloomington Hospital. Top-notch care, for sure, but it meant the guy's condition was serious. My eyes widened as I swore silently. I hoped it wasn't Mr. Ward, the man who had traded plates with Adele. He hadn't looked very well to begin with. Buck had eaten the omelet, but our local lieutenant was in excellent health and apparently also enjoyed a cast-iron stomach. My generous, polite, prayerful older customer might not be so lucky. If he died—and even if he didn't—the food inspector was going to be over here faster than green grass through a goose, as Buck loved to say.

I stood in such a rush my chair almost tipped over. At

the counter, Danna was already back, unloading an armful of dirty dishes.

"Danna, where's the box the mushrooms came in?" My words tumbled out in a low, urgent tone.

She peered at me. "Outside the service door. What's up, Robbie?"

"Please put on gloves and get the box. Put it in a plastic bag and . . . um—"

"And bring it in? Sure. How about if I stick it in the back of the walk-in?"

I could only nod.

"I gather something was wrong with the mushrooms," she murmured.

"Something is definitely wrong, and it's possible it was the mushrooms," I said.

Turner stared. "That's bad for a restaurant, Robbie."

"And for our poor customers," I said. "Yes. It's very bad."

CHAPTER 10

"**B**uck, do you still want your sandwich?" Turner asked, pointing to two loaded plates. "Wanda's plate is ready, too."

"I might as well," Buck said. "I'll take and bring my cousin's over. Thank you, young man." He grabbed the lunches and headed back to eat with Wanda.

"Enjoy your meal," Turner said.

Buck called back his thanks.

"I'll be right back," I said to Abe. I followed a blue-gloved Danna to the service door.

Outside the rain had stopped. Diamonds of sunlight sparkled in pools of standing water. Drops from an over-flowing gutter hit the top of a trash can with an annoying persistence, and steam hovered above the dark pavement as if from a subterranean wizard's cauldron.

Danna raised the lid on the recycling bin and lifted out

the box the mushrooms had come in. "Do you think we're going to have to close?"

I held open the clear plastic bag she'd brought out with her. "I expect so."

"That's not good. And the week hasn't even started."

"We'll manage, Danna. We did when we had to close before."

"If you say so."

Inside, I watched as she deposited the evidence—maybe—in the walk-in before I rejoined Abe.

"You've never had a case of food poisoning here, have you?" Abe asked.

"Never in two and a half years. I had to close those two times in my first fall. First when a very bad person reported that we had rats in here. We didn't. That's when I last saw the health inspector. And then I had to close when someone had the nerve to break in and leave a body behind the pickle barrel."

"I remember. That's when I was first falling in love with you." Abe's cheeks pinkened. "I didn't think I had a chance, because of the guy you were seeing."

"And it's my good fortune he didn't work out." I failed to muster a smile. "I'm sorry, Abe. You know how happy I am. Right now I'm worried about my customers, and my livelihood."

"I know, sugar."

"Even that Christmas when Oscar confiscated my hot chocolate packets, I didn't have to close." Oscar being State Police Detective Oscar Thompson. I gazed across the room. At least Buck was focused on his sandwich and not on his phone. If he received an alert that my customer had died, even Hollow-Leg Buck would abandon his lunch. "I wonder if I'll have a visit from Elizabeth Lake before we close today or after."

"Who's that?"

"Health inspector for Brown County." I smiled grimly. "She has to do her job, but she's kind of too strict. I hope poor Mr. Ward doesn't die. Even if he makes it, my restaurant is in trouble."

"This Mr. Ward ate the mushrooms, I gather."

"Yes." I told him how he'd offered to swap plates with Adele. "He didn't look very healthy to start with."

"Does he have a first name?"

"I don't know. Samuel goes to church with him, but they were all formal with using 'mister' and last names."

"I think I've heard of a Jeremiah Ward. Older fellow?"

I nodded. "And he looked unwell, with jaundiced skin. He was eating by himself." I gazed at the front door, expecting Lake any minute.

"Shall we try the chocolate while we can?" Abe pointed to the plate, where the two chocolate halves lay awaiting our taste buds. "Believe me, I am not making light of the situation. But, bad mushrooms or not, Phil is still going to bake us a cake in a month."

"You're right." I sampled my piece. The creamy mocha had the right coffee-chocolate balance, with a touch of Kahlúa, if I wasn't mistaken. The rich, dark chocolate cake was to die for.

"That's kind of heaven," I said.

"Agreed." Abe licked his lips even as he smiled. "But all of them are, right?"

"I know. But does one stand out for you? Do you have a favorite?" I knew how much he liked carrot cake, and his reaction to the lemon had been beyond favorable. My choice would be the chocolate, but I'd be happy with any of them.

"Should we do rock-paper-scissors? Rock is carrot, paper is lemon, and scissors are chocolate."

I snorted. "It sounds like you love all three as much as I do. How about this? We have a three-layered cake, and . . ." My voice trailed off as the cowbell jangled.

Six windblown women came in, dressed for hiking.

I stood and smiled. "Hello, everyone. That big table is open," I said, pointing. "Someone will be right with you."

They made their way toward the eight-top, chattering and shedding jackets. The bell jangled again, but this time Elizabeth Lake was the newcomer. I grimaced.

"That's her?" Abe asked.

"That is her."

Wanda rose and hurried to the door. The two women spoke, one slim and blazer-clad and the other robust-figured and uniformed. They conferred, with glances in my direction. Wanda appeared to be pushing back about something. I crossed my fingers that she was taking my side. When I'd last seen Inspector Lake, she'd made me lock the door but had let the customers currently in the restaurant finish their meals and leave before she posted the sign. It was nearly two and we would be done in half an hour, anyway. Would she do that this time, too? Wanda gestured toward the walk-in and kept talking. Buck must have told her what I'd asked Danna to do.

I exhaled. "I'd better go talk with them."

"You'll get through this, sweetheart." Abe grabbed my hand and squeezed it. "And I'm here for you."

"I know. Thank you."

I shifted my focus to Wanda, raising my eyebrows and trying to telegraph an *Am I open?* message.

"You're good," the detective murmured to me, barely moving her lips. "For now."

Lake kept her mouth shut. All righty, then.

Danna caught my eye with a questioning look. I nodded and pointed at the group. Bracing myself, I turned to the inspector.

"I guess you're here about the mushrooms, Ms. Lake," I said.

"Yes. Detective Bird convinced me against my better judgment to let your restaurant stay open until your normal closing time. After that? I think you know the drill."

Thank you, Wanda.

"Actually, Inspector, I've never had a case of reputed food poisoning, so I don't know the drill." I stressed *reputed*.

She cast a glance upward as if exasperated at my blatant ignorance. Two and a half years ago she'd worn a no-fuss haircut falling a little below her ears. Now she sported a wavy shoulder-length do at odds with her tailored blue shirt, the dark blazer, and the black slacks and flats.

I waited.

"After your last customer has left, I will post the establishment as closed," Lake said. "I trust you remember that part of the process?"

"Yes." That nightmarish part. How could I forget?

"I understand you've retained the container the food in question came in. What about any dishware or cooking implements used to prepare the omelets?"

"It's all been washed." I flipped open my palms. I couldn't do anything about that. "We stopped serving the omelet at eight-thirty because we ran out of mushrooms. Buck didn't tell me about the people falling ill until he and Wanda came in for lunch at—when, Wanda? I think it was about one-thirty."

"That would be correct."

"So, no, Ms. Lake. All I have is the box."

"What is the name of your supplier?" Lake asked. She'd drawn out a tablet from her briefcase and jabbed it with her finger.

"It's the FH Foods Company."

"Tell me what else was in the omelets. Was any of it used in other dishes?"

Huh. I looked at the inspector, thinking. "Let's see. Fresh rosemary and thyme. Eggs and Gruyére cheese. The cheese would have also gone into sandwiches, grilled and otherwise. You'll have to ask my assistants. We all cook. Has anybody gotten sick from eating lunch here today?"

"Not that we've heard," Wanda said.

"Good. I can't imagine the herbs making anybody sick," I continued. "And they were used in very small quantities in the mushroom omelets."

"We should take the rest of that cheese, whatever it's called, to be safe." Wanda wasn't one to bother with names in other languages.

"Not a problem," I said.

Buck ambled toward us. Had he ever looked so sorrowful?

In a grievous tone, he said, "Jeremiah Ward has died."

CHAPTER 11

The front door of Pans 'N Pancakes was now emblazoned with a big orange sign reading, *By order of the Brown County Health Commissioner this establishment is hereby CLOSED to protect public health and safety.* Below was more verbiage, but that was the really visible part. Visible to anyone from the bottom of the steps. To any car that drove by. To news reporters who got wind of the death.

I sat with Danna and Turner at three o'clock, plates of odds and ends in front of us. Danna had the last catfish sandwich, I was good with two turkey burger patties on one bun, and vegetarian Turner was about to dig into a grilled cheddar and tomato. Abe had had to go, but promised to call later, and Buck took off shortly after his announcement of the death. Wanda and the inspector stayed until the last customer had left. After Lake posted her notices and left, Wanda departed with the bagged mushroom box and the rest of the Gruyére in its wrapper. My team and I had finished cleaning up and storing all the food a couple of minutes ago.

"I feel awful about that man dying." I rubbed my forehead. "And for his family."

"I agree," Danna said. "What a way to go."

"Did somebody say he was already sick?" Turner asked.

"He looked kind of yellow, but I don't know for sure," I said. "But even if he was ill before he ate here, the thought that our omelet killed him makes me feel awful."

"Remember during the pandemic?" Danna asked. "The first to die were people who already had health problems."

"Right." Turner took a bite of his sandwich.

"I don't know about you guys, but I'm ready for a commiseration beer. Anybody?" I asked. They were both over twenty-one.

"Now that the rain is over, I have volleyball in an hour, so, no thanks," Danna said. "It's our first outdoor game of the season, too."

"Hit me." Turner pointed to his chest.

"You like a pilsner, right?" I asked on my way back to my apartment. "Danna, grab yourself a root beer or whatever."

Turner nodded. A minute later, Birdy dashed past me into the restaurant as I returned with two bottles. I'd planned to let him in, but if he wanted to pretend he was getting away with something, more power to him.

I poured the beer into the glasses. "Here's to Mr. Ward." I raised my glass.

They echoed the sentiment.

"We would have been closed tomorrow, anyway, but it looks like you both are going to have a few days of enforced time off," I said after we'd clinked. "I'll keep paying you, of course."

"Thanks," Danna said after she swallowed. "How long do you think it'll be?"

I shrugged. "Not a clue. I hope it counts in our favor that we've never had a case of food poisoning here before. Oh, we need to let Phil know so he doesn't bring more desserts."

"I'll text him," Turner said. "If it was localized to the mushrooms, doesn't that make it the supplier's fault and not yours?"

"I sure hope so." I sipped my IPA. "I had a thought. If we can get the names of the people who got sick, we can offer them gift certificates."

Danna wrinkled her nose. "Do you think they'd want to eat here again?"

"Ugh." I hadn't thought of that. "Maybe not. But they could use them in the store."

"Want me to put something on our Facebook page?" Turner asked. "Like, if you ordered the mushroom omelet today, please see the proprietor next time you come in."

"I think it's too soon for that," I said. "We aren't sure it was the mushrooms, and we definitely don't want to advertise food poisoning."

"Robbie," a frowning Danna began. "You said Ms. Sand stole your graters. Whatever caused the food poisoning, do you think it was, like, sabotage?"

"I have to admit that crossed my mind." I worried the corner of the label on my beer bottle. "The Sands used to own a food wholesale business. And you know what else?"

They both waited for me to speak.

"Their son-in-law took it over. I met him earlier. That big guy who sat with the Sands and Corrine. Orland Krueger."

"Is it the company we use?" Danna asked. "FH?"

"Yes," I said. "Now that I've met them, I think the initials must stand for Francis and Hattie."

"Maybe they asked him to deliver bad mushrooms to make all our diners sick," Turner said. "What did they look like, anyway?"

I glanced at Danna.

"I don't know," she began. "They looked like mushrooms. Brownish with little white specks on top, white underneath. I'm not really up on types of mushrooms. When I sliced them, I thought I smelled radishes, even though there weren't any around."

"Me, neither," I said. "A box that says *Gourmet Mushrooms* from a reputable food supplier? I take them at their word."

"We should be able to," Danna agreed.

"Adele told me yesterday that Francis has an old grudge against her. And Hattie apparently stole my graters. Could they all be in this together?"

"Wait," Turner asked. "She stole your what?"

"The new pile of graters I picked up on Saturday. They went missing today."

"Did you confront her about them?" Danna asked.

"No, with everything that went on with the inspector, I let it slide."

Turner was already busy on his phone. He looked up.

"You nailed it, Robbie." He held up his cell and read from it in a dramatic tone. "*Krystal Sand married Orland Krueger in a lavish ceremony held at the Story Inn attended by over two hundred guests.* It mentions Francis Sand, too."

"When was the wedding?" I asked. The Story Inn was a renovated general store and restaurant a lot like mine, except it was situated in the middle of nowhere south of here in the county. They'd built a new barn a few years ago and had been marketing the place as a wedding venue and function mecca.

"Let's see." Turner swiped through the article. "It was last September."

"Lavish, huh?" Danna asked. "You wouldn't think owning a food wholesale business would make somebody rich."

"I don't know. Did I tell you guys about Francis's son?" When they both shook their heads, I told them about his death.

"That's sad," Turner said.

"It is." I nodded "That's the grudge Francis holds. He'd asked Adele to help the kid, but she wasn't able to."

"It's not her fault," Danna said.

"Absolutely not," I said. "But if Francis wanted to get back at Adele, he could have thought ruining my business would be one way to do it."

Turner tilted his head. "Kind of a long shot."

I laughed. "No kidding. Back to the wedding: Maybe Krystal is his only other child and he's been saving up for her marriage celebration for a long time."

Danna worked her own phone. "Wow. A wedding that

big at Story can run you big bucks." She looked up. "Dude must have deep pockets."

I drained my beer. "It's always possible that bad mushrooms got into the box totally by accident and we're spinning our wheels. Or it wasn't the mushrooms at all." Except my gut told me otherwise.

CHAPTER 12

I dug into a steaming plate of lasagna at Abe's table that night at seven. I hadn't arrived as early as I'd hoped, and the dinner was all ready when I came in. A fat candle gleamed in the middle of the table, and a tossed salad filled a wooden bowl next to it. His colorful woven place mats dressed up the antique dining table. I savored the rich tomato sauce, the creamy ricotta, the smooth comfort of wide pasta noodles, and the earthy taste of mushrooms.

"Mmm," I said. "This is so good."

"Sean made most of the dish." He sipped his wine. "I only advised."

"He couldn't stay?"

"No, it's a school night. I took him home an hour ago. But we had a good day. We went mushroom hunting this afternoon, and then came back to cook together."

"Please tell him I said it's the best lasagna I've ever had."

"I will. Sean asked me to teach him how to cook. He took a smaller pan of it home with him, but sans morels. And speaking of mushrooms, did the inspector give you any sense of how long your restaurant will need to stay closed?"

"Not a clue. And we're not sure it was the mushrooms that made Mr. Ward and the others sick. But I can't imagine what else it would have been."

"You'd be closed tomorrow anyway, right?" he asked.

"Yes. Now I might have a whole string of enforced days off. Which does not make me happy."

"I know, hon. That place is your dream." Abe smiled fondly at me.

"It really is." I gazed at the lasagna. "So you both picked the mushrooms we're eating?" I shuddered.

"Yes. And don't worry, I know what I'm doing. Morels are easy to identify and they aren't easily confused with anything poisonous. I'll give you some to take with you."

"I don't doubt you. Wait, though. You said Sean took home a pan without mushrooms?"

"Yes. He likes finding them, but he actually doesn't like the taste."

"Kids," I said. "He'll probably grow into it."

Abe frowned into his glass.

"Is the wine bad?" I hadn't tasted mine yet.

He looked up. "No, it's fine. It's his mom. Jan has decided she's all done with cooking."

"Really? With a growing teenager at home?"

"Yes. I feel bad for him."

"Right, because the alternatives are lots of expensive takeout or a bunch of unhealthy ready-made dinners."

"Or a kid doing all the cooking. Not that he's a little kid anymore. But you know what I mean. He shouldn't have to take over a parental role like that."

I reached out my hand to his and squeezed. "At least he wants to learn. Your dad taught you to cook, right?"

He nodded. "But I didn't have to take over family dinners when I was fifteen."

"Would Jan let him come and live here?" I took another bite.

Abe set down his fork. "Robbie, we're going to be married soon. You don't want a teenage boy around the house, do you? He can be noisy and smelly and rude. And we wouldn't have as much privacy."

"Abe O'Neill, he's your son. Remember when you asked me to marry you, and I checked with Sean before I said yes?"

He bobbed his head once.

"I'm marrying you—and your family. If Sean needs or wants to live here, naturally that's fine with me. He'll be off to college in a few years. And it's not like he'll be sharing our bedroom." I gazed in his eyes. "I mean it. I would welcome him. I like the kid, you know."

Abe sniffed and swiped at his eye.

"Hey, eat your dinner." I smiled at my sentimental fiancé, then devoured another bite of my own meal. "Speaking of Jan, what does she do for work? You'd think I would know, but we rarely talk about her."

"She's a programmer. A software engineer."

"Which means she's smart."

"Very. That's where Seanie gets his math genes," Abe said. "Jan also quilts and has a kind of side business restoring antique quilts."

"How does she feel about you remarrying? She hasn't found a new husband, has she?"

"She hasn't. As far as I know, she hasn't even dated anyone. I suspect she's not that happy about us, even though she and I have been divorced for twelve years now."

Maybe she hadn't dated because she still had a thing for Abe. I tasted the wine. "Ooh, this is good."

"The Oliver vineyard has really upped its game with their red varietals."

"Tell me again why you and Jan split up?" I was sure we'd discussed the reasons for their divorce earlier in our relationship, but the details were fuzzy. I'd only met her once in passing. Last year, Sean had been with Abe at the store, and Jan had picked the boy up after she got off work.

"She changed after we were married. Maybe we'd been so smitten with each other at the start that I hadn't noticed, but after she wore a ring she never wanted to go out, to have fun, to socialize. It was like she wanted me all for herself."

"And you're an extrovert." Kind of like me. "You like being around people."

"I do. It was more than that, though. Seanie was born fifteen months later. After that she stopped being intimate with me. She gained a lot of weight and claimed I wouldn't be interested in her. But it was all in her head. I still desired her. She didn't believe me. We were young, and I didn't want to give up that part of my life."

"And why should you? I assume you tried counseling?"

"I tried. She refused. I'd read about postpartum depression and wondered if it was that." He shook his head.

"She finally told me she wanted to split up, and that she wanted primary custody of Sean. I agreed as long as we had joint legal custody. I was worried about her, and I hoped having to take care of him would keep her on a more even keel."

"She's done a good job," I said. "Sean's a great kid."

"He is. And she's never stopped me from spending lots of time with him. Lately I don't think she and Sean have been getting along anywhere near as well. Her brother seems to be the only person she really clicks with."

"If she isn't good at relationships, maybe having a kid who is nearly an adult man is hard for her to handle."

"And he has his own relationship these days," Abe said with a grin. "Totally gone on a brilliant—and cute—girl in math club."

"Good for him."

"It is." He took a deep breath and let it out. He smiled. "Sugar, enough of the depressing talk about my ex. Do we still have things on the to-do list for our happy day a month from now?"

CHAPTER 13

Abe had pulled a noon-to-nine shift at the electric company. We slept in and enjoyed a leisurely breakfast. Rosy-cheeked, I made my way home at around ten. Being with Abe, whether at his place or mine, felt like a refuge. We hadn't had any real conflict in our time together—not that life with him was boring, by any means. Tension with other people and circumstances arose in my life, but not with Abe. He was comfort and safety, exactly what home should be. I couldn't imagine another soul I'd want to marry and spend my life with.

With a pang, I wished Mom was still alive to know Abe and be at our wedding. I knew how much she would have liked him and approved of our union. I didn't have much of a belief in heaven being a place where deceased loved ones looked down on us from. I was pretty sure my mother's spirit, wherever it rested, was sending us her blessing.

A wind had picked up again and blew in more clouds from the west. I pulled my sweater closer around me. As I neared my store, my thoughts returned to the purloined graters. I'd successfully kept the theft out of my mind during most of my ride with Lou and my visit with Abe. Now? I pictured Hattie Sand's bulging bag. How could she be so brazen as to steal from me? She couldn't think she'd be able to display my graters in her own store. The green-handled one was especially memorable, and I would recognize the others, too. Francis had offered to give me a tour of their store today. I planned to take him up on it later.

I passed the bakery in downtown South Lick. The aroma of fresh-baked bread nearly steered me inside, but I'd had a big mushroom omelet and toast with Abe. Plus, Birdy would be waiting for me to give him his morning treat. I kept going, rounding the corner onto Main Street. As I neared the end of the built-up area where Pans 'N Pancakes was, I slowed. A tall, boxy green van sat nearly in front of the antique store. I stared. On the side was painted *KK's Sandos* in big red and yellow letters. Under that was *Breakfast and Lunch*, accompanied by paintings of colorful sandwiches brimming with ingredients. A breakfast sub loaded with glistening egg and bits of ham. A meatball sandwich on a bulky roll, green lettuce and red tomato peeking out underneath.

A breakfast and lunch food truck? Across from my store? This KK had the nerve. I checked for cars, then hurried across the street, circling around the truck to the sidewalk. A menu was painted on the side, listing a half-dozen sandwiches under headings of Breakfast and Lunch. The side window was up. A napkin dispenser, a squeeze bottle of ketchup, and salt-and-pepper shakers sat on the narrow counter. Nowhere did I see a food permit posted. I didn't know the regulations about food trucks. But I had to think that they needed a permit to prepare and serve food to the public. Brick-and-mortar restaurants like mine sure did.

Inside, a woman with an apron tied behind her chopped vegetables with her back to me. A strawberry-blond pony-tail was threaded through a gray twill ball cap. The smell of frying onions wafted out.

"Excuse me," I said.

She turned and set her hands on the counter, leaning down to see me. "Good morning. Welcome to KK's Sandos. What can I get you?" A smile with an overbite split her thin face. A strand of hair escaped her hat, which had *Brown County State Park* embroidered on the front.

"Nothing. How long do you plan on parking here?" I knew I sounded brusque. I couldn't help myself, but tacked on a smile to soften the tone.

She pulled her head back a little. "Uh, as long as I want. Why? Do you have a problem with that?"

"I'm Robbie Jordan. I own the *breakfast* and *lunch* restaurant across the street." I stressed the words, which were also subtitled on my clearly displayed sign. I gestured with my thumb. "So, yes, I have a problem with you being here."

She blinked. "I'm Krystal. Nice to meet you, Robbie. I guess. Also, it actually looks like your restaurant is currently closed."

The big honking orange sign. "Yes, but that's temporary."

"Whatever. The food truck law lets me park in any valid parking space. I'm sorry if you feel offended."

Offended wasn't the half of it. "Do you have a permit?"

Without speaking, she pointed to a framed document hanging above her work counter inside the truck. I couldn't read it from here, but it looked a lot like a permit to serve food.

"Good luck, then." I shut my mouth before I said more.

I stepped into the street without looking. An approaching car beeped at me, but slowed so I could cross. From in front of my store I watched it pull to the curb. Four young men piled out, disappearing behind the van. To order hearty breakfast sandos, no doubt.

CHAPTER 14

"Seeing that food truck sure burst my bubble of bliss, Birdy," I said after I was back in my apartment.

The little black-and-white one didn't care. He was in his own happy place, chowing away at the two tablespoons of wet food I'd doled out.

I changed out of the swingy knit dress I'd worn over leggings to Abe's and threw on a long sweater and my slippers. I paced my very small living room, thinking.

I didn't care if this Krystal person parked her truck over there on Mondays. I wasn't open anyway. Regardless of the day, she'd be out of luck when it rained or snowed. Who would want to stand outside in bad weather and wait for their sandwich? And, while I offered the option of takeout meals—as opposed to taking home leftovers—it wasn't my primary business and almost nobody ordered them. Maybe I needed to relax and not worry about her. People who wanted a to-go *sando*, as she put it, might prefer the quick in and out of a food truck.

Still, I was a bit steamed. The courteous thing to do would have been to pay me a visit, tell me her plans, and ask for my blessing, so to speak. I thought about the food trucks I'd seen in Santa Barbara when I was out west for my reunion. The best one was operated by a former classmate. They'd all been situated in a parking lot near the public pier and offered distinct fare: hot dogs vs. Asian noodle dishes vs. creative hot pockets vs. tacos. None of them were in direct competition as far as the food went. Farther out on the pier, sit-down restaurants served meals and drinks, but they tended to be pricier and served a different clientele. A breakfast and lunch truck across from South Lick's only breakfast and lunch restaurant was another thing, entirely.

I drank a glass of water and tried to let my stress slide off. It was stupid to let a probably harmless food truck take over my mood. Another good bike outing would do a world of good for my peace of mind. Abe couldn't come with me to Adele's. Maybe Lou wanted to take a ride out to the farm this afternoon. We three ladies could talk wedding stuff into the bargain.

Sinking onto the couch, I texted her about riding at three. She replied in an instant that she'd love to. Next was to check out the plan with Adele—by voice, not text.

"Hey, Auntie," I said after we greeted each other. "I'm afraid Abe can't make dinner tonight."

"That's a crying shame. But you can?"

"How about if Lou and I ride out to your place later in the afternoon, instead?" I asked her. "We can have a visit and go over the last-minute list."

"You and your maid of honor? Sounds good to me, hon."

I cringed at the term. Lou and my high school friend Alana, who would be coming out from California, were both going to keep me company during the ceremony. But archaic terms like *maid of honor* and *bridesmaid* didn't make sense to me. I did have the sense to keep my mouth shut about it to Adele.

"I might could whip up a snack or two," my aunt added. Her idea of a snack was fresh-baked bread or a rich cake. Or both.

"Perfect," I said. "See you in a few hours."

My phone dinged as soon as I disconnected from Adele. My cleaning service sent a text to say they wouldn't be able to be in today. I'd decided early on to give myself a real day off and not spend it cleaning. The service, actually a one-woman business, came on Mondays to deep clean the store's bathrooms and floors.

Sorry. My kid took ill. Have to stay home.

I texted back.

Hope he feels better soon. No worries.

I'd have to find time today for a quick extra mopping and swiping down the restrooms. My phone dinged again, with a text from the food delivery service. *Right.* I'd placed an order yesterday, and they would never give me an exact time for the drop-off. Sometimes even their three-hour window was wrong. I'd completely forgotten to cancel the order after the orange sign went up, and now I didn't even need it. I hurried into the store, leaving the door to my apartment open, and unlocked the service door on the side of the building.

"Good morning," I said, standing aside for the delivery person. This time it was a young man, not the taciturn woman who usually brought my order.

"Robbie Jordan?" He jiggled his leg as he handed me the device for me to scribble my signature with my finger.

"That's me." Gone were the days of signing a paper receipt in ink on a clipboard, which had been the system only three years ago when I'd opened. That said, I did use an app to order, which was a lot more convenient than phoning in a list of food I needed.

I scrawled something vaguely resembling my name and handed the device back. I followed him and his handcart, which held a stack of boxes, into the kitchen. I always tried to order in for the week, but often we needed to place a second order by Friday. "Please leave them by the walk-in."

He slid the boxes off the cart. "I'll be back with the rest," he said.

Birdy wound, purring, around my ankles.

"Don't get run over, Birdman," I told him as I started unpacking buns, butter, and bell peppers—otherwise known as mangoes by longtime locals.

The delivery guy wheeled in another stack.

"Thanks," I called to him as he left.

He waved a hand without looking back. This company must specialize in delivery people of few words. *Company*. I stared at the boxes. They weren't labeled with a company name. That was strange. Previous boxes had been marked FH Foods. At least none had "Gourmet Mushrooms" written on the side.

For now, I had food to put away and then a catfish special to try out for whenever we could reopen. And maybe a little research on food truck regulations in Brown County.

CHAPTER 15

"Lemons, check. Melons, check," I said to Birdy as I continued to unpack the order. "Milk, cheese, eggs, yogurt. Got 'em."

Birdy, now ensconced on a chair and having a good wash in an impossible yoga pose, glanced up, then went back to the job at hand—licking his not-so-private parts.

I stared at the pile of empty boxes. "But no carrots. No potatoes. No mustard. And no pickles. Again? What the heck?" I was sure I'd ordered those items. I hurried over to my desk and drew the iPad out of the drawer. Firing up the app, I checked yesterday's order. I wasn't wrong. I could do without carrots, but potatoes and pickles? They were a must-have for a place like mine. I still had some mustard, but running out would not go over well with diners. I punched the company's number.

Which went to voice mail. I left a clear message about

what I needed. "And I need it today." This was the second time in a row they'd screwed up an order. In a pinch I could pick up those items at the grocery store. But not in bulk and not for a good price. At least I didn't need the missing foods urgently.

But I knew doing some cooking would fix it, or at least take my mind off it. I finished stashing the food, then got out the catfish fillets, cornmeal, flour, and eggs. I set the oven to preheat to 425 and went to work.

The fillets were thin and flash frozen. With a hot oven, they would cook quickly. I didn't need to defrost them. I mixed cornmeal, flour, seasoned salt, black and lemon pepper, and paprika in a ziplock bag. I added a pinch of cayenne. Being a native southern Californian, I loved a flash of spicy in my food. Many residents of southern Indiana were not so used to hot food, or so fond of it, so I restrained myself from adding more.

I'd eaten so much good food during my two visits to California last year, and I had brought home recipes, or the idea of them. Pans 'N Pancakes had featured chicken empanadas, veggie quesadillas, and Mexican chocolate mini-cakes after I came back. Orange scones and avocado huevos rancheros, too. We should reprise some of those specials.

I beat two eggs into a shallow dish and added a few drops of habanero sauce, again restraining myself from making it too spicy. After the oven dinged that it was up to temperature, I lined a baking sheet with parchment paper, sprayed it with olive oil, and went to work. I dipped both side of a fillet in the egg mixture, then shook it in the bag of dry mix until it was coated. I placed the fish in the egg mixture again, turned it, and laid it on the paper-coated pan. Rinse and repeat.

As I worked, my thoughts went right back to KK's Sandos. The woman had said her name was Krystal, so that had to be the first half of KK. She'd parked almost directly in front of the Sands' new store. Yesterday I'd met Orland Krueger, their son-in-law. Krystal Sand was the bride from the article Turner had read from. I flashed on the woman in the Reds cap who'd come out of the antique store with Francis yesterday morning. I'd barely seen her, but she'd been tall and had light hair. Like Krystal's. And that overbite had looked familiar to me. Did Francis or Hattie have one? I couldn't remember. Francis was certainly tall, too. She had to be the Sands' daughter, and that was why she'd parked there. I had to admit her food truck name was clever, working her maiden name into a nickname for sandwiches.

I sprayed the tops of the fillets liberally with oil and slid the pan into the oven, setting the timer for twenty minutes. If they weren't done by then, I would reset it for longer. I wanted to research food truck regulations. But in a kitchen, cleanup always came first. By the time all was clean and wiped down, the timer dinged. I peeked, poked, closed the oven door, and set the timer for ten more minutes. The crust wasn't crispy yet, and one thick fillet was still translucent, not the opaque that would indicate it was cooked. Fresh fillets would probably go faster. I made a note on the pad of paper where I'd been keeping track of my ingredients and amounts.

A quick search on the iPad at my desk on both state and county sites yielded nothing about where food trucks were allowed to park. If Krystal had a license, she must be complying with necessary regulations for keeping food safe, both cold and hot enough. I needed to give up on any notion of forcing her out of my territory. I sniffed.

Something was smelling good in here, and my big break-fast was a more distant memory than it had been.

I pulled out the pan at the second ding. The one thing I hadn't cleaned up was a small cutting board with wedges of lemon. I slid a piece of fish onto a small plate, doused it with lemon juice, and grabbed a fork. I didn't budge from standing at the counter to sample my experiment. The first bite was perfect; Crunchy on the outside, with tender, flaky fish inside. It could use a sprinkle of fresh parsley, I thought. And for diners who wanted the sand-wich—sando, as it were—version, I could make up a tasty mayo sauce with a touch of dill, mustard, and more lemon juice.

Houston, we have a special. Peace of mind, not so much, but that would come with time. I finished the fillet and left the rest to cool. It was about time to take Francis up on his offer of a Sands Antiques tour.

CHAPTER 16

A flag reading *Open* flew to the side of the antique store's front door, which stood ajar. I skirted half-a-dozen people waiting in line at the food truck for their sandwiches, and I avoided looking at Krystal as I entered the shop. Inside was a hall and a staircase. A table held a collection of carved duck decoys, their paint restored and the wood polished.

I went through the arched doorway to my right, where it looked like they'd removed an interior wall to create a long, spacious room. In the front were gleaming end tables, antique sofas and love seats, glowing brass lamps, and bookshelves with very little on them. At the far end were two dining sets, a hutch, and a sideboard. The only thing that indicated this wasn't a home—albeit one with a surfeit of furniture—was the desk with an iPad on a stand and a discreet sign displaying several credit card logos.

Francis, his back to me, talked with a man and a woman in the dining area. I wandered through the front of the store, admiring the furniture, but I wasn't in the market for any of it. I'd be combining households with Abe soon. The few fine pieces I owned, crafted by my mother with simple, smooth lines from lighter wood, appealed to me much more than any of these.

I didn't want to bother Francis while he had paying customers, so I returned to the hall in search of the kitchen. A sign at the base of the stairs directed people to the second floor for bedroom furniture. Women's voices drifted down from up there. Hattie's, perhaps? That was fine with me. I'd rather search for my graters without being under her scrutiny. I aimed myself toward the back of the house, passing framed Audubon bird prints hung on the wall. On my right, a swinging door had been propped open, revealing a kitchen empty of shoppers.

The space had been renovated, but in a style reflecting the period when the house had been constructed. White subway tiles, a deep sink of black sandstone, varnished wooden counters, and white glass-fronted cabinets fit the era. A crock of wooden spoons sat on the counter next to the AGA six-burner stove, on top of which were arrayed a Dutch oven, skillets of all sizes, and two big soup pots, all made of seasoned cast iron.

Against one wall was a Hoosier cabinet in cream and pale green. An ingenious storage cupboard, it included a flour bin above a built-in sifter. The cabinets and drawers all stood open, as did the rolltop compartment at the waist-level counter section, where pie tins, cake pans, canisters, and rolling pins were displayed. A big stoneware mixing bowl brimmed with vintage cookie cutters, plus some that were so shiny they looked new. Was this also a not-so-antique shop?

At the back of the kitchen was what looked like an addition, with a wall of windows, an oak table and chairs, and a built-in padded bench. A bunch of daffodils in a blue-and-white pitcher added yellow cheer to the table set with blue place mats and flowered plates. I realized I didn't know if the Sands had moved here from Gnaw Bone. If they lived in this building, it was going to be a challenge to keep a place like a kitchen always clean, devoid of personal items, and ready for customers.

Francis came into the kitchen through a different door with the couple he'd been talking to.

"Here's where we have the—" He stopped when he saw me. "Robbie, I didn't know you were here."

I smiled. "You were busy. I didn't want to bother you. You have some very nice pieces in the front, and this is a lovely kitchen."

"Thank you." He seemed touched. "We worked hard on it."

The woman of the couple seemed excited by the Hoosier cabinet. The man fingered the Dutch oven.

Francis eyed them, then said to me, "I can show you around later, if you'd like."

"No worries. I'll wander a little. I have to get back to Pans 'N Pancakes soon." Not really, but I'd rather poke about on my own.

The woman turned. "Do you own that darling country store acrost over there?"

"I do. We're closed today, but we sell vintage cookware and serve breakfast and lunch every day of the week but Monday. You would be most welcome." After I was allowed to reopen, that is. I didn't look at Francis, but I thought I spied his frown out of the corner of my eye. Tough. It might be petty of me, but I'd been on Main Street selling antique cooking implements first.

"We'd love to, wouldn't we, hon?" She glanced at her husband, who wasn't listening. "We live in Pittsburgh, but our daughter's in Bloomington. She just had her fift baby. Five little children. Can you believe it?"

I'd never met anybody from Pittsburgh, but I guessed *fift* was how they said "fifth."

"I hope to see you in Pans 'N Pancakes, ma'am." I headed out the door I'd come in by. At the back end of the hall was another propped-open door. This one led outdoors, my exact destination.

From the stoop, I surveyed the rear of the property. It didn't look much different from the back of mine, with a small clearing and cloud-darkened woods beyond, and a big old barn to the side. I followed a flagstone walkway to the wide barn door, which had been slid all the way open. The barn also flew an *Open* flag from a pole in a holder. The wind whapped the flag harder than a granny beating her rugs. While the part of the house I'd seen had been thoroughly renovated, the barn's fading, peeling paint and splintering boards made the structure look beaten down instead of quaint.

Stepping inside, I found a flea market atmosphere. Wide boards on sawhorses on each side of a passageway wide enough to hold a vehicle held a mishmash of glassware, lamps, and tools. Each table sported a sign with a per-item price. Drinking glasses at a dollar each. Five dollars per lamp. Small tools a dollar each, with bigger ones priced at four. More painted duck decoys, except these were chipped and the colors were faded. But no cookware.

Nobody seemed to be working in here, so I ventured farther into the gloom. Where were my graters? A few bare light bulbs illuminated the recesses of the barn about as much as the light from a waning moon. I squinted to see what was displayed in the dimness.

There. The last table on the left, in front of what had been stalls for horses, held a pile of choppers, graters, and other kitchen implements. I pulled out my phone and turned on the flashlight app. My green-handled box grater was nearly hidden at the back behind a heavy meat grinder. Fishing the grater out by the handle, I shone the light on each side. Sure enough, at the bottom I spied the blue price label from the young man selling his grandma's possessions. I hadn't noted particulars of the rest of the batch I'd bought on Saturday, but the graters near this one looked too familiar for it all to be a coincidence.

Hearing a creak from the front of the barn, I peered in that direction. Maybe Francis coming to give me the tour? But I didn't see anyone.

I stared at the grater in my hand, which seemed to have taken on more importance than it might deserve. I could simply grab it and leave. But really, I needed to confront Hattie—and Francis—with her theft. Maybe she was a compulsive stealer—otherwise known as suffering from the illness of kleptomania—and couldn't help herself. Did her husband know? How could he not?

I glanced around. Still no one. I set the grater back on the table, switched off the flashlight, and activated my phone's camera, making sure the flash would go on. Picture taken, I slid the phone into my pocket and turned to go.

"Whoa," I exclaimed.

Hattie stood three feet away with her fists on her hips.

Her nostrils flared and her glare was sharp and suspicious. "What are you doing back here?" She picked up a curved, lethal-looking chopper from the table and moved closer, holding it blade out.

I took a step back. "I toured the downstairs of your store, and I wanted to see what you had out here, too." Why was she reacting this way? "Isn't all this stuff for sale?"

"It's going to be. Most of it." She stroked the side of blade carefully with her finger even as she stared at me.

"I saw the *Open* flag and prices up front, and I thought you were open for business." I had to keep this normal. Or try to.

"We'll be open when we're ready."

Why was the barn flying an *Open* flag? We were getting into crazy territory here. I swallowed down the thick feeling in my throat. "Why don't you go ahead and put that chopper down?"

She blinked and looked down at the chopper as if she didn't know how it got into her hand. She set it down.

I let out a breath. Close one.

"We're still getting set up." She frowned. "What were you taking a picture of?"

Busted. "This nice array of stuff." I edged toward the front.

Should I confront her now that she seemed more normal? No. Not in the dark back of a barn with a woman who had gone a bit *Psycho* on me. Nobody knew I was here. And it was only an antique grater. A purloined, pretty antique grater hidden as if on purpose. It made me wonder what else Hattie was hiding back here.

CHAPTER 17

Lou and I dismounted our bikes in front of Adele's house at a little past three. I was panting.

"That wind was coming straight at us," I said. "Looks like it might rain later." Ash-colored clouds rolled in from the west.

"We were riding uphill, too." She unclipped her helmet and hung it from a handlebar. She snapped her fingers. "I just remembered. Len wanted me to ask you about working in your restaurant. He's interested in learning how to cook professionally."

Did I want someone else in our kitchen? "Can I think about it? I'd love to help him out. But the three of us are a pretty well-oiled machine these days, and I'm afraid a fourth person might get in the way."

"I hear you."

"Let me talk to my team, okay?" I removed my helmet, too.

"Sure."

I'd opened my mouth to ask her about Len when Adele appeared around the side of the cottage, holding a trowel. That conversation would have to wait.

"Hey, there, girls," Adele said. "Glad you made it. Some wind, ain't it?"

"It sure is." I bussed my aunt's cheek. "I'm glad I wore long pants and a windbreaker."

Lou, not even breathing hard, greeted my aunt. "I made sure Robbie got a good workout."

I was in good shape, but superathlete Lou left me in the proverbial dust.

"Why, that's dandy," Adele said. "I baked us up some goodies. Come on the heck in."

We leaned our bikes against the low split rail fence that surrounded the flower garden in front. In the summer it turned into a tangled riot of color. Right now it was a lovely mix of bulbs in bloom, a bright pink azalea, and lilac buds getting ready to pop their purple scents into the world. We followed Adele in the side door.

A couple of minutes later we sat around Adele's worn kitchen table. A spread of fresh bread, butter, and slices of a blueberry cake filled the middle of the table and we each had mugs of hot cinnamon-spice tea.

"Anybody want to top up their tea with a splash of fun, be my guest." Adele poured a little Four Roses bourbon—the fun in question—into her mug, then sat back.

"Hey, it's downhill all the back to town, right?" Lou grinned and poured for herself, then held the bottle over my mug.

I nodded. "Why not? It's my day off." I took a sip. I set my mug down and patted my lap. "Come sit with me, Chloe." Adele's über-sweet white cat jumped onto my lap and settled into her characteristic loud purr. The woodstove radiated warmth, as did the weathered face of my aunt. I'd been coming here to visit since I was little, when my mom and I would spend vacations with Adele. In the half-dozen years since I'd lived in Indiana, Adele and her sheep farm had become my anchor.

"We heared the news about poor Ward," Adele began.

"I feel awful about his death," I said.

"What?" Lou asked. "Who is Ward? Did he die after eating your food?"

"He's a gentleman who ate a mushroom omelet at the store yesterday morning," I began, then told her about others getting sick and Mr. Ward dying.

"That's awful," Lou said.

Adele nodded.

"Seems someone might have planted toxic mushrooms in my food order." I scrunched up my nose. "What I don't know is why. Adele, is Samuel here?"

"No, but we can get him on the horn." She punched a number on her house phone and clicked it into speaker mode.

After some preliminaries, I asked, "Samuel, does Mr. Ward have family?"

"He does, God rest his soul, but his son and family live in Cincinnati, and his daughter is up in Kalamazoo with her kids. Jeremiah's wife passed some years ago."

"I would love to send them a card and flowers, or a donation. Does your church have their address?"

"I will look into that for you, dear," Samuel said. "You

know, he was suffering from liver cancer. I believe his life was not fated to last much longer, regardless. You must not blame yourself."

Liver cancer. I'd been right about him being ill. No wonder his skin was yellow.

I swallowed. "But I'm still responsible."

"You know, hon," Adele chimed in. "My scanner confirmed that some other folks fell ill, all due to them mushrooms, or whatever it was."

Adele and her police scanner, which she'd refused to relinquish after she left the position of South Lick fire chief.

"It's true. Including Buck, but not seriously," I said. "He said he has an iron stomach. Anyway, Wanda and her department will investigate. She took the box the mushrooms came in and some other food items. The board of health closed my restaurant, of course."

"That's no good," Adele said. "For how long?"

"I don't know. I wish I did." I swallowed. "Thanks, Samuel," I said. "I'm glad neither of you ate the mushrooms."

Adele said she was, too, and told Samuel she'd see him later before disconnecting.

"To change the subject, we rode by lambs cavorting in your field," Lou said. "Do you keep them, or do they turn into dinners?"

"Some of both," Adele said. "I proposed a roast lamb for the wedding, but Robbie here said that would be too close to home."

I shook my head. "Way too close. A pig will be fine, Adele."

My aunt chortled. "So what all we got to talk about

today, celebration-wise? You have your dress and shoes, Roberta. The pig is ordered, along with the guy who is going to roast it."

Adele was the only person who called me by my legal name, which I got because of my father, Roberto.

"The caterer is all set for everything else," Lou said.

"Abe told met the band is looking forward to playing in the barn," I said. "They'll need to come out the week before and check out final logistics."

"Good," Adele said. "I heard from Roberto and Maria, and they're all set with tickets and whatnot."

My father and his wife, who lived in Pisa, Italy. "I'm so glad they're coming. And I've hired the bus to shuttle people from South Lick out here and back."

At a bark outside the screen door, Adele rose to let in Sloopy, her border collie.

"Hey, Sloops," I said. When he yipped and trotted over, Chloe leapt off my lap. *Ouch.* Claws and stretch riding pants weren't a good combination.

"Didn't you say you had an idea for centerpieces, Robbie?" Lou asked.

"I do, and I had a thought about a corsage for this guy, too." I stroked Sloopy's head until he lay next to my chair and went to sleep. We spent the next twenty minutes hammering out all the month-before details. I finished off two pieces of bread and butter. I gave in to the blueberry cake, too.

"Adele, is this all butter?" I asked. The cake was rich and smooth and not too sweet.

"Well, hon, it is a pound cake. Pound of butter, pound of flour, pound of sugar, pound of eggs. I didn't go quite that far, but it's good, ain't it?"

"Yes, ma'am." Lou nodded as she popped in her last piece.

I caught sight of a box grater next to Adele's stove and frowned.

"Why the frown?" she asked me.

"How well do you know Hattie Sand?" I asked her.

"I've known her for a long time, but we ain't close. Why?"

"Remember that set of graters I bought Saturday?"

"'Course."

"I displayed them in the store Saturday after we got back, and yesterday they all went missing."

Lou's eyes widened. "You mean somebody stole them?"

"Maybe." I took a minute and explained about Hattie and Francis opening the antique store. "They both ate lunch with Corrine in Pans 'N Pancakes yesterday, and Hattie spent some time browsing the cookware before she sat down. I checked out their store and barn this morning."

"Lemme guess," Adele said. "You up and found them graters in the store."

"Well, in the back of the barn, but yes, on their property. Hattie surprised me right after I'd taken a picture of the most distinctive one, the box grater with the green Bakelite handle. I know it was mine. It was like she was sneaking up on me, and she looked furious. She grabbed a big, sharp chopper in a threatening way."

Adele whistled. "She's a little bit of a thing, but that's one lethal weapon."

"What did you do?" Lou stared at me.

"I guess I talked her down. After a second she put it back and looked kind of bewildered at herself."

"That's Harriet, all right." Adele nodded knowingly.

"Harriet?" I asked.

"Sure. We growed up together. Harriet Shaber, she was back then. She's always had this itty-bitty stealing problem. She actually served a bit of a sentence for larceny. I thought she'd hit the straight and narrow once she shacked up with old Francis about twenty years ago."

Apparently not.

"Do they still call it kleptomania?" I asked.

"No." Lou shook her head. "It has some official name now. Probably *compulsive stealing disorder* or something like that."

"I know it's an illness," Adele said. "In my experience? Once a klepto, always a klepto."

CHAPTER 18

I surveyed the contents of the walk-in cooler after I got home from Adele's at about six. I wished I knew how long I'd be closed. I'd asked Inspector Lake, but she'd declined to say.

The eggs would keep for a while. Actually, almost everything in here would, and now it didn't matter about not having potatoes and mustard. Things like lettuce and peppers would be okay for a few days. Even though the bread might get stale, it wouldn't spoil. I'd already shifted any meat to the freezer. Customers had eaten half the cupcakes, and I could give the rest to Abe for him and Sean. I shivered from the cold, picked up the only open gallon of milk, and shut the door behind me with the satisfying *clunk* of the heavy latch.

"Birdy, come here." I poured a little milk in a saucer and set it on the floor, then stashed the gallon in the small under-counter fridge. I'd take it back to my apartment when I was done in the restaurant and use it for cereal or even a soufflé. "Milk, kitty," I called when my cat didn't materialize.

Birdy sauntered over from wherever he'd been, stopping to lick an urgently needed area on a rear paw. I wandered around the store, neatening a display of hats here, moving a cake pan there. Mostly I felt at loose ends. Normally I'd be doing breakfast prep right now. But I wouldn't be serving breakfast tomorrow morning at seven.

I sank into the chair at my desk and thought about poor Mr. Ward. Dead from eating an omelet he hadn't even ordered for himself. Dead from being a gentleman for swapping meals, for being a man who loved mushrooms. In truth, likely also dead because he was already ill. No one else had expired from ingesting the mushrooms, thank goodness. But I still felt his death press down on my spirit. His children must be mourning. His grandkids missing their Peepaw, an affectionate nickname for grandfathers around here.

Slouching in the chair, I idly scrolled through a few emails on my phone. Birdy hopped up on my lap. He was always happy to find me sitting down and immobile. I checked the store's Facebook page.

We also needed to tell people we were closed tomorrow. And the day after and the day after. *No.* I was determined to take this one day at a time.

Pans 'N Pancakes closed on Tuesday due to circumstances beyond our control. Check this page for updates.

I copied the message, then posted it. I located my standard picture of the front of the store and posted that to Instagram, pasting in the same words to go with it, plus a few of the obligatory hashtags. I couldn't do much more than that.

Bang. I sat up straight. More bangs. Someone pounded at the front door. Who could that be? Six o'clock, well after our normal—and clearly posted—closing time. And the big, honking orange poster should have scared anybody away. Where I sat, I was out of sight of the glass in the door. I crept along the side of the restaurant and peeked out a front window, which was mostly hidden by the drinks cooler in front of it.

Orland Krueger stood on the covered porch, hand raised to pound again, a dripping fedora-type hat on his head. He'd looked menacing even at lunch Sunday. Now? I could be wrong, but he sure looked upset. He knocked with enough force to rattle the door, and that was saying something. It was a heavy old antique piece of beautifully worked wood, with *heavy* being the key word.

No way was I opening my store to an apparently angry man way taller and bigger than I was. No possible way.

CHAPTER 19

Rain pelted the windows at eight-thirty that night. The storm clouds I'd seen had blown in fast, and the rain now seemed to be hunkering down in my part of the southern Midwest. The sun didn't officially set until now, but I'd already had the lights on for an hour.

After I'd calmed my nerves from Orland's furious knocking earlier, I'd come back here to my apartment, locking the door to the restaurant behind me. So far I'd changed into yoga pants and an oversized sweatshirt, eaten a plate of Sean's lasagna, played with Birdy, and done a crossword puzzle. I'd also texted Abe even though I knew he was at work.

Come for dinner tomorrow night? Want to see you and talk about stuff.

As soon as I sent the message, I remembered he had Sean Tuesday nights. *Shoot.* I loved Sean's company, but

Abe and I wouldn't be able to talk as freely. I yawned. I could go to bed, but eight-thirty was early even for me, and my alarm wouldn't be going off at five-thirty tomorrow morning to open the restaurant.

I poured a couple of fingers of Four Roses into my nightcap glass and sat on the couch, tucking my feet up next to me. Birdy made short work of nestling in on my other side. When he'd first showed up outside my back door and adopted me, I tried to pull him on my lap. He made it clear he preferred to snuggle next to my thigh. I wasn't complaining. Any respectable cat ordered its life to suit itself, not the resident human.

I could suit myself by researching Orland Krueger, a man I needed to know more about. I reached over to where I'd left my phone on the coffee table and managed not to disturb my kitty. I poked and thumbed and swiped. The search was made easier by Orland having a unique name. Mr. Google didn't turn up anyone but our local, heavy-browed Krueger. He was originally from Minneapolis and had an undergraduate degree in music. But he'd also played basketball. He was indeed a cobweb rig, although he looked too heavy now to move agilely on a basketball court.

Searching on, I read that he'd taught music at a private Indianapolis high school. That he'd bought a small ranch house in Zionsville about ten years ago. And that he'd run for mayor of the north-of-Indy suburb, but lost the race. How he ended up buying a food supply business in Brown County? Or meeting Krystal Sand? That I couldn't discover.

I wondered if Abe had ever run into Orland among the local bluegrass circuits. One more thing to ask him tomorrow. While I was poking around, I might as well see what I could learn about Krystal herself. Turner had mentioned a Krystal in his culinary class. Unlike Orland's, her name wasn't unique, although it wasn't common. I did learn that she'd graduated from IU Bloomington with a degree in business, and that she'd participated in a Young Entrepreneurs program in Indy some years ago. And that was all I could find.

I set down my phone and switched off the lamp. Outside, the wind in the trees must be setting off the motion-detector light at my back door. Dark shapes waved in the illumination. Skeletal fingers scratched at the window. I knew they were branches, but I shuddered, nevertheless.

Ill-intentioned people—villains, that is, otherwise known as bad guys—had tried to invade my personal space more than once since I'd moved in. Someone adept with lock picks had broken into my store to leave a body and later attacked me in the walk-in. A crazed person came after me with one of my own vintage kitchen implements—a lethally sharp one. A desperate murderer had traversed a hidden tunnel that led to the second floor to recover a possession from long ago.

I had tight windows and new, secure locks, and the tunnel had long since been securely blocked off. If someone got past all that, my sole defenses were my wits, muscles, and cell phone. Lots of people in this region, including my aunt, owned guns for self-defense. I wasn't one. To me, it seemed like a recipe for trouble.

The scratching didn't let up. Was someone outside now? But who? The person who maliciously included toxic mushrooms in my delivery, maybe. One of the four in the Krueger-Sand clan? I shook my head. It was an extreme stretch to imagine any of them doing something so nefarious. Still, any reputable food service would only use reputable sources of farmed or wild mushrooms. Someone out to get me—or Adele—had apparently delivered poisonous fungi. Wanda had to be on the case. At least I hoped so.

The tall case clock ticked in the dark. And ticked. And ticked. I stared. Was it glowing? I could swear it was. Maybe I'd never sat in the dark with it. The numbers and the arrow-shaped tips of the hands emitted a faint green light.

A clock's ticking should be comforting. This one had kept time for more than a century. Life had continued, second by second, minute by minute, hour by hour, since forever. Why did I find the relentless *tick-tock* threatening? Why did my pulse beat too fast in my neck? I tried to time it, but my clammy fingers slipped. My throat was too thick to—

Bam. A loud crash sounded near the back door. I screamed. Birdy leapt off the couch and raced into my bedroom. I grabbed my phone and rushed into the kitchen. I hunched down and crept into the back hall, where the outside light shone in through the pane of glass in the door. I raised my head to peer out. I collapsed back onto my rear end.

A big limb had split off the nearest birch tree. It lay across my back walk. No human had caused the noise. I was safe.

I didn't care what time it was. I was going to bed. I planned to sleep with a pillow over my head and a cat on my feet. Enough with the suspense, already.

CHAPTER 20

Eight-fifteen in the morning shouldn't be too early to reach a human in a public office, but nobody had picked up. "Please call me back." I left my number for the county Board of Health and jabbed the disconnect icon. In old movies I'd seen characters slam down the receiver when they were unhappy with a call. Such an act must have been infinitely satisfying. Poking an icon on a little screen didn't have anywhere near the same effect.

I needed to know when I could reopen, when I could return to making and serving food. When my store could resume its important function as the community watercooler—and pay for my employees' and my wages at the same time.

I stared at my phone. Maybe the sheriff's office was the authority who would decide, not the health inspector.

I happened to have Wanda's personal number on speed dial. Our relationship had become a lot more cordial in the last year than it had been when I'd first met her. I hoped she wouldn't mind my not going through official channels.

Except she didn't answer my call, either. I swore to myself, then left a similar message as I had for the Board of Health. "Wanda, I need to know when I can open my restaurant again. Please call me. Thanks."

I paced my little living room. I'd whipped up a dozen whole-wheat blueberry muffins at seven this morning, simply because not cooking didn't seem right. I couldn't open the restaurant, but I was happier when I was busy. Maybe I should start packing for my move to Abe's. That task didn't seem urgent, though. In a way, all I had to bring was clothes, plus Birdy in a cat carrier and his food and litter box. I already kept a toothbrush and basic cosmetics at Abe's, since I frequently spent the night. And I wasn't in a hurry to clear out my apartment. I planned to leave essential furnishings here, anyway.

Instead, I poured a second cup of coffee in the kitchen and carried it to my laptop. I wasn't interested in continuing with the FH food supply company. It was possible the toxic mushrooms had been a mistake. Maybe that was why Orland came by yesterday, to tell me how it happened. I didn't care. I shuddered to remember his stormy expression. Other businesses must exist to supply small restaurants like mine. My fingers flew on the keyboard as I searched.

I found two that looked promising and filled out their contact forms. Where else could I wander on the Internet? I traveled to where Turner had gone on Sunday, to the

Krueger-Sand wedding at the Story Inn. The article in the *Brown County Democrat* society section was short, but included an interesting nugget at the end.

Later in the evening the groom and another man became involved in an altercation. It was resolved without incident. The couple was due to leave for their honeymoon in Vermont the next morning.

Orland Krueger in an altercation on his wedding night? I wasn't surprised, but maybe I wasn't being fair. I didn't know the man. I'd only met him once, and I might have misinterpreted his expression yesterday. One of the wedding guests could have turned argumentative. Orland wasn't necessarily to blame.

I heard knocking at my back door. I would have been alarmed if my phone hadn't also indicated an incoming text. I swiped it open to read that Buck was at the door and hurried to let him in.

"Buck, good morning. Do you want to come in?" I gazed at his face, which looked worried, and at the sunny day behind him, with cardinals calling and finches flitting in the trees. A study in contrasts.

Hat in hand, he waited a moment to speak. "All righty, if you don't mind. But I won't stay."

I led him into the kitchen. "Coffee? And I made blueberry muffins, if you have time."

He rolled his eyes. "You know me too dang well, Robbie."

I laughed. "Sit down. The coffee won't take a minute." I set two muffins—I did know him, and one wouldn't be enough—a knife, and my orange Fiestaware butter dish in front of him. I ground beans and flipped the switch on my four-cup drip machine. I sat, too. "What's going on?"

He swallowed. "Seems the Ward family wants to press

charges. The district attorney is pushing for negligent homicide."

"Against the food supplier. Good. They should be more
careful."

"No, Robbie. Against you."

I stared. "Me?" My voice rose to a near shriek. "Buck,
that's crazy. I didn't know those mushrooms were toxic.
Why aren't they charging FH Foods?" He couldn't be serious. Could he? Sure, ultimately I was responsible for
the food we served, which was why we were so meticu-
lous about cleaning. And why I'd thought I was using a
reputable food service.

The coffee machine sizzled and dripped. Birdy hopped
onto Buck's lap.

"Seriously," I continued. "I feel terrible that the man
died, but I didn't even know him."

"I know it don't make sense. But you and me, we've
been friends for a while now. I wanted to give you a
heads-up. You might should find yourself a lawyer."

"Are you kidding?"

He wagged his head back and forth with a baleful
look. "And by the way, the lab results came back. It was,
in fact, the mushrooms what killed him."

I paced to the door and back. "Is Oscar on the case?"

"Nope. Because the county Board of Health's involved, it's the sheriff's business."

"Detective Henderson?"

"Noperoo. Not her, neither. Anne's off on maternity
leave."

"Who's handling it?" I asked.

"My dear cousin happens to be in charge."

Wanda. I'd been right.

CHAPTER 21

I called Corrine and asked her for a criminal lawyer recommendation. In my several brushes with murder over the last few years, I'd never needed a lawyer for myself. As mayor, Danna's mom no longer practiced law, but she still held the license, and more important, she knew everyone. She'd promised to get back to me with a name.

"But lemme tell you what I think, hon," she said. "That charge is gonna be dropped sooner than a blacksmith's hot iron. It ain't goin' nowhere. Mark my words. I never heard of such a ridiculous claim as you being negligent. Heck, they might as well charge my girl and young Rao into the bargain. It's all hogwash."

"From your mouth to the judge's ear," I replied. I would believe it when the charge was dropped and not a minute before.

I suited up for another bike ride and pedaled south toward Story. For most of the ride I fumed about what Buck had told me. Negligent homicide, indeed. I felt terrible for Mr. Ward's children, to lose their father before his time, even though the illness might have taken him soon, anyway. But how was I supposed to know bad mushrooms had been delivered? After Buck left, I'd spent a little more quality time with the internet and discovered that criminal negligence meant "acting with conscious disregard of the risk of death." So negligent homicide was disregarding a cause of death I had no way of knowing about. What was I supposed to do? Taste every food that ever came into my store?

Unclipping my bike shoes, I dismounted in front of the Story Inn, then checked my phone. I'd left at nine-thirty, and the seventeen miles had taken me about an hour and a half. Although the food truck seemed to be parked permanently in front of the antique store, oddly KK's hadn't seemed open when I cycled by. How could Krystal advertise breakfast and not be doing business at nine-thirty? I couldn't guess.

I clomped up the couple of steps past flower boxes brimming with tulips in all hues. The two ancient gas pumps still stood sentinel, as rusty as ever with their squat crowns of lights. Yesterday's rain had blown through, leaving today looking fresh and clean, with a sunny breeze and cool temperatures.

I popped my head inside the former general store. Unlike my restaurant, this one served lunch and dinner. I picked up the delicious scents of meat, herbs, and I wasn't sure what else. A white-aproned woman laid silverware on a square table.

She glanced my way. "Help you? We don't open 'til eleven-thirty." She spoke with a classic southern Hoosier twang.

"I wondered if I could talk to the person in charge of weddings here?"

"That'd be Georgia. Keep going down the road a piece 'til you hit the function barn." She gestured vaguely to her right. "She's around there somewheres."

I thanked her and turned for the door. My step slowed when I spied the wall lined with vintage cookware, tomato cans with colorful labels, a washboard, even a vintage mailbox. I scolded myself and kept going. Their antiques were part of the decor, not for sale. And I'd ridden down here for more than the exercise.

I swilled a few gulps of water from the bottle clipped onto the cycle's down tube before wheeling my bike back along the small road between the dozen small buildings that had been homes and shops a hundred years earlier. Now they were all either lodgings or offices for the inn, which owned the entire former town.

By the time I reached a large wooden structure on my right, all that stretched ahead was a patch of woods with a canopy of branches reaching over the lane. In the era when the town was thriving, Story Road was a throughway to Bloomington to the west. In the mid-sixties, Lake Monroe reservoir was created by damming a creek south of the college town, which filled the valley northeast of the dam. These days if you kept going on the lane you'd eventually walk into water.

A great blue heron beat its wide, strong wings slowly overhead on its way to fish in the reservoir for the day. My bike safely leaning against the outer wall of the function barn, I peered into the building, which was open on one side with wide steps leading up to it. The rafters soared to a peak above, and large windows splashed the wooden floor with light. The barn boards looked pre-weathered. At the back a door was open to a small room, where a woman sat at a desk facing away from me. Her puffy blond hair fell above her shoulders.

"Excuse me," I called as I clomped over the floor toward her. "Are you Georgia?"

Startled, she whirled in her chair, then gaped. "Robbie?"

Georgia turned out to be Georgia LaRue, someone I'd last seen working as a South Lick library aide.

"Hi, Georgia. Do you work here now?" I asked. Now that I thought about it, she hadn't visited the restaurant in a while. She used to come alone at noontime with a book to keep her company over lunch.

"I do. The position opened up last summer, and it pays better than the library. Have a seat." She gestured to another chair. "What can I help you with? Are you finally marrying that handsome brother of Don's?" She had a romantic relationship with Don O'Neill, who ran the South Lick hardware store, but they'd kept it quiet until recently. Georgia's husband had passed away this winter after living with severe dementia for several years in a nursing home.

Smiling, I sat. "I am, but that's not why I stopped by. I heard you had a big wedding here last fall. Krueger and Sand?"

"We did, and it was big, all right." She pressed her lips together and frowned. "It was the first one I ran solo. Trial by fire, Robbie."

"In what way?"

"Well, first, they'd invited two hundred people. Who

even knows two hundred people? We rented an enormous tent, set it up right out front." She pointed to the field in front of the event barn's open wall. "They wanted a sit-down dinner, a live band, an open bar, the works."

"You had a lot of logistics to organize."

"That I did. Thing is, those people were impossible. But the boss said to accommodate them. We use their food wholesale business in the inn, so . . ." She spread her hands. "Krystal is Mr. Sand's only kid, and they wanted to do it up right."

I'd been correct about the couple not having other children.

"And Jan," she went on. "Sheesh. You know, Abe's ex?"

Jan? "What did she have to do with the wedding?" I asked.

"She's Krueger's sister."

My eyes popped wide open. "She is?" I'd had no idea what her maiden name was. When I thought back to when I'd met Jan, I remembered she'd been tall.

"Yepperoo. Guess you didn't know. Anyhoo, their parents have gone on ahead."

I smiled to myself at the local euphemism for dying.

"Jan pulled the worst kind of mother-of-the-groom behavior, except she's the sister, not the mother." Georgia crossed her legs and smoothed the cloth of her dark slacks. "Orland's twin sister, no less."

Twins. *Wow.*

"And everybody knows the bride's family is supposed to run the wedding, not the groom's," Georgia said.

True. In my case, I had asked Abe's mom, Freddy, to be as involved in our festivities as she wanted. She was a classical cellist and had offered to bring her string quartet to play before the ceremony. Abe and I had been delighted at the suggestion. Freddy also quilted. She was busy making small mats for the table centerpieces to go on. So far she hadn't been a mother-of-the-groomzilla in the least.

"Krystal's mom also passed, and she didn't seem to care for her stepmom much," Georgia added.

"Since Krystal's mother is deceased, maybe Jan felt it was her place," I said. "I didn't know she and Orland were twins or even related."

"They are, and they seemed to really like each other. They were joking and dancing together and generally getting along every time I saw them. Not all siblings do. But boy, did Orland ever get into a fight with one of the guests. Man has a temper on him."

"That's not good. Do you know what it was about?" I asked.

"No. I stayed well out of it, and a couple of guys got them separated." Georgia tilted her head. "Why are you interested in that wedding?"

I supposed she might well ask. "Some kind of bad stuff is going on lately. The Sands opened an antique store across the street from me, complete with antique cookware. Krystal has a breakfast and lunch food truck out front of it, which is in direct competition with my restaurant. Orland Krueger took over the Sands' food service business, and it's the one I use for the restaurant. And a man died from eating mushrooms I served in omelets on Sunday."

"How terrible." She frowned. "Were the mushrooms delivered by Krueger's outfit?"

"Exactly. And now the Board of Health has closed the restaurant."

Georgia whistled. "I can surely see why you want

more info about that gang. Francis sure did dote on his little girl, the bride. But do you think one of the family did it on purpose? The bad mushrooms, I mean."

"I have no idea." Right now I wasn't feeling too encouraged about being able to find out, either. Jan seemed like more of a loose cannon that I had realized. Was she trying to prevent Abe and me from marrying?

Georgia leaned over and patted my knee. "Robbie, you're smarter than anyone I know. I've seen your puzzle brain in action. You'll figure it out." The phone on her desk rang. "You stop by any time now, hear?"

"Thanks. I will." I tried to keep my stiff-soled bike shoes from making too much noise as I made my way out.

"Story Inn weddings and events, Georgia speaking."

I glanced back to see her give me a wave. I wasn't feeling anywhere near as confident as Georgia had been that I would get to the bottom of this fiasco.

CHAPTER 22

I pushed myself riding back. A good, hard ride was the only way to temporarily clear my mind of wretched thoughts. I flew by the poor, vandalized Stone Head statue, who'd had his head with its inscrutable *Mona Lisa* expression stolen one too many times. I passed the covered bridge that was no longer open to cars. I cycled past peas and spinach coming up in a large home garden on one side and gazed on the other side into the woods that were part of Brown County State Park.

Before turning left on Route 46, I paused, setting my foot down. I could turn right and get myself a world-famous Original Gnaw Bone Tenderloin sandwich. I wasn't sure if it was actually world-famous, but the sandwich definitely rocked deliciousness. I still had a few miles to go, though, and pushed on as soon as the route was clear.

It was after one o'clock when I pedaled slowly down

Main Street in South Lick. Once again, a line for Krystal's food truck had formed on the sidewalk in front of the Sands' antique store. The smell of something frying tickled my nostrils and made my stomach gurgle. I'd burned plenty of calories. I might as well get a so-called sando and check out the opposition's cooking at the same time.

I left my bike on the front porch of my store. The hefty woman at the end of the line was about Abe's height and wore a sweater that strained over her back. She turned at the sound of my bike shoes on the pavement. I blinked.

"Jan?" I smiled. "You might not remember me, but we met last—"

"Hi, Robbie." She didn't return my smile. "Of course, I remember you. Abe's fiancée." She clamped her mouth shut as if she was about to say more and common courtesy told her not to. The sun brought out red highlights in her light hair, cut in a stylish ear-length bob that fell around a puffy face. She carried a large quilted bag with an old-looking quilt peeking out the top, a bag that resembled Hattie's big bag.

"Are you here to try out your sister-in-law's cooking?" I kept a smile plastered on my face. Abe had said Jan wasn't happy about our wedding, and I didn't want to get her back up.

Jan looked a little taken aback that I knew Krystal was her sister-in-law, but she didn't pursue it. "She's a good cook. Are you here to check out the competition?" Her tone was snarky.

"I just rode nearly forty miles, and I'm hungry." The answer about checking out the competition was, "Yes," but I wasn't about to let her engage me. "It smelled so good when I rode up, I couldn't resist."

"She's planning on opening a restaurant next year," Jan said.

Good. Then she would move her truck. The three people in front of the window turned away holding sandwiches wrapped in white paper and open bottles of soda. They perched on the stone wall a little way down and began to unwrap their meals. Jan stepped forward, gazing at the short menu next to the window.

"What can I get you, Jan?" Krystal leaned her elbows on the counter.

"Give me a fried catfish, okay, with extra chips? And a root beer. I'll eat here, so a boat is fine."

Fried catfish. I groaned silently. A special I planned to offer as soon as I could. Well, anybody had the right to fry up catfish. And a "boat" must mean an open cardboard container, not wrapped to go. Not something I had to deal with in my restaurant.

"You got it," she told Jan.

I took a step forward.

Krystal spied me and straightened. "Robbie? Are you here for food or to harass me some more?"

Jan faced me, eyes wide. "You harassed Krystal?"

"I did not." I let out a breath. "I asked her if she had a food permit and how long she would be parked here. Krystal, I'm sorry if you felt harassed. That wasn't my intention."

"Your restaurant is closed now, isn't it?" Krystal folded her arms. "You don't see any orange Board of Health posters on my truck."

"I seriously only came to get a sandwich. I'm hungry and it smells great." I held up both palms. "If you don't want to serve me, that's fine."

"A sale's a sale, right?" Jan murmured to her sister-in-law.

Krystal pressed her lips together and looked away. She unfolded her arms and focused on me again. "All right, what do you want?"

I ran my gaze down the menu. "A meatball grinder, please. With the works."

"Anything to drink?" Krystal asked.

"No, thanks."

Inside, Krystal turned her back to prepare the sandwiches. Jan poked and swiped on her phone. She looked up at me.

"I understand you and Abe are going to tie the knot soon."

"We are." I wanted to tell her Sean had given me his blessing. But she must know that. She must have asked him how he felt about his dad remarrying. Or maybe not. I had asked Abe if he wanted to ask Jan to the wedding. He'd said she would probably consider it a slap in the face, so we hadn't sent her an invitation.

"I wish you, uh, many years of happiness." She almost started to say something else, then once again closed her mouth.

"Thank you so much." I pointed to her bag. "Abe told me you repair antique quilts. Is that one of them? Are the Sands going to offer it for sale?"

"I *restore* them. It's different."

"How so?"

She cast her gaze skyward and tossed her head. "You wouldn't understand. But to answer your question, yes. My brother's in-laws are going to sell the quilts I bring back to life."

"Using your hands to restore old objects to their former beauty must provide a nice counterweight to working on a computer all day." I worked with my hands to create works of culinary beauty and yumminess. I couldn't imagine my livelihood depending on sitting still and staring at a screen day after day.

"One catfish, one meatball," Krystal announced, setting the food on the counter. "Jan, I've got yours covered. Robbie, that'll be nine-fifty." She set her fists on her hips, as if daring me to challenge the price that was nearly double what any other sandwich takeout place in the area charged.

As I reached around to the pocket in the back of my cycling jacket for my money, I glanced at the menu. No prices. *Huh*.

"Thanks, Krys." Jan stuck her two bags of chips in the quilted bag and picked up her sandwich boat and bottle of pop, as they called it around here. "Take it easy, Robbie."

As Jan headed around the corner of the store, Orland pulled into the driveway in a panel van labeled *FH Foods*. She waited for him as he climbed out.

"Hey, favorite bro." Jan held out her arms for a hug. "Did you miss me?"

"My twin big sister?" He hugged her in return. "Always. But don't think you being seven minutes older means anything."

"Only everything." Jan laughed and elbowed him. They both disappeared down the drive.

Glad he hadn't spied me, I picked up my wrapped lunch and tried to hand Krystal a ten-dollar bill. With flared nostrils, she scowled in the direction her husband and sister-in-law had gone. A crow screeched from the tall pine behind the antique store. An old pickup truck driving by clunked as it hit a pothole. Krystal switched her gaze to me. She folded her arms again and looked like she was about to speak.

A young couple in running clothes jogged up. "I'm so excited to have a food truck in town," the flushed-cheek woman said to the man she was with.

Krystal handed me my change as she smiled at the runners.

"Thank you," I said. I might have had more to say, too, now that Jan was gone. I wanted to ask her about Orland, and why he'd been pounding on my door yesterday. But now was not the time.

Krystal ignored my thanks, instead focusing on the couple. "Welcome to KK's Sandos. What can I get you?"

CHAPTER 23

As any chef does, I mentally dissected my meatball sandwich as I ate it in my apartment kitchen. The meatballs were well seasoned, but a little dry. The sauce seemed heavy on ketchup—pronounced *catch-up* around here—rather than marinara, and I would have used a crustier roll. The puffy one Krystal served the sandwich in was falling apart as I ate. But the cheese was real provolone, not American, and all the flavors ended up meshing well. I was too hungry to be picky.

I drained my glass of milk and went to shower off my biking exertions. With water flowing over me, I cursed out loud, realizing Corrine hadn't gotten back to me with the name of a lawyer. My outing and my visit to the food truck had nudged the words *negligent homicide* out of my brain. Now they flooded back in. Or had I not checked my phone? Maybe I didn't have to worry. Corrine had seemed positive the charge would be dropped. It was possible it already had, and that was why she hadn't messaged me the lawyer's name.

I rubbed shampoo suds into my plentiful hair with more vigor than I really needed. I wanted to be done with this shower and back at the lifeline that was my phone. Another thought rushed in. Orland Krueger was Sean's uncle. Had I talked with Abe about Orland? I knew I hadn't told him about Orland beating on my door yesterday. But had my guy ever even mentioned Sean's uncle on his mom's side? Maybe not. I wondered if Sean had been at the Story wedding. If Orland ended up being convicted of including the poisonous mushrooms in my order on purpose, Abe's son would have a criminal for an uncle.

I rinsed my hair and applied conditioner, a requirement for long, curly locks like mine. I hoped Orland wasn't the bad guy. But if he wasn't, that left Francis. Or Hattie. Or Krystal. Or . . . Jan?

I again swore out loud. Sean's mom a criminal? That would be awful for him. I rinsed out the conditioner, switched off the water, and stepped out. Still, unlike in some of the previous murders, this one seemed like an attempt to discredit me and my restaurant, rather than intentional homicide. That is, first-degree murder.

Five minutes later, in leggings and a cotton sweater, I brushed out my hair, shook it, and fluffed it with my fingers. I had neither energy nor need to style these curls. They did what they did, and I dealt with it. Exactly like I was about to deal with my current predicament.

A trip to Nashville was the first step. I needed to talk with Wanda and thought I would pick up a couple of steaks at Tuckaway Butchery to grill for dinner. *Wait.* I frowned. Abe hadn't replied about my dinner invitation. I checked my phone and exclaimed. Three new texts had popped up during my shower.

Abe wrote asking if it was okay to bring Sean for dinner, to which I replied, **Always.**

I swiped open Corrine's text.

Ted Greaney is the best. He's waiting for your call. He's there til 5.

She included the number. I texted back a quick thanks, then took a deep breath and called him.

After we got basic greetings out of the way, I said, "South Lick police lieutenant Buck Bird said the county sheriff's office was going to charge me with negligent homicide." I told him about the mushrooms. "But I don't think I have been. I mean, nobody has come by, that I know of, or called me in. What do you think I should do?"

"You have some options." His voice was low and gravelly. "You can engage me to make inquiries."

"May I ask what that would cost me?" I didn't know how long my restaurant would be closed. I wanted a good lawyer if I needed one, but I didn't have unlimited money at hand.

He cited an hourly rate that made me choke.

"But it might be best to sit tight and wait," he added. "It's a bit like the proverbial hornet's nest. Don't stir it up if you don't have to."

"Okay. But I can call on you if I am charged?"

"I'm happy to help."

"Can I ask you a question?"

He cleared his throat. "At your service."

"Why would they charge me and not the company who delivered poisonous mushrooms to me?"

"It's possible they are pursuing separate charges against the supplier."

I hadn't thought of that. "Thank you. I won't keep you. I'll let you know either way."

"Please. If you hear they are withholding the charge, I'd like to know."

"What will I owe you for this call?" I cringed, waiting for his answer.

"Not a cent. You're a friend of Corrine's, and anyway, I always offer a free initial consultation."

Whew. "Thank you."

We said our goodbyes and disconnected. "Don't disturb the hornet's nest." I was entirely capable of following that advice. My tense shoulders felt lighter. I guess I didn't need to pay Wanda a visit, after all.

I swiped open the last text. And groaned. It was from Wanda.

Was looking for you earlier. Please stop by the Nashville sheriff's barracks at your earliest convenience.

My relief landed in the wastebasket with a *thud.*

CHAPTER 24

My heart raced all the way to Nashville. It was only five miles away but took me twenty minutes to get to the county seat because of the winding, two-lane road. I pulled into a parking space in the nearly empty lot a few rows back from the Brown County Law Enforcement Center, but I stayed frozen in my seat. I'd never been inside the two-winged building, and I didn't want to do this alone.

I scolded myself. "Who's going to hold your hand?" I said out loud. I had no desire to go running to Abe, and I wasn't about to call—and pay for—Ted Greaney if I didn't have to.

I opened the door to my little Prius, but once my feet hit the pavement, I sat without budging. What was wrong with me? I'd never been a shrinking violet. Never held back from doing all the hard things. I had bought my own property, done my own renovations, brought to life my dream of owning a restaurant. I'd confronted murderers, for goodness sake. And now I didn't want to go in and talk with a friendly detective?

No, I told myself. I don't. I sat and watched a red-shouldered hawk alight in a pignut hickory tree across the busy state road. It flapped its wings before settling into the classic, nearly upright stance of raptors. The wind blew a cloud over the three o'clock sun as if to match my dark mood.

I blew out a breath. Maybe I had a choice here. I found Wanda's text and thumbed a message.

Am in the sheriff's parking lot. Do I have to go in?

I sent it. And waited. And waited some more.

A sheriff's SUV pulled into the lot. The brown vehicle with the gold five-pointed star on the door slowed as it passed me, then nosed into the row closest to the building. Two men in brown uniform shirts and tan pants climbed out; one burly, one lean. The burly one strolled over to me.

"Can I help you with anything, miss?" He set one hand on his thick duty belt. He held his other arm away from his body in that position all officers of the peace seemed to love.

"No, thanks. I'm waiting for Wanda." I was about to make up a story about how she was bringing me something but closed my mouth at the last minute. Never lie to an officer of the law.

"What's your name? I'll tell Sergeant Bird you're here."

"Robbie Jordan. Thank you. I'd appreciate it."

His dark eyebrows rose under his Smokey the Bear

hat, but he only nodded and followed his partner into the building.

Ugh. He'd recognized my name. That could be a bad sign. Where the heck was Wanda? I'd been waiting fifteen minutes. I'd give her five more, then I was so out of here. I glanced down at my phone. No new message. At a flash of light, I looked up.

Wanda pushed through the glass door, which had caught a ray of the reappeared sun. She hurried toward me.

"Sorry, Robbie." She sounded breathless. "I was on a call. Old George told me you were waiting for me."

I rose. "I texted you that I was out here."

"You did? Dang it. My cell's been acting up." She edged it out of the back pocket of her snug tan pants. She poked and swiped at the phone. "Welp, you sure enough did."

I waited for her to arrest me, or whatever she was going to do. "So, you said you wanted me to come in. I'm here."

"Oh, that." She batted at the air. "I shoulda canceled that request. Seems the magistrate says we ain't got cause to charge you with nothing."

A breath rushed out of me. I set a hand on the roof of my car so I didn't collapse. "You don't?"

"Nope. I was glad to hear it, too. They might be looking at action against the supplier, though. That's where it rightly belongs, IMHO."

In my humble opinion. I suppressed a nervous giggle at Wanda pronouncing the texting acronym out loud. Wanda's opinion had never been particularly humble, but right now I was relieved not to face criminal charges. Corrine had been right.

"Thank you," I said. "I'm free to go?"

"Yes, ma'am."

"Is anybody talking about the possibility that some-body had those mushrooms delivered to my restaurant on purpose?"

She stared at me. "You mean like to poison all your customers?"

"Sort of. What if somebody wanted me to have to close? Or was hoping to make my diners sick—or even kill one of them?"

"They surely accomplished that, didn't they? But you got a itty-bitty hole in that logic, you know. How would this supposed bad guy know that particular person would eat the mushrooms?"

"It's a stretch, I acknowledge that. But seriously, what if it was a crime and not an accident? Would that be your department or Buck's?"

"It'd be in South Lick's jurisdiction, I spose, with the help of the state police if they need them. You should know the drill. I've been involved up to now only be-cause the county health department is."

"I guess I'd better talk to Buck, then. Does my store have to stay closed?"

"That's up to the health inspector, Robbie. She'll let you know."

I looked at her more closely. Her uniform shirt didn't fit as tightly as it used to, and she had more definition in her round face.

"Have you lost weight, Wanda?" I must not have no-ticed in my restaurant because too much was going on.

"Yeah. It's a pain in the rear end, but I been hitting the gym every day and trying to watch my diet."

Right. She'd ordered her fritter the other day with salad instead of bread. "You look good. It's great you're thinking about your health. Keep up the good work."

"I got me a ways to go, but I have a purpose and a deadline." She uncharacteristically blushed. "Me and Oscar are getting hitched in September."

I almost gaped but caught myself. "I'm so happy to hear that." I reached out and hugged her, a first for us. "Congratulations." The state police detective was a bit older than she was, but I didn't know by how much. It was none of my business, anyway.

"I thank you." She stepped back, looking embarrassed. "Hear you and Abe are tying the knot next month. I might have to hit you up for some wedding tips."

"You can ask me anything. Can you join us at the wedding? We'd love to have you." I told her the date. "With Oscar, naturally. It'll be out at Adele's farm. A pig roast and barn dancing and everything." I hadn't invited her previously, because we'd never socialized, but our home-grown wedding could accommodate two more people with no problem.

Wanda blinked fast. Were those tears in her eyes? "That's awful nice of you. We'd be plum delighted to help you all celebrate."

"Good. I'll let you get back to work now."

We said goodbye and I watched her head back to the building with a spring in her step. Wanda was in her mid-thirties. I wondered if we'd see a little Bird-Thompson baby next year. More curious things than that had happened, for sure.

CHAPTER 25

"Knock, knock," Abe said after he opened the back door to my apartment.

"Come in, gentlemen." I stirred the morels on the stove, then turned for a quick kiss.

Sean followed him in, with one hand behind his back.

"Wine." Abe held up a bottle.

"And flowers." Sean brandished a big bunch of yellow and red tulips.

"Perfect. Thank you both. Abe, you know where the opener is if you want to let the wine breathe. I'm sipping a little white, and there's probably enough for one more glass in the open bottle in the fridge."

Sean bent over the stove and inhaled. "Are those, like, the morels we gave you?" He straightened, looking delighted.

"They sure are," I said. When I'd realized I still had

them in the fridge, I'd had a twinge of unease. Did I ever want to see a mushroom again? But I trusted Abe to find safe ones. I told myself not to be ridiculous and got to work cleaning them. "Don't they smell heavenly?"

Abe nodded.

"How are you cooking them?" Sean asked.

"A slow, gentle sauté in butter, then I'll add a little sherry and a few herbs. Rosemary and thyme, mostly."

"I don't like mushrooms, but that sounds like a good treatment." Sean nodded his approval as my big pot of water came to a boil.

"Sean, can you light the grill on the patio? We'll let it heat up for a few minutes, but the meat is ready." I'd already made a green salad and seasoned the steaks, which sat waiting on a plate.

Sean ambled out. I poured a box of orzo into the pot and stirred, then turned the heat down so it didn't boil over.

From behind me, Abe wrapped his arms around my waist and nuzzled my neck. "I missed you."

"I missed you, too," I murmured, twisting to face him. "We have a lot to catch up on." My gaze fell on the table. "Oh! The asparagus."

Abe stepped away, laughing. "We have to catch up on asparagus?"

"No, silly. But when I was at the butchery, a local organic farmer came in with fresh-picked bunches. I had to get one. But I haven't decided how to cook them." I'd already popped the ends off, so they were ready to go.

"We can grill them. Do you have one of those vegetable pans for the grill? The thing that prevents veggies from falling into the fire?"

"Good idea. Yes, I do. It came with the grill." I'd gotten the small gas grill when I moved in here. Charcoal was good, but gas was much quicker. "The asparagus is so fresh, it won't need much cooking." I stirred the orzo again, then drizzled the asparagus with olive oil, turning the stalks so they were coated. I found the square metal pan with the holes in it and laid the asparagus on it.

"I think it's hot enough," Sean announced from through the screen door.

"Shall I?" Abe asked, picking up the plate of meat and the asparagus pan.

"Please." I lowered my voice. "But let Sean tend it and come back in, okay?"

"Sure. He's good with a grill."

I added a splash of sherry and the herbs to the mushrooms, stirred the orzo, and dug out a big vase for the flowers. Abe returned and took a sip of the wine he'd helped himself to.

"I almost got charged with negligent homicide today," I told him as I trimmed the flowers.

His eyes went wide. "Almost?"

"Yes. This morning Buck stopped by and said I would be. I asked Corrine for the name of a criminal lawyer." I rushed to tell him the sequence of events before Sean came back inside. "I took a bike ride down to Story this morning, and by the time I was back and showered, Wanda had texted asking me to go to the barracks in Nashville. Before I went, I spoke with the lawyer for a few minutes."

"What's his name?"

"Ted Greaney."

"He's a good guy."

I wasn't surprised Abe would know him. He knew almost as many people as Adele did.

"Knows his stuff," he added. "He and my dad fish together."

"Anyway," I continued, "by the time I got to talk to Wanda, she said the magistrate had decided not to charge me." I lowered my voice. "But they might charge the food supplier. I didn't know until today that Orland Krueger is Jan's brother. That means he's Sean's uncle." I set the full vase on the table.

"Yes, he is." Abe frowned.

"Dad?" Sean called. "Turn them now?"

Abe checked the clock and raised his voice. "Yes."

"Orland was here at the end of the afternoon yesterday pounding on the store door. He looked mad or upset or something."

"Did you let him in?"

"Absolutely not. He didn't even see me."

The timer dinged for the orzo. Sean would be in soon with the steaks and asparagus. I wanted to talk wild poisonous mushrooms with Abe, but I didn't want to upset Sean. That talk would have to wait.

"I'll tell you more about Orland when I get a chance." He pointed at the orzo pot. "Want me to drain that?"

"Thanks."

A few minutes later we three sat around my table, Abe and I with glasses of red, Sean with a big glass of milk.

"Here's to the chef," Abe said, raising his glass.

"To the chef," Sean echoed.

"You both helped."

We dug into our steaks, which were nicely medium rare. The grilled asparagus was a perfect addition, and the morel sauce flavored the little torpedo pasta bits, even though I'd saved out a big portion of orzo for Sean tossed only with olive oil.

"Mmm." Abe pointed with his fork to the morels. "I approve."

"Thanks," I said. "You guys picked them. Where did you learn about mushrooms, Abe?"

"Him and my mom used to hunt them," Sean piped up.

"That's true," Abe said. "Jan taught me when we were first going out."

"Do you have to also study the bad ones so you won't pick them?" I asked.

"Sure," Sean said. "My mom knows all of them. Her and my uncle always went when they were kids."

"*She* and my uncle, Seanie," Abe corrected.

The teen rolled his eyes and forked in a huge mouthful of orzo.

"Your Uncle Orland?" I asked.

Sean nodded. My unease flooded back in. He'd confided that to know safe mushrooms, one must also have to recognize the poisonous ones. And both Jan and Orland did.

CHAPTER 26

I stared at the crossword puzzle in front of me on the kitchen table at seven-thirty Wednesday morning. Birdy bathed on the floor next to the refrigerator. I'd been looking at the same clue for what seemed like an hour, but I wasn't thinking about it at all. I was antsy from not working. From having my routine interrupted and no purpose to my day. I pushed the paper and pen away and picked up my coffee.

"Birdy, let's go say hello to the morning." I unlocked the back door and held it for the cat. I sprawled in one of the lawn chairs on the small flagstone patio while he froze, eying a bird in the blooming redbud tree at the edge of the woods. I still wore my Santa Barbara jammie pants—printed with grinning tacos and flying avocados—and a sleep shirt, but I didn't care. Nobody could see me back here. The sun had only been up for half an hour, but so far it was shaping up to be a good day, weather-wise, if a little cool.

I wished I felt good. I had no complaints physically, but the state of my life right now was not so hot. My livelihood was on hold, with a direct competitor parked across the street. A man had died from eating my food, and others had gotten sick. If somebody had delivered bad mushrooms on purpose, I didn't know who.

Come to think of it, the delivery person who brought the box of mushrooms had been new. Could he be responsible? I wondered if there was a way to find out without contacting the company directly. But shouldn't the police be handling all these details? I didn't know if they were or not.

Birdy crept closer to the tree with his special stalking gait, slow and smooth. His gaze never left the prey. I wasn't worried about the bird. They always flew off in time. Did I have a way to stalk a solution to my woes? Maybe.

I brought a pad of graph paper and a pen outside and sat. I knew writing it all down it would help clarify my thoughts. I could even make it into a crossword puzzle, but first I needed to make lists.

I started with Krystal Sand Krueger. She wanted her food truck to be a success. If I had to stay closed, or if I got a reputation for serving unsafe food, that would only help her business. I added Orland Krueger. He owned the food supply business, and I now knew he also had years of experience identifying mushrooms. He would be the most direct link to the box that delivered the bad ones. He could have slid them in to help his wife, with or without her knowledge.

I tapped the paper. I needed to know more about the FH Foods business. Where did they bring the food from?

Did they have security at their warehouse and on their trucks? I'd need to get one of the delivery people to talk to me.

Back to my list. I couldn't omit Francis Sand, one of the former owners of the business. He would want to help his daughter, and he also held a grudge against my aunt. Hattie Sand was more of a long shot, but she was also a former owner. She might have a weird notion that my selling antique cookware threatened their antique store. Either one of the Sands would know how to interrupt the delivery company's supply chain.

And then there was Jan Krueger O'Neill. She hadn't seemed happy about Abe and me marrying—and she knew about mushrooms, too. Orland was her brother. He could have told her about his new enterprise, given her a tour. She could have figured out how to include the toxic fungi in my order. Or the two of them might have acted together. For Sean's sake, I hoped not.

Of all of them, Krystal had the biggest financial stake and therefore the strongest reason, at least on the surface. But jealousy could also be a pretty strong motivator, and so could a decades-old grudge.

For me, it was time for breakfast, a shower, and a purpose. I laughed as Birdy made a dash—and the bird took flight. I had all day ahead of me, and I planned to see if I could make a few ideas take flight, too.

CHAPTER 27

By nine o'clock I pushed through the door of First Savings Bank to the sidewalk after depositing the weekend's considerable till. I crossed Main Street, with the police station being my next stop. I wanted to pick Buck's brain about the poisoning.

I stuck my hands in my jacket pockets. *Aha.* So that was where I'd left my multi-tool. I must have stuck the useful little folding tool into the pocket for my trip to the fair with Adele last Saturday. You never knew when you might need a knife blade, a screwdriver, or even a corkscrew.

Before I turned onto Walnut, I glanced back at the bank building. It was one of several in South Lick built in the Art Deco style a hundred years earlier, with rounded edges, vertical lines, and a clean, smooth style. I was glad it had been preserved and not torn down. They'd turned the upper floors into condos and kept the downtown area alive.

I turned to head toward the station and spied Buck ambling toward me. He gave me a little wave.

I waited to speak until he was close. "Exactly the man I was on my way to see."

"Mornin', Robbie. What's on your mind?"

I glanced around. "Could we sit down somewhere for a couple minutes?"

"Why don't you come with me? I was headed over to the bakery for some breakfast, seein' as how I can't eat at your place. We can get something to go and sit over by the gazebo. If you don't want nobody listening, that is."

"I don't, really. It sounds like a plan."

Five minutes later we perched on a bench in the square by the gazebo, which was the former site of the town's Jupiter spring, which had been the name of a sulfur spring in the 1800s. The town had been famous for its spas, and Adele had told me Jupiter Water was sold as a laxative nationwide until about 1950. The spring was closed after lithium, which occurred naturally in the water, became a controlled substance.

We each set our coffees on the bench between us. He'd ordered a ham, egg, and cheese breakfast sandwich with extra ham, plus two jelly doughnuts. I'd given in to a chocolate cruller, a weakness I rarely indulged in. Buck had insisted on paying for all of it.

As I bit into the deliciousness of a cakey, sweet, fried piece of chocolate heaven, I gazed at the gazebo. Columns, set in limestone blocks, supported an octagonal covered structure that itself supported a domed top. Ornate metal grillwork included the word *Jupiter*. With any luck, a few answers would spring up, too.

"I expect you're wanting to be talking about them bad mushrooms." Buck took another giant bite of his sandwich.

I nodded and swallowed. "Did you hear I'm not being charged?"

"I did. That's a good thing. But this question of the poisoning needs solved."

"I'll say. And soon. Wanda told me it's your department's responsibility now, because my restaurant is in South Lick."

"Appears to be."

"So, do you have a plan?" My knee jittered. The pace of life around here was slow, and Buck took it even a notch slower. I was way more action-oriented than patient, but with Buck, patience was a prerequisite.

"Working on it."

I gazed at him over the top of my coffee and waited. He'd been forthcoming with me in the past about cases. Would he be now?

He downed half a doughnut in one bite. Three couples riding tandem on fancy, well-tuned motorcycles purred by. A fat pigeon waddled up and pecked at the crumbs Buck had dropped on the pavement below the bench. I waited.

When I couldn't stand it any longer, I said, "Do you want to hear my list?"

"Ayup."

I ran through the Kruegers, including Jan, and the Sands, ticking them off on my fingers. "They all have a connection to the food service business. Orland and Jan know a lot about mushrooms. And Krystal is competing with my business."

Buck swiped at his mouth with the napkin. "I was

thinking of moseying over to the food truck for my breakfast, but I didn't want to hurt your feelings."

"As long as I'm closed, you wouldn't." Well, maybe a little. Or a lot. "Anyway, it seems like the thing to do is look into the food service company. Who could have substituted a box of mushrooms in my order? When did they do it? Things like that."

"I would agree. Problem is, the company is situated over to Nashville. I've got to work with the department there, and Chief Seastrom is off on a sabbatical somewheres. Old Ben and I been friends for a while. His replacement ain't being overly cooperative."

"Seriously? Isn't he obliged to help?" I wanted to stamp my foot, but that would only scare away the pigeon. "What if whoever did it tries again? How can I run a restaurant with someone trying to sabotage the food I serve, or worse?"

"Welp, I'm sure you can order your supplies from some other outfit." He lowered his chin and looked at me as if over the top of his glasses—which he didn't wear.

"True, and I've already checked out a couple of others. Shouldn't whoever sourced those mushrooms be brought to justice, though?"

"I reckon so."

I caught a flash of red out of the corner of my eye and looked to see Corrine clicking briskly toward us on her red heels with a blazer to match.

"Howdy, there, you two. Solving the problems of the world?" She sank onto the bench kitty-corner from ours and set down her large leather Kate Spade handbag.

"Not of the world, exactly," I said.

"Did you talk to my buddy Ted?" Corrine asked me. "You know him, Buck. Ted Greaney."

Buck bobbed his head.

"Yes, on the phone, thanks. Then Wanda told me I'm not going to be charged, so I didn't need to hire him. It's good to have the name, though."

"I hope you never need to use his services, hon." Corrine picked a speck of lint off her black skirt. "Have you heard when my girl's going to be able to get back to work? She's getting antsy setting around the house."

Danna and me, both. "No," I said. "I wish I knew. It's up to the county health inspector."

Corrine rose. "I'll see if I can put a bug in her ear. Y'all take care, now." She bustled off.

The mayor of South Lick might speak with a twang, but she was definitely a woman of action.

"Don't you worry none, Robbie." Buck dusted off his pants and provided the pigeon with several more meals' worth of crumbs. "I'm working on them suspicious mushrooms. Between old Corrine and me, we'll put things to rights." He stuck his hands in his pockets and ambled off.

"Thanks for breakfast," I called after him.

He gave a wave without looking back. Would they be able to put things to rights, as he'd termed it? I sure hoped so.

CHAPTER 28

L ou and I bumped over the right side of the double covered bridge into Brown County State Park at two-thirty Wednesday near the end of our ride. I'd been at loose ends and had asked if she was free.

Now she wanted a pit stop, and I always loved the quiet of the park. I sat on a bench outside the visitors' center and listened to all kinds of spring birdsong I couldn't identify. A woodpecker battered a tree nearby with a great din. Little black-and-white birds pecked at the holes of a bird feeder hanging from a pole at the entrance to the building.

I took a long swig from my water bottle and tried to focus on the present. Which was pretty lovely. When Lou perched on the bench next to me, I pointed to a flash of red on a tree. "That's one noisy woodpecker."

"Pileateds are the biggest ones we have here."

"*Pilleeated*?"

"It means it has a crested head. They aren't uncommon in our woods."

"I don't think we have them in California. Not that I ever saw."

She pointed as the bird flew to a dead tree a few yards from us. "Don't move."

We watched as it made a racket jackhammering its head over and over at the hollow trunk. When it paused, I admired the poufy red top of its head that came to a point in the back like a streamlined bike helmet.

She nudged my elbow. "So wedding prep seems in good shape. Am I supposed to throw you a bachelorette party or something?"

Lou had agreed to be one of my two attendants. She'd promised to make sure we didn't lose Abe's ring, that my hair looked okay, and that I didn't freak out.

"I think we're in good shape. We went over a lot with Adele on Monday. As for the party, just . . . no. How archaic is a bachelorette party, anyway?"

"Yeah. We'll do whatever you want. At least we got you a dress."

We'd gone shopping with Adele in January. The Indianapolis bridal shops seemed to specialize in either strapless numbers in satin with trains or overly fussy lace-trimmed gowns. I hadn't liked a single one. We'd made a second trip to an international import shop Lou knew in Bloomington and found exactly what I wanted.

"And I love it." The dress, made in Mexico, was of a fine white cotton. It had cap sleeves, a full skirt, and white embroidery. Most important, it fit me perfectly and flattered my full-hipped figure and my small waist. I planned to wear it with blue espadrilles and a wreath of flowers in my hair.

We watched the woodpecker without speaking for another moment.

"So, Lou," I began in a gentle voice. "How come I didn't know about Len?"

She leaned her elbows on her tanned knees, staring at her clasped bike-gloved hands.

When she didn't speak, I went on. "Adele mentioned that Len was Leah. You can talk to me about it, you know."

"I know, and I'm sorry." She sat up straight and twisted to look at me. "These last months have been a tricky time. Leah started the process when I was away last fall. My parents, bless their hearts, have been super-supportive. Me? I felt hurt she didn't confide in me. I mean, I know she's a lot younger. That is, *he*. See? I keep slipping up. It's so much to get my head around."

"I can only imagine. You've had a little sister for almost twenty years. Now you have a younger brother."

"Right. And he's awesome." She stared at her hands again, fiddling with the Velcro fasteners on the gloves. "He needed to do this. Other girls were mean to Leah, and boys made fun of her. She never was very girly. My sister was so depressed, she even tried to end her life. Luckily my dad found her in time. Len and I had a really good talk yesterday. He told me it had been excruciating to live in a body that wasn't the gender he knew he was meant to be."

"Wow. I haven't been close to anyone who felt that way. It's good your parents are being supportive."

"That's helped a lot."

I stretched my arms above my head. The bird flew back into the woods. "Adele told me about a young man who died in a car crash some years ago. He'd been badly bullied for being effeminate. She'd tried to mentor him when she was fire chief, but it didn't help."

"It's not her fault he died."

"How could it be?" I asked. "I've met his father a couple of times. He and his wife have opened an antique shop across from my store. The father—Francis Sand—still blames Adele for his son's death."

"Why?"

I explained about Francis asking Adele to help the kid, and what had happened then.

Lou stood, extending one heel to stretch her calf and hamstring. "How long ago was it?"

"Over twenty years."

"That's a long time to hold a grudge. I'm sure no parent ever gets over the death of a child. Still, it sounds like this Francis could use some counseling help."

"I would agree."

"Hey, have you heard when you can reopen the restaurant?"

I shook my head. "No."

"Some friends of mine own a restaurant in Bloomingulch. They had a lady die a few years ago from something she ate at their place."

"I read about that. They apparently use the same food supply company I did. I've changed to a new one, believe me. Did they have to close, too?"

"I don't remember," Lou said. "I can ask Chris."

"She and Paul came in to eat the other day." The day Mr. Ward died. "It was nice to meet them."

"They're good people, and she and Paul are a great team. Chris bakes the most amazing desserts, and he leads up the kitchen staff."

The woodpecker flew off, beating its broad white-patched wings. "What have you been up to?" I asked her.

"Well, I'm defending my dissertation next week."

"You are? I didn't know. That's so exciting. I'll be able to call you Dr. Perlman."

"You will. And graduation is the week after. You can meet my folks. They're coming down from Lafayette, and I'm going to throw an epic party."

"Tell me where and when, and I'll be there," I said. "How long have you been working on that doctorate, anyway?"

"Five years. Five freaking years out of my life." She laughed. "But it's been fun, and hey, that's how you and I met, right?"

"Exactly." I'd met Lou in Bloomington when I was looking for my father and she was doing research in the hospital's medical records. She'd helped me out, we'd realized we both loved cycling, and we'd been friends ever since.

"May is going to be one big party, ending up with your wedding," she said. "Does your friend in California have her plane tickets?"

"Yes. Alana is coming a week early to help and to hang out." I'd loved seeing her—my BFF since before I could remember—again last year when I'd gone back to Santa Barbara for our tenth high school reunion. She'd just gotten engaged and we'd pledged to be at each other's weddings. I had gone back for hers last September and was looking forward to spending more time with her next month.

"I know you didn't want to have a bachelorette party," Lou said. "But the three of us should go do something fun after Alana arrives. Ask Adele along, too."

"I'd like that."

"Hey, remember when I asked you about Len shadowing you? He went and talked to that food truck lady across the street from you. She's glad to have an extra pair of hands, and he's interested in the food truck angle. You don't have to worry about overloading your team."

I swore under my breath. I'd forgotten all about Len's request. "I'm so sorry. With everything that's been going on, I forgot. I'm glad for him that he landed a gig. Although I hope Krystal moves the darn truck somewhere else. We should get moving." I threw a leg over my cycle.

She mounted her bike but kept one foot on the ground. "So are we going to see some mini-Abes and mini-Robbies in the next year or three?" She grinned.

"Give me a little while to be married, okay?" I gave her a mock glare. "Don't get me wrong, I definitely want to have a couple of kids, and Abe's on board. But maybe not ten months from now."

CHAPTER 29

By eight-thirty that evening, my frustration at not having my restaurant open yesterday or today was eating at me. The bike ride should have relaxed me. I should have already finished prep for tomorrow and be heading to bed. Worst of all, South Lick shouldn't have a malicious mushroom-poisoning person at large.

I stared at the lists I'd started this morning, but couldn't think of a thing to add. I picked up my *Times of London* Sunday puzzle book and a pen, but, just like this morning, after I read a clue over and over for a minute and a half, I set it down. Instead, I found an episode of the *Great British Baking Show* I'd never seen.

I switched off the television half an hour later. I'd been watching the show without absorbing any of the drama or even the baking methods, something that normally interested me. I paced around my small home, which was starting to feel more like a cage. I slowed at the bookcase in the living room. On one shelf sat a framed picture of Lou and me. In cycling gear and on our bikes, we'd grasped hands and held them in the air at the end of a hundred-mile ride raising funds for the local cat shelter. We both grinned and looked triumphant. The next day I could barely walk, but it had been worth it.

I poured myself a little bourbon and plopped down on the couch again. I pressed Lou's number, crossing my fingers that she'd be home and available to be a sounding board for my thoughts.

But no such luck. The call went to voice mail.

I sat thinking. I sipped my drink and took a deep breath. Stroking Birdy on the couch next to me, I said, "It'll be fine, right, Birdman?"

In the absence of any response from my feline friend, I welcomed an incoming call from Abe.

"I got off work a little while ago," he said. "How was your day?"

"Frustrating. Yours?"

"I worked. I'm done. Not much new, but I did wonder if my darlin' would like some company tonight."

"That's the best thing you've ever said to me."

He chortled. "Even better than asking you to be my bride?"

"That was good, too. Come on over, please."

"All you have to do is open your back door. I'm standing right here."

I smiled. My evening just got awesomely brighter.

CHAPTER 30

In my store Thursday morning at eleven, my heart broke to see it empty of customers. The restaurant was an indoor ghost town without the aromas of bacon frying and biscuits baking. It was too quiet, with no forks clinking on plates, no beef patties sizzling, no lovely murmur of diners conversing and laughing. The store seemed lonely for diners and employees, friends, family, and strangers.

I grabbed the feather duster and wandered through the cookware shelves, flicking dust off the items and the shelves. Maybe they would let me reopen without serving food. But would anyone come in? The pots and pans and implements, Adele's knit hats, the few new trinkets I sold, all were really what retailers called a loss leader. The for-sale items drew people in, who then decided to stay and eat.

I had to do something, anything. I'd already gone for a bike ride, showered, and cleaned my apartment kitchen. I grabbed my iPad and slumped in the easy chair next to my desk. If I ordered one thing from FH Foods, I could talk to the delivery person. I'd have to figure out how to phrase my question. But maybe I could at least learn about how the business operated and how a box of bad food got slipped into my order. I brought up the app. I didn't want to order anything fresh that would spoil, or anything expensive. I scrolled through until I saw the heading *Pickles*. That was it. Surely they were sealed by whomever made them. And even if they seemed tampered with, it wouldn't break the bank for me to toss them. I ordered a gallon jar and submitted the request. I usually got back an automated delivery window right away, but not this time. Maybe their software was down.

What else could I do? I wasn't sure Buck would get the answers I wanted, but right now I was at a loss. The big clock on the wall read eleven. Did I have any wedding-related things to accomplish? I checked the app we'd been using for planning and swore. I'd forgotten to get back to Abe about the cake last night. Sending him home with the cupcakes had also slipped my mind. Since our cake deliberations had been interrupted when we were sampling the cupcakes a couple of days ago, we still needed to make a decision.

We—Abe, Adele, Lou, and me—were using a shared spreadsheet. I opened that and added a note to Abe about needing to let Phil know about our choice. Abe and I could finalize that tonight. Oops, no, we couldn't. He'd pulled another noon-to-nine shift. Maybe we could talk after he got home, but I was usually pretty tired by then.

I texted him but didn't get a response right back. I'd

stashed the iPad in the drawer when I heard a knock at the front door. Not a pounding like Orland had done, but simply knocking. My cell rang from an unfamiliar number. I connected against my better judgment. In a fraught time like this, it could be good news. Or bad.

"This is Inspector Lake. I am at the front door of your establishment."

Good news, I hoped. "I'll be right with you." I hurried over to unlock the door. "Please come in." Was this going to be my lucky day?

"That won't be necessary." She didn't smile as she removed the laminated orange sign from the door and slid it into a leather folder. "You may reopen whenever you wish." She turned to go.

I gaped. "That's it? But have you figured out how those mushrooms got in here? Are charges being brought against the supplier?"

She faced me. "I'm not at liberty to discuss further details, Ms. Jordan. I have removed the stop order. Good day." She trotted down the stairs.

Well, glory be and hallelujah. I couldn't stop smiling. From the doorway, I watched her drive off. A honeybee buzzed around the purple and yellow pansies in my planter. I touched the back of the nearest rocker on the porch and listened to it creak back and forth. I even smiled at the three cyclists who rode up to the food truck and dismounted.

But I had work to do. I turned toward my store. I wrinkled my nose and faced across the street again. Right before I turned, I'd caught a flash of light from an upper window in the Sands' antique shop. I peered in that direction but didn't see anything. I must have been mistaken. I shut and locked the door, even though I felt like dancing on the porch and yelling, "We're open!" Instead, I phoned Danna.

"The inspector just came by," I said. "The order is lifted. We can open tomorrow. How does that sound?"

"Awesome. How else? Do you need help setting up?"

"Yeah, maybe. I'm going to call in what we need from a different supplier. How about I text you when I get a delivery window and you can swing by then?"

"Perfect."

We discussed logistics and an order list for a few minutes before ending the call. I texted Turner about tomorrow, receiving an immediate **Great news!** back from him. I shot off a quick text to Abe. One more, and then I'd get to the order.

I called Phil but he didn't pick up. I texted, instead.

Any chance of brownies tomorrow? BoH says I can reopen.

He shot back a quick, **Sure.**

Now I was glad I hadn't given away the cupcakes. They'd still be fine tomorrow. iPad in hand, I returned to the easy chair to do the order. Zipfoodery's app was different, so it was slow going as I navigated through. I avoided ordering mushrooms. It would take me a while to return those normally tasty fungi to our menu, and I would make sure my staff and I knew how to identify the bad ones.

I was delighted to have part of my life—an important part—restored to normal. But picking at the back of my brain was the worry at not knowing who had maliciously messed with my delivery. And would someone try to sabotage us again?

CHAPTER 31

By noon I was cutting butter into flour, baking powder, and salt for biscuit dough. I'd taken the frozen meat out to thaw and put opera on the speakers. This was my happy place, prepping for breakfast, thinking about a special, doing the work of a restaurateur. We could offer the catfish sandwiches tomorrow, too.

The FH delivery would be here any minute. The new company, called Zipfoodery, had given me a four-hour window of two to six PM. I'd had to call to convince them to fit me in today, but they seemed pleased to have a new business account. They seemed professional despite the silly name, and they offered a wider selection of products than FH did.

Maybe I was expecting too much from the FH delivery person. My regular one was a woman of few words, and the young man earlier this week had been taciturn, as well. Today was the last free day I had to figure out more on this crazy case. If I couldn't get whoever brought my pickles to talk to me, maybe I'd have to head over to the FH Foods office in Nashville. I grimaced. Or not. The last person I wanted to run into was Orland. I would have to settle for online research.

I cracked and dropped in the eggs, incorporating them with a fork, then lightly stirred in the milk. Biscuits needed a gentle hand. I gave the dough a quick knead to bring it together and formed flat rounds. Once they were snug in plastic wrap, I stashed them in the walk-in.

I was mixing up the dry whole wheat pancake ingredients when the doorbell on the service door buzzed. Before opening the door, I checked the peephole to make sure it was the delivery person. I swore. Orland loomed outside, holding a gallon jar of pickles. This was not going according to plan. Should I open the door? Pretend I wasn't here? I clutched my phone like the lifeline it was. I'd been attacked by big men in my store before. I couldn't allow a repeat of that. But maybe all he was doing was bringing me what I'd ordered.

He buzzed again, leaning on the button. All right, already. I flipped open the bolt and pulled the door toward me.

"Hello, Orland." I fought to keep my voice from shaking. "I was expecting my usual delivery person."

He extended the jar of pickles. "I was in the neighborhood. I can't pay someone to deliver one item." He spoke slowly and overpronounced the words.

"That was all I needed." I took the big jar and smiled. "Thanks."

"I heard your stop order was rescinded."

"Yes, we're reopening tomorrow." How had he heard that? From Krystal, no doubt, or her parents. I was sure they were keeping tabs on me. I watched what they did, too. Or maybe he'd noticed the sign was off the door.

"And all you needed was one jar of pickles?" He narrowed his eyes.

"Yes." All I needed from his company, anyway. I could communicate later by email about wanting to close my account. "You have a good day, now." I stepped back.

"I had nothing to do with those mushrooms, you know. Nothing." His dark gaze bore down into my face. He took a step toward me.

"Good." I shut the door as fast as I could and secured the bolt. I wanted to scream, "But they came from your company!" Instead I sank down to sit with my back against the door, hugging the jar. That could have been an entirely innocent visit. Orland delivered my order and told me he didn't have anything to do with the mushrooms. Why had I felt threatened? Because my gut told me so. I blew out a breath. It didn't matter. I was safe.

I left the pickles on the floor near the service door. Who knew what he might have done to them? After I scrubbed my hands, I returned to my pancake mix, willing my hands to stop shaking. After I finished mixing, I stored it in the big plastic tubs we used. I was coming up short on brainstorms for a breakfast special. I knew our regulars would be delighted we were open again. Nobody would care if we didn't offer a special for breakfast or lunch. Or maybe Danna would have an idea for something easy.

I returned to the iPad and the easy chair. I hoped I could pick the brain of whoever delivered the Zipfoodery order about their process. Maybe it would resemble FH's. In the meantime, I'd see what I could learn from Mr. Google. I shut off the music so I could concentrate.

I was getting started when I heard a scratching from the door to my apartment. *No.* Had Orland gone around back and somehow gotten in? I'd come straight in here from town. I knew the door between my living space and the store was locked. My pulse raced. More scratching. Now it was fainter. I hadn't seen any vehicles parked out front. But if it was Orland, he could have parked across the street.

I peered out the side window, which was toward the back of the restaurant, not near the service door. No vehicle in my driveway as far as I could see. The scratching stopped. I made my way closer to my apartment door and nearly jumped when I heard it again. A plaintive meow followed the sound.

Laughing out loud, I unlocked the door. This was no tall, angry man. Birdy sat on the narrow table next to the door where I dumped mail and keys. He tilted his head as if to say, "You're having fun out front, why can't I?" He jumped down and kitty-sauntered into the restaurant. My favorite kind of intruder.

CHAPTER 32

I sat at the big table in the restaurant folding store napkins and towels at one-thirty. When I'd opened my apartment door to Birdy an hour ago, I'd also taken a half hour for a lunch break. A cheese sandwich on sourdough, a glass of milk, and a quick crossword had done wonders to calm my nerves after my encounter with Orland. While I sat in the kitchen, I remembered that I never finished the store laundry on Tuesday. It still sat wrinkled in the dryer. I spritzed a bit of water on the cloth and ran the dryer again to smooth out the laundry as I ate. All our store napkins, towels, and aprons were a deep royal blue. They barely showed stains and eliminated the waste of paper napkins.

Last winter I'd resolved to hire a laundry service, but I hadn't been able to find a reliable one that didn't also break the bank. Anyway, folding relaxed me and freed up my mind to think in the same way as cooking did. I hadn't gotten to my internet research yet, but I had all afternoon. Birdy snoozed, Sphinx-like, on the chair next to me. With any luck the food delivery would be here promptly, and I could quiz the delivery person about how they worked.

My hands slowed. I'd never run a search on Francis. Instead, I'd relied on Adele's memory of him and past events. The linens weren't going anywhere. I pulled out my phone and tapped in his name. I found obituaries for a half-dozen people by that name. Two men were in Luxembourg, a Francis Sand lived in New York, and . . . bingo, the Hoosier edition.

Huh. This Francis was apparently an avid birder. He'd won a contest for who saw the most unique breeds of birds in one year. That might explain all those Audubon prints on the hall walls and even the duck decoys in the store. I came across an obituary for Theodore Sand, who had died "unexpectedly." It mentioned Francis as being the surviving father. As president of FH Foods, he'd given a speech to the Nashville Chamber of Commerce. But I didn't see a record of the company's sale to Orland Krueger anywhere. It must have been a private deal. Or maybe Francis was still the titular head but had turned the day-to-day business over to Orland.

I dug more deeply into FH Foods and found a whole lot of boring. I was about to set down the phone and get back to the folding at hand when I clicked one more link.

"Whoa. Get a load of this, Birdy."

He cracked an eyelid, decided it wasn't worth the effort, and returned to his nap.

It was an article from four years ago in the *Herald-Times* about a woman dying after eating at Phat Cats Bistro, a well-known Bloomington restaurant. *Huh*. The restaurant of the couple who had eaten here on Sunday, Chris and Paul. Thank goodness the mushrooms had run out before they'd ordered.

Authorities have determined an ingredient in the meal caused the death. Police are questioning the owners of the company who supplies the majority of the restaurant's food. As of the time this publication went to press, no one at FH Foods had replied to multiple requests for an interview.

Wow. I couldn't believe FH was still in business. Would Buck have dug this up? Bloomington, home of the state's flagship university, was in Monroe County, not Brown County. I kept digging for a follow-up story but didn't find one. Strange. I peered at the date. This had happened before I'd opened my restaurant. I hadn't even thought of researching FH Foods before I started using them. I'd selected the company because it was as local as it could get, and I liked the ordering software.

I copied the link for the story and texted it to Buck. I added a note.

FYI. Couldn't find follow-up story. Hope you can.

Come to think of it, I hadn't researched Zipfoodery's safety record, either. No time like the present. Google didn't dig up any dirt on them, thank goodness. Phone stashed, I got back to the folding. I finished the towels and aprons and started smoothing and folding the napkins. The last step would be to roll a fork, knife, and spoon in each. It was more work up front, but it made setting tables go much faster when we were busy. Danna could help me later if I didn't finish.

My phone buzzed with a text. Maybe Buck had news.

But it was from Phil, saying he was out front with brownies. That made me smile as I hurried to unlock the door.

"That was fast." I held out my arms for the trays he carried.

"Just call me Mr. McFeely."

Mr. McFeely being the postman on the Mister Rogers show. "Speedy delivery? I haven't thought about him in years."

Phil nodded as he trotted down the steps. "Be right back with more." He returned with two more wide trays, these bearing cookies.

I set my load on the counter. "Can you stick around?"

"Sure."

I locked the door again. "Beer?"

"You bet. I earned it."

When I came back from my apartment with two beers in pint glasses, Phil had taken over my folding station. "Hey, you don't have to do that."

"I know. I love me some folding."

I handed him his beer. "Cheers, and thanks. How did you bake that stuff so quickly, anyway?"

"I had the cookie dough all mixed up and in the fridge when you got closed. And brownies go fast."

"I appreciate it."

"Plus, I have a rehearsal for Ravel tonight, so I wanted to get the baking out of the way." Phil had a rich operatic baritone, and he'd been getting more and more parts lately.

I grabbed the silverware caddies and brought them to the table for rolling.

"Did they let you reopen because they figured out who supplied the bad mushrooms?" he asked. "Turner told me that was what happened."

"No. The inspector came by this morning to take down the sign. They decided not to press charges against me, so they didn't have a reason to keep the restaurant closed."

"Wait. Press charges against you?" Phil's voice rose.

"Crazy, huh?" I filled him in on what had happened. "How was I supposed to know the mushrooms were bad?" I sipped my beer. "Phil, you hang out in Bloomington a lot. Have you ever eaten at Phat Cats Bistro?"

"It's a bit out of my grad student price range, but my parents took me once. Incredibly good food, and desserts to die for."

I shuddered at the phrasing.

Phil laid another folded napkin on the growing stack. He could fold faster than I could roll. "Why do you ask?"

"The owners ate here the other morning. Lou knows them. Someone died from food poisoning after eating at their restaurant a few years ago. At least they're still in business."

"And they use the same food supplier you do?" His blue eyes widened in his dark face.

"Yes. FH Foods. I've now switched to an outfit called Zipfoodery."

He snorted. "Some name."

"I guess they want you to think they zip the food right over." I checked the clock. "They're bringing my order this afternoon, in fact. They might be here any minute, but it could be as late as six."

"Back to Phat Cats. I do remember now about the food poisoning. I read about it at the time."

"I could only find one article. What had the person eaten, do you know?" I asked.

"Was it mushrooms?" He frowned, concentrating on

his memories. "It wasn't. I remember now. It was oysters the person ate."

"Raw oysters?" I shuddered. "Sorry. I love sashimi and sushi with raw fish. But only in California. Raw oysters creep me out."

Phil laughed.

"Plus, it's the Midwest. We aren't anywhere near an ocean. Who eats raw oysters in Indiana?" Still, it got me thinking. The bad oyster could have been the same kind of accident as the bad mushrooms. Or both could have been delivered with malice aforethought.

CHAPTER 33

Zipfoodery didn't arrive until five-fifty—with only ten minutes to spare in the four-hour window they'd given me. Phil had left a while ago. At least they made it. The delivery person was a lean, muscled woman about my age wearing a green T-shirt with the company's name emblazoned on the front.

I introduced myself at the service door and showed her where to unload the boxes and bags.

"Thanks so much," I said after I scribbled my name on her tablet with my index finger. "Can I ask you a couple of questions?"

"Sure. This is my last stop. You're new to ordering from us, right?"

"I am, and I appreciate your company accommodating me at the last minute. Do you want to sit down?"

She glanced at her phone. "Okay. But only for a couple of minutes. My dog's going to want his run, and I am, too."

We sat at the closest table.

"I'm wondering how your business works," I began. "Where do you get the food I order?"

"For the produce, the boss goes up to the big market in Indy every morning super-early, before dawn, usually. The rest of it we stock and reorder when we need to. A lot of restaurants use the same things over and over. You probably do, too."

"Sausages, hamburger buns, butter. Yes, we do."

"We're a clearinghouse, I guess you'd say. You know, if you had to order from fifty different places, that'd be all you would have time for. We just do it for you."

I nodded. "So, when I put in an order, you or someone else selects each item in your warehouse or wherever."

"Right. I pick—that's what we call assembling all your items—as well as drive."

"I understand."

"Why do you want to know all that?" She stood. "Simple curiosity?"

Should I tell her? I didn't see why not. "The company I had been using delivered poisonous mushrooms to me earlier in the week."

She whistled. "Seriously?"

"Yes. A bunch of people got sick and one actually died. I'm trying to figure out if it was done on purpose, and if so, could they have slid a box into my order during the supply process."

"That's possible, for sure. We have plenty of holes when the truck is sitting open or two people are picking. It could totally happen. I mean, it wouldn't, not at my place. We're good people, all of us." She shook her head. "I don't blame you for making the switch."

"Thanks for explaining what goes on behind the scenes. That helps."

"I gotta split. Catch you next time." She made her way out the service door, moving with the easy gait of a runner.

Lots of holes in the process. *Great*. Right now I needed to get going on my own process. I had food to put away and more prep to accomplish. I texted Danna that the order was in. She replied within seconds.

Want me to pick up burritos on the way?

I hadn't even considered dinner, but it was after six o'clock. I was going to have to eat sometime, and we had a decent Mexican takeout place in town.

Sure! Chicken, please.

My stomach grumbled even thinking about food, especially a chicken burrito from Paco's Tacos.

I'd grabbed a couple of pilsner lagers from my apartment and moved all the cold foods—milk, cream, OJ, ground beef patties, strawberries, and more—into the walk-in by the time Danna let herself in the front. She locked the door behind her and set the sack of dinner on a table. My mouth watered to see the logo on the bag, a cheery red chili pepper waving a gloved hand.

"Dig in." She headed to the sink to wash her hands.

I did the same. We were cooks and already took handwashing seriously. After what happened last year, I was extra-diligent. I grabbed plates, glasses, and napkins and joined Danna, who was sliding the plump wraps out of their own wrappings.

"Here." She handed me one. "I got the beef. They both have extra guac."

"You know me too well." I poured the beers and handed her one. "Thanks for thinking of food."

"Sure. Oh, and he gave us these." She set a couple of little plastic containers of salsa on the table between us.

I took a bite and savored the perfect mix. The shredded chicken was flavored with cumin and chili powder. The grated pepper Jack cheese was partially melted around spicy black beans, and the smooth guacamole tied it all together. "Mmm."

"Paco knows his stuff."

We ate, chatting between bites. She told me her boyfriend was on a trip to Maryland to see his grandmother. I related the story of the inspector surprising me in the morning.

"Did it feel awesome to have her take down that ugly sign?" Danna asked.

"Absolutely." I sipped my beer. "I talked with the woman from the new place who delivered the order a little while ago." I explained what I'd learned about the supply process. "If FH operates the same way, anybody could have slid that box of mushrooms into the order."

"But if the delivery person also did the picking . . ." She surrounded the last word with finger quotes. "Wouldn't they notice an extra box when they unloaded the truck?"

"Maybe. Or maybe at FH the driver only drives."

Danna swallowed a bite. "Did you ever think Abe's ex might have done it? Even though she and Abe split up a long time ago, maybe she didn't want you to marry him."

"That has occurred me. And she apparently knows her mushrooms."

"I just remembered that FH was the supplier when I cooked for that sleazebag who owned the diner in Nashville. Remember?"

"That guy. Ugh."

"A thousand ughs. But hey, he's the reason I started working for you."

"Am I ever glad you did." I laughed. "I needed an assistant when I first opened, and you showed up. Did you meet Francis or Hattie at the time?"

"I did. They came in to eat one day. Sleazebag knew them. He told me their meal was on the house, so not to give them very big portions." She rolled her eyes and popped in her last bite of burrito.

"Was anybody ever poisoned at the diner?"

"Not that I know of. Other than by eating too much fried food, that is. The dude insisted on reusing the oil for way too long."

I finished my burrito, as well. "I hope there's no connection between FH and Zipfoodery. When I told the delivery person what happened, she said nobody at her place would do something like that. I'm terrified of serving bad food again."

"Hey, that was the first time in three years, right? It's not going to happen again, boss. By the way, I updated our Facebook and Instagram pages to say we'll be open tomorrow."

"Thanks. I did Google the new place and couldn't find any reports of food poisoning anywhere."

"Good. It'll be fine. Did you trial the oven-fried catfish?" she asked.

"Yes, and it was yummy, even with those frozen fillets. Think we should go with them for today's special?"

"I don't see why not."

"Let's do it," I said. "We have a huge bag of them."

"Now, do we have any cream cheese?" Danna asked.

"I bought five pounds."

"Perfect. I was thinking about making some yummy cream cheese pastries for a breakfast special."

"Have at it," I said. "I'll get the rest of the stuff put away. I already did the biscuit dough and the pancake mix. I'll trim the berries."

She wadded up the paper trash, rose, and lobbed it with a high one-handed shot into the trash can across the room. "Three points!"

I smiled. "But Danna? Let's not offer omelets tomorrow, okay?"

She folded her arms. "No, that's not okay. Not offering mushrooms is one thing. But nobody's going to die from a ham-and-cheese omelet, Robbie. Trust me. It'll be fine."

CHAPTER 34

Danna left by eight. We were all set for tomorrow, all except for my unease. Danna had to be right. Nobody else would get sick from the food we served. But what if . . . no, I couldn't let my mind go to that dark place. And she was probably right about serving omelets. Personally? If I were a customer and had heard about what happened to poor Mr. Ward, I wouldn't order even a cheese omelet. I might not even come here to eat. But we did have to keep omelets on the menu.

I wiped down the counter in the kitchen area for a second time. I took a clean towel and wiped it dry, for the calming motion more than anything. Even though I'd hated having to be closed, in a way it was less worrisome than my fears about reopening. I let out a little *eek* when my phone rang. I hurried over to the table where I'd left it and let out a breath when I saw the display.

"Hey, Adele." I sank into a chair.

"Heared you got the old go-ahead to open on up. Good news, hon."

"I did. I'm sorry, I should have called you."

"Don't you worry your head none about that. Are you going to keep using Francis and Hattie's outfit for your food?"

"No way. I got a delivery from a new place a couple hours ago."

"Glad to hear it."

"Do you remember reading about a food poisoning at a restaurant in Bloomington a few years ago?" I asked.

"Yes, indeedy. I knew the lady a tiny little bit, the one who passed. A bad oyster, I do recall."

"FH Foods supplied that restaurant, too."

"Well, if that don't beat all." She made a *tsk*ing sound. "I'm surprised they're still in business."

"That makes two of us."

"Welp, gotta run. Our show is on."

"What are you watching?"

"*Seinfeld*." More distantly, she said, "I'm coming, Samuel."

"You do know that show went off the air years ago, right? Like maybe decades ago."

"'Course I know." Adele laughed. "We're watching reruns, but they come on right now. You take care. Love you, hon."

I was in the middle of echoing her sentiment when she disconnected. No streaming at will for those two. They stuck by the old model of watching TV. Adele and Samuel watched shows at their scheduled time or not at all. If *Seinfeld* aired at eight-thirty, that's when they were going to see it. Speaking of shows, I'd heard about a new

Netflix series I wanted to see. A good drama should get my mind off poisoned food.

And speaking of taking care, I hadn't locked the door after Danna left. I switched off lights and moseyed over to the front door, idly glancing out the window. The sun was starting to set here on the western edge of the eastern time zone. I stared at the second floor of the antique store, where a sash was open. The window didn't have a screen on it, either.

"What the—?" My jaw fell open at the sight of a telescope on a tripod in the opening.

A telescope, which, because of the slope on this side of the street, pointed straight into my store. I felt the steam coming out of my ears. Francis Sand, birder, had a lot of nerve spying on me. I grabbed the door handle. I wanted to march across the road and throw rocks at that thing.

"No, you will not," I scolded myself aloud. It would be dark soon. I didn't need an angry confrontation right now, with nobody here to back me up. That would be a very bad idea. What I could do was snap a picture, and I did.

I locked the door and pulled down the window shade to cover the glass. I hadn't used the old green shade once since I'd opened, and a puff of dust came with it.

At my feet, Birdy meowed. I scooped him into my arms. "You haven't had dinner, you poor thing. With any luck, mosquitoes will bite that stupid man all night. Let's get out of here."

We headed into my apartment, but it was hard to settle down. I closed all the blinds and curtains. If Francis or Hattie felt like snooping into my private life as well as my business, they were out of luck. I was cocooned and safe, but that didn't make me any less steamed about the telescope. What kind of a weirdo aims a telescope at his across-the-street neighbor? I grabbed my phone. Buck needed to know.

The Sands aimed a telescope into my store late today. Is that legal?

I kept it vague about which Sand. I had no idea if it had been Francis, Hattie, or both. Or Krystal, for that matter.

After I sent the message, I thought about tomorrow. Krystal and I were going to be in near-direct competition again. And I'd been here first. She must be doing pretty well, though, if she wanted to hire Len as a helper.

All my unease rose up anew. Starting in the morning, I was again going to be responsible for the health of every single person who ate the food we served. How could I be sure it was safe? I picked at a thread on the sofa's arm. I had a bigger question. Who had made sure I served toxic mushrooms?

CHAPTER 35

Danna was already in the restaurant when I stumbled in at six the next morning.

"I wanted to get a head start on the pastries." Flour covered her hands as she rolled out dough.

Yawning, I poured myself a cup of coffee. Abe had stopped over after work again, and we'd stayed up late talking. Among other topics, I had described the brownish-on-top mushrooms with white specks and white underneath.

"Did they blush when you pressed or cut them?" he'd asked. "Turn a rosy color?"

"I don't think so. Danna worked with them more. She said she smelled radishes when she cut them, but she didn't have any radishes around."

His nostrils had flared. "Did they have gills?"

"Maybe. Why?"

"You might have served *Amanita pantherina*. Panther-cap mushroom. It's toxic, but it looks similar to a couple of other edibles, including *Amanita rubescens,* the one that blushes. Panthercaps are especially poisonous for someone with an underlying health condition."

"Like Mr. Ward," I'd whispered, to which he'd nodded.

We'd talked longer. I'd told him about the telescope, and he thought it was as outrageous as I did. We hadn't gone right to sleep once we hit the bed, either. Now I was short on slumber, and it had totally been worth it.

I peered into a mixing bowl and inhaled. "Cream cheese, vanilla, and sugar?"

"Yep, but not too sweet, and the dough is like a pie dough. I'm going to make little roll-ups, kind of like cannoli, but baked instead of fried."

"Have at it. Let me know how I can help."

She gave me a white-dusted thumbs-up. "Hey, why's the shade down on the door window? You never do that."

I didn't want to explain about the scope. "Just feeling on edge, I guess." I headed over to raise it.

By seven, I was fully caffeinated. Bacon and sausages sizzled on the grill. That and the smell of freshly baked biscuits and cream cheese pastries combined into an aroma from heaven. The tables were set, I'd mixed up the pancake batter, and we were ready to roll. I'd kept myself too busy to let my concerns about food safety rise up.

I unlocked the door and flipped the sign to *Open*. Buck waited on the porch along with a half-dozen other regulars. I stepped back to let them in, then glanced at the day. Steely clouds forecast showers later, if not a downpour. I hugged my arms against the chilly air. I didn't see an *Open* flag flying at KK's Sandos, and the telescope had disappeared behind a closed sash. None of that was under my control. I turned back to what I could do something about, namely running a popular restaurant.

I poured coffee and took orders, shuttling them over to Danna, and ended up at Buck's table. He hadn't answered my text last evening, not that I'd expected him to at night when he was off duty.

"Mornin', Robbie. You must be real glad to be open again."

"I am, for sure. What can I get you to eat? And did you see my text? Do you have any news on the poisoning?"

"Whoa, now, girl. One question at a time. I'm so hungry you could drive a two-ton pickup loaded with rocks through the hole in my stomach." He squinted at the Specials board. "Give me some of them pastries, a side of biscuits and gravy, and a kitchen sink omelet." He glanced around and lowered his voice. "Hold the mushrooms, though, will you?"

I cocked my head. "We don't have a single one in the house. No worries on that account." I scribbled down his order. "I'll go put this in. But I'd love some answers when I come back."

"I didn't see no telescope over there while I was waiting. Just saying."

I pressed my lips together and pointed myself to the kitchen area where Danna wielded her two spatulas like the pro she was. I stuck Buck's order up on the carousel.

"Buck wants breakfast for three, as usual."

She laughed as she flipped a pancake.

"Danna, if Hattie Sand comes in, we need to make sure she's not out of our sight, okay?"

"Because she stole stuff."

I nodded.

"I'll do what I can," she agreed. "But if it's before Turner shows up, we might not be able to manage that."

"I know. Let's hope the Sands are sleeping in." A couple of hungry diners entered, setting the bell to jangling, followed by a dozen more. I started a new pot of coffee and grabbed the full one after I called, "Sit anywhere that's open," to the newcomers. I followed them to their tables, poured, took orders, and hurried back to the grill when Danna hit the bell. And it was only seven-fifteen.

When Buck's order was ready, I carried it over.

"Thanks, Robbie. I was like to faint."

"No, you weren't." I set down the plates. "So, is it legal for someone to aim a telescope into a neighbor's windows? Isn't there a Peeping Tom law or something?"

"You claimed it was aimed into the store, not your bedroom. Correct?" He bit off fully half of one the cheese pastries, spilling powdered sugar down the front of his uniform shirt.

"Claimed?" I set my fists on my hips. "I know what I saw, Buck. And yes, it wasn't aimed into my private living quarters, but why should that matter?"

Chewing, he held up a hand and swallowed before speaking. "You can file yourself a civil claim for invasion of the right to privacy."

Huh. "But it's not a criminal act?"

"You'd have to ask that lawyer you lined up."

"What does a civil claim even mean?" I asked.

"As I recall the law, you can ask for monetary compensation for the embarrassment, humiliation, and mental pain that a person of ordinary sensibilities would have suffered under the circumstances."

"Is that a direct quote?"

"'Matter of fact, it is." He grinned. "You give me a

call if you see them peeping again. Even better, take a picture and send it to me on the text."

I smothered a snort. Buck could cite the law, but he texted with his index finger and was a little behind on the terminology. "I took one last evening. I'll send it to you." I would need more proof than one cell photo if I went to all the trouble to take the Sands to court, something I wasn't sure I was prepared to do. "Have you heard any more about who put those mushrooms in my order? Does Wanda know anything?"

He wagged his head back and forth. "Not yet." He forked in a huge, messy bite of biscuit. The gravy dripped partly back onto his plate, partly onto the table, and partly down his chin.

Jeez. I liked the guy, but his eating habits could use some serious revision. And nothing had been discovered. Planting those mushrooms—panthercaps, if Abe was right—here had to be a crime, although I didn't know what the exact label would be. Malicious food substitution? Homicidal poisoning? Negligent sourcing? And why was it taking them so long to find the culprit? Was Buck losing his edge? Too many questions. Zero answers. I turned away.

A diner across the room caught my attention. Another held up his coffee mug, which was presumably empty. Danna dinged the ready bell. Time for this restaurateur to get to work. I should have told Buck the name of the mushrooms. I'd text it to him when I got the chance.

By seven-forty, every table was full, with a party of three waiting. The cowbell jangled again. I groaned inwardly to see Francis and Hattie enter the store. She again carried a large quilted bag hanging limp. Exactly what I did not need. I glanced over at Danna, who flipped her hands open in a "What can we do?" gesture. Turner wouldn't be here until eight. I couldn't babysit Hattie's compulsive stealing disorder, if in fact it was that and not malicious theft.

Rather remarkably, the first couple who had come in at seven were finished and on their way to the door. I had a solution.

I hurried over to the Sands. "There's a two-top opening up. Please come sit down, and I'll clear it for you."

"You go ahead, hon," Hattie said to Francis. "I'll browse the shelves for a few minutes until Robbie here has our table ready."

I scrambled frantically. "I'm sorry. Nothing's for sale today, and that area is off limits. I'm doing inventory." I clasped my hands, raised my eyebrows, and smiled. No bloody way was she getting her sticky fingers on my cookware.

CHAPTER 36

Turner slid through the door at a few minutes before eight as I was taking Francis and Hattie's breakfast order over to them. Francis read the newspaper while she studied her phone.

"Two over easy with home fries, sausages, and biscuits, and a cheese omelet with wheat toast and fruit, correct?" I set the first order in front of Francis and the second at Hattie's place.

"Yes, thank you." Francis folded the paper.

"You're not getting breakfast at the food truck, I see," I said.

"Krystal's closed today," Hattie said with a frown. "Some gizmo in her setup broke."

"That's too bad." I watched Francis stick his fork into both yolks. The yellow ran out in tiny rivers toward the potatoes.

"I was thinking maybe you tampered with it," Hattie added.

"Me?" *Seriously?* "I would never do something like that."

"Maybe, maybe not." She cocked her head as she reached for a little jar of jam from the caddy.

Sheesh. "Francis," I began, "I wanted to ask why you had a telescope aimed into my store last evening."

He whipped his head to give Hattie a look of alarm. She focused on spreading strawberry jam on her toast and didn't glance up at him—or at me.

"Do you mind telling me?" I cocked my head.

"Why, no, not at all." Francis swallowed. "I was trying to get a good look at a Cooper's hawk in the big tree next to your store. The scope wasn't aimed in here."

As if. "Interesting. I didn't know we had that kind of hawk around here." I gazed at Hattie once more, which she apparently didn't notice. "Well, enjoy your breakfast."

"Thank you," he said. "It looks delicious."

I made my way around the room. I delivered two tickets and took orders from three gentlemen. I cleared a four-top and shifted the dirties and the orders to the kitchen area. But my mind was on that look Francis gave his wife. Had he lied to cover up for her? Maybe he hadn't even been home.

I greeted Turner, now aproned up.

"Morning, boss," he said. "Where do you want me?"

"Danna, want a break from the grill?" I asked.

"Sure. It's all yours, bro." She took off her grease-splattered apron. "I'm also gonna take a quick break in the you-know-where." She pointed her chin toward the restroom. "And then I'll do up more biscuits."

"Sure," I said. "The pastries are popular."

"Ooh, pastries?" Turner asked.

"You better grab one before they run out," Danna told him. "There's only one more pan."

Turner checked the orders and poured out three disks of pancake batter, followed by a disk of beaten egg for an omelet. "Robbie, I dropped by the food truck before I came in. I thought I'd say hi to Krystal, but it was closed up tight."

"Her stepmother said a gizmo had broken, whatever that means."

"That's not a good sign during Krystal's first week," he said.

"No, it isn't. Hattie accused me of breaking the part, which is complete fantasy." I slid the plates I'd rinsed into the dishwasher.

"You? That's total fantasy and crazy talk, Robbie."

"Yeah. But I do wish Krystal would park the thing somewhere else."

Turner laughed as he flipped the pancakes. "Who wouldn't?"

Danna came back and slid into a clean apron. The three of us went through a lot of them in a day. From the start I'd maintained it was important for whoever was serving to look relatively clean, and the aprons were well-sewn and of a nice, sturdy twill, so they held up well under multiple washings. I'd ordered them from a company called Hoosier Aprons in Evansville. They'd cost a bit more than ones made in China, but I felt good that they were fabricated not only in this country but by workers in this state.

"I think your friends from across the street want more coffee," she said.

Francis held his mug aloft. I grabbed the carafe.

"Thank you," he said. "I noticed a Zipfoodery truck here yesterday. Are you multiple sourcing now?"

"No, I've decided to move my account to them."

"Oh?" He narrowed his eyes. "You don't like my son-in-law's service? That company has been in the family for a long time, you know."

"It was time for a change." I didn't have to defend my decision to him. "Can I get you anything else?"

He only shook his head. "Only the check."

I fished it out of my pocket and laid on the table, face-down.

Hattie finally looked up. "When will your cookware section be open again?"

"I'm not sure." I spied another customer wanting coffee. "Please excuse me."

After I filled mugs several tables away, I glanced back. Francis and Hattie talked intently in low voices. He scowled at her. She glared back. I wasn't going near those two again if I could help it.

CHAPTER 37

We'd had a bit of a lull midmorning, as we often did, but the lunch rush was more intense than ever, and it started early. We'd been right about people being happier that we'd reopened than worried that they'd be poisoned. And I was too busy to fret. The fake-fried catfish sandwich proved very popular. Even though Danna forgot the first breading stage, they came out crisp and delicious with the hint of lemon.

By twelve-thirty I was beat. Danna and Turner didn't look so fresh, either. A four-top had opened up when Adele and Samuel pushed through the door, dripping with rain. Nobody else was waiting, so I beckoned them over, giving the surface one last swipe before they arrived.

"Howdy, hon." Adele shook out her jacket before kissing my cheek. "Land sakes, that rain is a real frog strangler."

I swallowed a giggle. "Hi, Samuel."

"How are you, Robbie, dear?" he asked.

"We've been busy, so I'm a little tired, but busy is good."

"Bless the Lord, it is." Ever the gentleman, he pulled out Adele's chair for her and waited until she sat to take his own seat, hanging his rain jacket over the back of the chair.

"What can I get you both to eat?" I asked. "For specials we have a yummy curried chickpea stew or a catfish sandwich."

Turner had worked a second lunch-special miracle with the chickpeas during the lull, plus the dish was both vegan and gluten free.

"And we have either brown rice or white rice to go with," I added.

"I'd like a plate of that with brown rice, please, with a glass of skim milk," Samuel said. "Adele, darling, what suits your fancy?"

"I got me a hunger for a catfish sandwich, sweetheart." She smiled at her honey. "And a co-cola, please, Robbie."

I smiled and wrote down the order. "Coming right up." To Adele, Buck, and certain older locals, all soda was "Coke," and I had to ask which kind of Coke they wanted. But "co-cola" actually meant Coca-Cola.

Turner was on break and Danna was back at the grill, so I kept up my customer service. Two more hours until we closed the kitchen. When the bell jangled, I turned to see Sean with Lou's brother, Len. Sean was out of school? And they knew each other? They seemed to. They were talking as they shed rain gear. I went to greet them.

"Hey, guys. Len, I'm Robbie. We met at the antique fair on Saturday." I smiled up at him and extended my hand.

He shook it. "I remember." He didn't smile back. His hands hung at his sides as if he didn't know what to do with them.

"No school, Sean?" I asked.

"Half day. The teachers had in-service meetings. We have b-ball practice, and Len's coaching our team."

Aha. "Cool."

"I told him you make the best lunches, so he picked me up. My mom's working, and that rain totally isn't biking weather."

"I'll say." I turned to survey the restaurant. "We're full right now, but—"

Adele waved her hand and pointed to the two empty seats at their table.

"Looks like you can sit with my aunt and her partner if you want." I gestured.

"Sure," Sean said. "Come on, Len. They're super-awesome old people."

I smiled to myself. Adele and Samuel were super-awesome for any age. "I'll be over in a minute to take your orders."

I loaded my arms with a turkey burger, a catfish special, and a grilled cheese and tomato that were ready. On my way to deliver the lunches, I glanced at Adele's table, where Sean seemed to be introducing her and Samuel to Len. Turner arrived at their table right before I did and was giving Len a high five.

"How's it going, man?" Turner asked him.

"All good," Len said, but he looked overwhelmed at all the attention. "You?"

"No complaints," Turner said.

"You guys know each other?" I asked.

"Len was in that same culinary class I took," Turner said. "The one Krystal signed up for, too."

I nodded. An interesting convergence. Maybe that was one reason Len contacted her about learning the ropes in her truck.

"Lou told me you were going to work with Krystal Sand, Len. It's too bad something broke in her kitchen."

"Yeah." He rubbed his chin. "I was going to start this morning."

"Hey, good to see you, dude," Turner said. "Come back any time." He turned toward the grill.

"What can I get you guys to eat?" I asked Sean and Len.

"I'm starving," Sean said. "I'll have a burger, loaded, plus a bowl of soup and coleslaw. And can I get extra chips and a glass of milk, please?" His teen boy appetite was every bit as legendary as Buck's.

"I'd like the chickpea special, ma'am, on white rice," Len said.

"Anything to drink?" I asked.

"A root beer, please."

"Exactly what I like to see." Adele beamed. "Nice, polite boys."

I suppressed a snort. "Coming right up."

By the time I came back with their meals, Samuel was regaling them with a description of a bird. "Yes, it was a magnolia warbler. One of the prettiest and most elusive, too, but we got a good sighting."

"You've been out birding, Samuel?" I asked.

"Why, yes. Brown County State Park is rich territory for migrating birds. In fact, it was your neighbor across

the street, Mr. Sand, who led us in search of spring war-
blers."

I set down the last plate. "When was that?"

"Yesterday evening, the last two hours before dusk.
Birds are quite active at that time."

"Telescope and all?" I asked, knowing the answer.

"No, this was strictly a binoculars walk."

So, I'd had a Peeping Tiffany, not a Peeping Tom. But
why?

CHAPTER 38

"I'd say that went pretty well." I plopped into a chair at three o'clock and set down my bowl of curried chickpeas and rice. My crew and I had about finished cleaning up and scrubbing down. Danna gave one last swipe to the grill, while Turner wrung out the mop at the sink. "Get yourselves some food, gang."

A minute later they sat, a turkey burger for Danna and a grilled cheese for Turner.

"You guys, I didn't tell you, but Abe thinks maybe the mushrooms were something called panthercaps. Danna, do you remember if they turned a rosy color when you cut or handled them?"

"They didn't."

"That kind is edible, but Abe said the panther mushroom is poisonous," I said.

Turner's mouth turned down at the corners. "Especially if you're already sick, like that old guy, right?"

"Yes." I pulled out my phone to text Buck the name of the mushrooms.

"Somebody either put those in our box on purpose or accidentally." Danna shuddered. "Hey, how did you keep Hattie Sand out of the cookware, anyway, Robbie? I never got a chance to ask you."

I raised my eyebrows. "I told her the whole section was closed, that I was doing inventory."

"She's the light-fingered one?" Turner asked.

"I believe so."

"That's a great ruse, but how long can you keep it up?" Danna bit into her burger.

"I don't know. I kind of hope she won't come back." I swallowed a bite of lunch and took a sip of water. "I didn't tell you guys about the telescope." I related what I'd seen. "Francis is apparently a serious birder. When I asked him about it this morning, he gave Hattie a funny look, then said he was looking at a hawk in the tree next to the store, not inside. But this afternoon Samuel told me Francis was leading a bird walk in the park at that time, and that he didn't have his scope with him."

Turner frowned. "What did she hope to gain by spying on the store? Was she waiting for you to leave the door unlocked so she could steal more stuff?"

"Believe me, I have no idea." I shook my head.

"It was kind of blatant, wasn't it?" Danna asked. "Right on the street like that."

"You bet," I said.

"Interesting that Len is going to sort of apprentice with Krystal," Turner said.

"Seriously?" Danna asked. "Wouldn't he learn more here?"

"Lou asked me if I would let him shadow us," I said. "I never got back to her. Partly I was afraid he would get in our way when we're super-busy. You know, having another person around who doesn't know how we work. With the whole mushroom thing happening, I forgot. If he knows Krystal anyway, that's probably better."

"Got it." Danna gestured toward the front of the store. "Speaking of the Sands, did you see their banner? Grand opening tomorrow."

"I didn't, but now I remember. On Sunday one of the two said they were going to officially open this Saturday." I moseyed over to the front door and peered out. Sure enough, a wide banner announced the opening and ribbon cutting at eleven o'clock tomorrow morning. The rain had stopped, with blustery clouds scudding overhead.

Turner and Danna joined me at the door.

"That ought to keep Hattie busy for the day." It had better, I thought.

"Yes, and it'll be good for us if the food truck isn't fixed by then," Danna said. "We should brainstorm specials."

"Look." Turner pointed. "There's Krystal and maybe a repair guy."

I squinted. "No, that's her husband, Orland."

"Well, he's got a toolbox and what looks like a part," Turner said. "Maybe hubby doubles as handyman."

"Either way, we should plan specials, as Danna said." I moved back to our table. "Let's sit down and figure it out so you guys can get home or wherever you're off to." For me, with Orland working across the street, this might be a good time to pay FH Foods a visit.

CHAPTER 39

By four o'clock I was pedaling hard up the hills of Brown County and coasting down. Puddles still dotted the back route to Nashville, and road spray wetted the back of my jacket. I didn't care. The air temperature had warmed with the sun coming out, and everything I wore could be tossed in the washing machine when I got home.

I rode past a stretch of woods with something fragrant in bloom. It bordered a small farm that had rows of blossoming apple trees, all pinks and whites. A riot of tulips in front, bright spots of reds, yellows, and even deep purple looked like a party in front of a white cottage-style farmhouse.

Riding usually cleared my mind. Today it wasn't having that effect. Buck hadn't come back for lunch, which he usually did. It was so frustrating not to have an answer about the mushrooms. Or the telescope, for that matter. I was nearing the country sheriff barracks. Should I drop in on Wanda again?

No. Buck had said she was off the case, that it was the responsibility of the South Lick PD. I kept going into the center of Nashville. I slowed when I spied Wanda at my favorite sweets shop. They had a walk-up window for ice cream, and I figured I'd earned a cone. Plus, it would fortify my nerves for visiting FH Foods.

I shouldn't linger long here, though. I definitely wanted to be in and out of the FH office before Orland returned. But even if he did, I would be in public. Other people would be around the company. I'd be safe. I could always say I'd come to close my account, a perfectly innocent thing to do.

"Hey, Wanda." I kept one hand on my bike and ordered a single scoop of Deadly Dark Chocolate in a sugar cone.

"Having a good ride?" Wanda held a little cup with a scoop of pale yellow in it.

"I am. Out for an ice cream?"

"Gotta maintain my girlish figure." She grinned. "And Italian ice don't have many calories." She was in uniform, so she was either on duty or just off.

I accepted my cone and paid, then stepped to Wanda's side.

"Wanda." I kept my voice low. "Do you have any information at all about those mushrooms? Buck won't tell me a thing."

She glanced around and spoke softly. "Not really. I do think him and the SLPD are doing their job, though. You shouldn't worry none."

"I'm worried. What can I say?" I took a too-big bite of the creamy dark treat, which gave me an ice cream headache. I rubbed my forehead.

She dipped a little plastic spoon into her cup of lemon ice. "At least it ain't murder this time around."

"It is if those mushrooms were purposely delivered to my restaurant." I stared at her. "And a man died, regardless. From what he ate in my restaurant."

"I know, and it's a crying shame. Good thing he didn't croak inside your place, right?"

"Oh, come on, Wanda. Death is death. Seriously, Buck hasn't told you anything?"

"Not much. I think he might be looking into your fiancé's ex, though."

Jan. "Really?"

"It was a little something he hinted at," she went on. "I don't rightly know. Her and her brother, they're pretty well known in these parts for their myco something or other."

"Do you mean mycology? Knowledge about mushrooms?"

"That's it," she said. "They started that BCMS a couple few years back."

"What does that stand for?"

"Brown County Mushroom Society." She dropped her cup, still half full, in the trash can.

"Whoa. You didn't finish your ice."

"I know. The first three bites are the best. Learned that in Weight Watchers." She smiled and gave me an easy nod. "I don't need more than two or three tastes."

"Good for you. That takes a lot of discipline." I licked

my Deadly Dark. Discipline was a foreign concept when it came to me and ice cream.

Wanda touched her forehead in a casual salute. "Catch you around, Robbie."

I waved, crunched down the rest of my cone, and rode off, my thoughts on the Brown County Mushroom Society.

CHAPTER 40

I dismounted in front of FH Foods, which was at the end of a row of businesses in a small industrial park on the outskirts of Nashville. The parking lot was smooth and dark, as if it had recently been repaved, and was sparsely occupied. A glass door labeled FH Foods Office was next to a loading dock. A wide, garage-type door at the end of the dock stood closed, even though an FH Foods truck was backed up to it.

After I leaned my bike against the wall and hung my helmet on the handlebar, I tried the office door. It was locked. I spied a doorbell set into the wall and pressed that. Maybe they didn't have a dedicated office person. I waited. And waited.

I supposed this was a ridiculous errand. It was Friday afternoon. The staff could be celebrating the end of the week in the back, having a beer, starting their weekend. Or they could all be gone for the weekend. I shouldn't have left it for so late in the day. I grabbed my helmet.

The door opened and a woman peered out. "Sorry for the wait. Office lady's gone. Help you with something?"

I did a double take. She was exactly who I'd been hoping to talk to. Not an office worker at all, this was my former taciturn delivery person. Whose name I'd never even asked, I was chagrined to realize.

"Hi. I own Pans 'N Pancakes. You used to deliver to me."

"Gotcha. Didn't recognize you. Bike clothes and such."

I was seized with nerves. This was harder than asking the new Zipfoodery woman about her process. "I . . . um, need to close my account."

"Come back Monday, then, or call. I don't handle accounts." She started to close the door.

"Wait. Can I ask you a couple questions?"

She tilted her head but came fully back into the doorway. "You got one more."

Cute. "Do you only drive deliveries, or do you pack the truck, too?"

"I pick and I drive, depending on what the boss needs." She folded her arms and leaned against the jamb.

"The new boss?"

"Krueger." She bobbed her head. "He's not bad. Works hard."

I struggled to phrase my next question. "Did you pick for my delivery on Monday? A young guy delivered it."

"Not really, but I helped the kid. He's new, we had a lotta orders."

"Could someone have slipped an item into my order

without you or the kid noticing?" I tried to keep my tone casual, but I wasn't sure I succeeded. "Added a box, say, to the truck destined for my restaurant?"

She stared at me like I had a mushroom growing out of my left ear. *Wait.* She wasn't looking at me. My insides turned to ice.

"Placing your order in person, Ms. Jordan?" Orland's deep voice asked.

How had he arrived so silently? I turned to see him looming behind me. I swallowed. "No. I need to close my account." He was the very last person I wanted to see, to talk with. My pulse beat hard in my neck and my heart thudded, but I mustered a little smile.

"And you come here in person at the end of the business day at the end of week to do that," he said in a skeptical tone.

I glanced at the woman and back at Orland. "I was out for a ride and thought I'd stop by." Was she going to tell him what I'd asked? Had he heard?

"That'll be all, Pat," he said to the driver.

She shot me a look I couldn't interpret, then disappeared inside. I was alone with Orland. He took Pat's place, folding his arms and leaning against the building. The casual stance was belied by his scowl and flared nostrils. Did I want to chat with him? Ask him if he'd fixed the kitchen in Krystal's food truck? Inquire why he had pounded on my door the other afternoon? Dig into the mushroom society? No, to all of it.

"Call on Monday when the office is actually open," he said with clipped words. "By the way, no one in my family had anything to do with what happened in your restaurant. No one, do you understand?"

"Thank you." I clipped on my helmet and slung my leg over the bike. *When in doubt, say thank you* was one of the best pieces of advice I'd ever gotten. I rode out of that parking lot almost as fast as Danica Patrick in the 2009 Indy 500.

CHAPTER 41

Back home, I was grateful my return trip had gone without incident. I'd been attacked while cycling before and never wanted to experience that again. I showered off my workday and my bike ride and combed out my hair. Abe's bluegrass group was performing at a Bloomington bar tonight. He'd invited me to go, but the band didn't go on until nine. With my alarm set for five-thirty in the morning, I'd declined, but accepted his invitation to eat out tomorrow night. I suggested Phat Cats, and he said he'd make a reservation.

Now at six-thirty, hungry me was on my own. Well, Birdy and I were on our own. He stared at his empty treat bowl, circled my ankles, and meowed his disapproval. I served him his dollop of canned food and watched bliss strike as he fell on it like he'd never been fed before.

For my own dinner, this Californian went with comfort food. I flash-fried three corn tortillas on both sides until they were soft. I topped one side of each with a smear of refried beans sprinkled with cumin and chili powder. I added grated pepper Jack cheese and salsa, then ran them under the broiler for a couple of minutes until the cheese melted. With the addition of avocado slices and a cold beer on the side, I was a happy expatriate.

I had breakfast prep to do later, but for now I could simply eat. And think. Pat had seemed like she was about to tell me something. Something important? I didn't know. I kicked myself for not finding out her last name. I wasn't finished eating, but I wiped my hands and found the FH Foods website on my phone. Unfortunately, it didn't list the employees by name anywhere.

I resumed eating, savoring the perfect combination of limed and flattened corn paste transformed by hot oil, beans, melted cheese, and smooth, rich avocado, the fruit of goddesses. The meal reminded me of my trip home for my reunion a year ago. Carmen Perez, owner of Nacho Average Café and B&B where I'd stayed in Santa Barbara, was planning to attend our wedding. She'd be accompanied by her mother, Luisa, otherwise known to all as Mamá. I couldn't wait to introduce them to Adele and Abe and my restaurant crew. Carmen and Luisa and I had connected in many ways. They'd even tried teaching me to make corn tortillas by hand. I'd been less than successful, but it was a fun evening.

When I'd ridden by the front of my store on my way home tonight, luckily I didn't see a telescope. Still, after I finished eating and went into the restaurant to work, I closed the shade on the door tighter than Scrooge's wallet, as Buck would say. I frowned as I got out the flour and butter. The lieutenant hadn't been anywhere near as forthcoming with this case as he had in the past. Was his boss cracking down on him? Or maybe he didn't have anything to share because he hadn't made any progress.

As I mixed baking powder and salt into flour for biscuits, my gaze fell on the round biscuit cutter. An antique with a red handle, it hung from a rack above the counter, along with the big pastry cutter and a dozen other kitchen utensils we used most frequently. And the biscuit cutter brought my thoughts to Hattie and her propensity for petty theft. Someone had said Hattie had served time in the past. Adele, maybe? That was it. She'd said Hattie had been incarcerated for larceny.

I looked at my hands, which weren't yet too covered in flour. I dusted them off and hurried over to the iPad on my desk. I had my fingers on the digital keyboard when my phone rang. I glanced at the display. I didn't know the number but connected anyway. You never knew when it might be a business call.

"Pans 'N Pancakes. This is Robbie."

"This is Pat. From FH."

My eyes whapped wide open. "Hi, Pat."

"You were asking about something sneaking into an order. Did you mean them mushrooms? I heard about your . . . uh, problem this week."

My problem. I'd had a problem, all right. "Thanks for calling. Yes, that is what I was curious about." *And still am.*

"I did see that box in the truck. Didn't look like our usual vendor's. Figured you ordered up something special."

"Did you see who put it in the truck?" I crossed my fingers.

"Nope."

"I don't suppose Francis or Hattie was—"

"Sorry, my ride's here. Good luck." She disconnected.

I stared at the phone. The box wasn't from their usual vendor. I should hope not. Shoot. I wished I'd had a chance to finish asking her if any of the three Sands had been around that day. That look Pat had given me after Orland showed up must have been because she didn't want to tell me in front of him. I saved her number, labeling it *Pat from FH*, since I still didn't know her last name. I could text her, but that really was Buck's job. I composed a text to him, instead.

Hope you're checking things out at FH Foods. A driver/ packer named Pat saw the box of mushrooms in the truck, says it wasn't from usual vendor.

I copied in her number.

I don't know her last name. Find out if any Sands were around FH on Monday. Ask the boy who drove and delivered my order, too. Don't know his name.

Should Buck be looking for Jan O'Neill, too? Probably, but I couldn't bring myself to accuse Sean's mom. In my mind, maybe. I didn't want to voice that suspicion to Buck. I sent the text and hoped he didn't think I was being pushy, telling him how to do his job.

Orland had warned me that nobody in his family was involved. But why should I believe him? Guilty people said things like that all the time.

What more could I do? *Oh.* I'd come over to my desk to check out Hattie's criminal past. I searched on Hattie Sand and Harriet Sand. Nothing came up except bits relating to FH Foods and the purchase of the building across the street from mine. What had Adele said her maiden name was? I was about to jab Adele's number when I remembered it: Shaber. Harriet Shaber. That key unlocked the stories.

But they didn't tell me anything. Yes, she'd served a term of one year for larceny under seven hundred and fifty dollars a long time ago and gotten off early for good behavior. Nothing since. She'd either learned her lesson—or figured out how not to get caught.

Except I'd caught her. She must be losing her edge.

I needed to get back to my prep, including store laundry, but while I was here, I poked around the Internet until I found the Brown County Mushroom Society website. Every page featured a warning in a banner at the top. *Never consume a wild mushroom unless its safety has been guaranteed by an expert.* They must have to do that for their own liability. The bottom of every page also included a legal disclaimer in small print.

One tab led me to a history of the group. Sure enough, Orland and Jan had founded it while Krueger was still her last name. I explored the other pages. The organization gave workshops, led mushroom-hunting walks, and sponsored cooking classes. One tab labeled *ID* displayed side-by-side color photographs of good and bad mushrooms, some of which looked identical to my eye, including the panthercap and the blushing one Abe had mentioned. I shuddered. No wonder they included that warning at the top. You wouldn't catch me going mushroom hunting, and it worried me that Abe and Sean did.

Another tab was labeled *Contact*. I tapped it, hoping for a list of staff or key players. Maybe I could find someone to ask questions of. Which questions, I wasn't quite sure. But all the page offered was a form, and I couldn't risk my request going to Orland or Jan.

I powered off the device and hurried back to the kitchen area. My job right now was not snooping. It was getting biscuits ready to bake in the morning, and I'd better get started.

CHAPTER 42

Turner and Buck pushed through the store door Saturday morning one after the other at a few minutes before eight. I waved from the grill. Turner hung up his jacket, while Buck came at a fast amble straight toward me. Did he have news?

I greeted him when he arrived. "How are you, Buck?"

"Welp, I'm on the right side of the grass, so that's something."

What? I peered at him. "You're on the . . . oh. You mean you're not buried under the grass." I giggled.

"Yep. I'm alive. Possibly not much more than that."

"I hope you feel better soon. Are you here for breakfast or to give me news?"

"A lot of one and a little of the other," he drawled. "Not news, exactly."

I wanted to shake the laconic out of him. Instead, I

turned a half-dozen sausages and folded an omelet. I loaded a plate with two sunny-side up, four pieces of bacon, and a pile of home fries, then slid the omelet and three sausages onto another. I hit the bell.

"Got your text," Buck went on. "Can we talk somewheres after I get some vittles into me?"

Turner started scrubbing his hands. Danna hurried up, giving me a frazzled look. She stuck four more orders onto the carousel and grabbed the plates that were ready.

"Sure, Buck," I said. "Go grab your table, quick. It's the last one open."

"One of you needs to bus," Danna muttered before turning away.

"I will," Turner said.

"Thanks," I told him. "You can swap out here after a while." If Buck didn't have real news for me, it wouldn't do us any good for me to go hover around his table while we were operating at maximum busy.

Yesterday my team and I had realized today was May Day. Turner had said that Scottish bannocks were traditionally served, but they seemed a bit plain. Instead, we'd gone with a strawberry-ricotta muffin for our breakfast special. It was too early for local berries, but we had a big flat of strawberries from Georgia. Spring herb quiche squares would be the lunch special, but made in large, flat pans instead of round nine-inch pies.

Danna came back with Buck's order. "True to form, Buck would like whole wheat banana-walnut pancakes, sausages and bacon, two muffins, and a side of biscuits and gravy." She stuck it onto the carousel. "The man's amazing. I can pack away a lot of food, but he leaves me in the dust."

"I know what you mean." I glanced over at the door

when the bell jangled. "There's Georgia. Do you know her?"

"Ms. LaRue from the library? Sure. I practically grew up in there, Robbie." Danna surveyed the tables. "She might have to wait until that couple leaves."

"Can you let her know?" I asked.

"Sure." She loaded up three more orders and waded into the fray.

Were no weddings taking place in Story on May first? It was supposed to be a lovely day. Or maybe Georgia had an event to run later, but had been pining for our cooking. Or . . . ooh, what if she'd thought of something to tell me, and that was why she was here? I'd told her about the death by mushroom. She caught my eye and gave me a little wave. I waved back and smiled. For now, though, I had six tables of diners waiting for their breakfasts, and Buck's order was the last one.

I was working the spatulas when the noise level in the store doubled. I turned to look at the door. A dozen men and women caroused in, with bells on. Literally. They all wore white shirts and pants, with blue sashes crisscrossed over their chests and backs. Rows of bells were strapped to their calves. I'd never seen such a sight. From their flushed cheeks and rowdy laughter, I'd have guessed they'd been drinking, but it was only eight-thirty in the morning.

"We've danced up the sun!" one of the men announced with a red-faced grin.

Turner arrived with an armful of dishes and mugs.

"Who are those people?" I asked.

He laughed. "They're Morris dancers from Bloomington. I actually know a few of them. They do this every year on May first. They start drinking before dawn and then do their traditional English dances as the sun comes up. They're harmless, mostly, even though sometimes they dance with sticks."

"Sticks?" I asked.

"Yes. Like two-foot-long dowels. I think traditionally they were swords."

"I guess sticks are an improvement." I gazed at them. "I hope they didn't drive here."

"Don't worry. They always have a couple of designated drivers."

"I don't know how I've lived three decades without ever hearing about Morris dancers." I rescued Buck's pancakes right before they burned, flipping them onto a cooler part of the grill. I peered at the group. "Is that Len Perlman?"

"Yeah, he's one of them. I love the group's, like, spirit. I might join up, myself." Turner straightened after loading the last dish into the dishwasher and gestured with his chin toward the front door. "On my way in I saw the *Open* flag on the food truck and the window was open, too. I guess Krystal's husband got her kitchen working again."

I only nodded. I couldn't do anything about that, and we obviously had plenty of business despite the competition. I loaded Buck's order onto plates.

"Feel like cooking?" I asked Turner.

"Sure."

We swapped out, and I loaded my arms with Buck's breakfast.

"That surely looks tasty, Robbie," he said after I set down the plates. He drowned the pancakes in syrup and took a huge bite.

"I'll be back in a bit." I made my way over to Georgia.

Danna had beckoned her to a clean table a couple of minutes earlier and had poured her coffee. "Good morning, Georgia. It's nice to see you back in here."

"Hey, Robbie. Seeing you the other day made me realize how much I miss eating here. I'm not running an event until later today, so I figured I'd get the best breakfast in town into me first." She gestured with her thumb toward the front of the store. "I checked out the menu over there. What Ms. Krueger is offering in her truck across the street is kind of a pitiful choice compared to what you all make. A ham-and-cheese omelet wrap and an egg-and-sausage muffin. That's it."

"Thanks for choosing us, instead. She serves a different clientele. Did Danna take your order?"

"No. Can I get me a muffin special, plus a ham-and-cheese omelet?"

I jotted it down. "Of course. Bacon or sausage?"

"Bacon, please." She beckoned me closer. "You know, I was thinking on that Krueger wedding I told you about."

My radar perked up. "Oh?"

"You said somebody here was poisoned by mushrooms." She spoke in a tone too soft to be heard by anyone nearby.

I leaned down to hear her and matched her volume. "Yes."

"The groom and his sister wanted our caterer to use mushrooms they'd picked themselves. She flat-out refused. Said she couldn't guarantee the guests' safety if she did."

"Interesting. I don't blame her. Can you tell me the caterer's name?"

"Sure," she said. "It's actually a restaurant in Bloomington. Phat Cats."

Whoa. "Really?"

"Yes. The woman, Chris, is the one who runs the catering business," Georgia added.

"I know. I met the couple earlier this week. They came in here for breakfast." Those two were popping up all over.

"Anyhoo, the Kruegers were pretty upset about it. Had a mess of their mushroom-club friends in attendance. I don't know if it means anything, but I thought you might want to know."

"Thank you. I appreciate that." I straightened. "I'll go put your order in."

CHAPTER 43

The next half hour was crazy. Danna, Turner, and I were operating at top speed and, thank goodness, top efficiency. A dozen people waited for tables, and everybody else seemed to be taking their sweet Saturday morning time with their meals. I didn't get back to talk with Buck until nearly nine.

"I don't have much time." I collected his dirty dishes, all pretty much wiped clean. How he didn't fall into a food coma every time he ate here was beyond me. "Do you have anything to tell me?"

"Not much. Got your text, but there wasn't nothing I could do about it last night. I thank you for the ideas and that lady's number."

"Haven't you already been looking into how the mushrooms got into my order?" I set my fists on my waist. "Talking to their delivery people and such?"

"Down, girl." He made a tamping-down motion with his hand. " 'Course we have. Just don't have anything definitive yet."

Turner hit the ready bell. Danna gave me that desperate look that meant she was overdue for a break. I mouthed, "Go," at her.

"Let me know when you do," I said to Buck.

"You bet." He was implacable. "See you at the grand opening across the street?"

"Possibly." I turned away. Was I steamed at the lack of progress? Maybe. Frustrated? Definitely.

I pointed myself toward the Morris dancers, who had pushed a table for four against the one that sat eight. A woman in flower-festooned long red braids poured from a metal flask into her coffee, then passed the flask to the ruddy-cheeked man next to her. He emptied it into his own mug.

"Folks." I cleared my throat. "You are welcome to bring your own alcohol to consume on the premises, but state regulations require me to pour it for you."

Braids smothered a giggle and slid the flask into her bag. It was hard to be too stern confronted with all these cheerful faces, and they weren't kids, either. Two of them had to be over fifty. Most were white and looked the English-Celtic part, but two Black women formed part of the ensemble. Len appeared to be the youngest one at the table. Still, I didn't want to get in further trouble with the county or the state.

"Sorry, ma'am," Ruddy Cheeks said, eyes twinkling. "It won't happen again. Next time we'll bring our mead in bottles and you can handle it. The food here is pretty amazing. We'll be back, for sure."

"Thank you." I smiled. "I hope next year I can get over to Bloomington to see you perform."

"We'll be at the midsummer solstice celebration in the Brown County State Park in June," Braids offered.

"And at the Oliver Winery Renaissance Faire in the fall, right?" Len asked her.

"For sure." She raised her mug and gave me an impish look. "We hit all the pagan festivals."

"Cool," I said. "Maybe I can catch you at one of those. Len, I thought you were going to apprentice with Krystal at her truck across the street."

"I am, but I told her I couldn't start until next week. She's barely open today, anyway, because of her parents' place having their big opening."

"Right." I surveyed the table. They all seemed to be still enjoying their meals, which seemed to have touched on every item on our menu, both regular and special. "Can I get something else for any of you?"

An older woman picked through her omelet, then beckoned me over. "There's no mushrooms in this, right?" she whispered.

I swallowed. "Not a one on the property."

"Good. We heard, and . . . well . . ." Her voice trailed off.

"You have nothing to worry about, I assure you." I kept my own voice low and confident. Possibly more confident than I felt, but she didn't need to know that. I glanced up to see Sean ambling toward the table.

"Hey, bro." Len held up his palm for a high five, which Sean returned. I couldn't remember if Len was over twenty-one or not, but his face didn't have the look of someone drinking with his breakfast. Maybe he was one of the designated drivers.

I greeted Sean, too. "Are you here to eat?" I asked.

"I'd like to, but I have family . . . uh, stuff to do across the street. My uncle and my mom roped me into indentured servitude."

Len's voice cracked as he laughed. "What, you have to put on a lacy apron and offer shoppers the hot hors d'oeuvres?"

"It's not that bad, but yeah, I have to help out. I saw your car out front and thought I'd say hi." Sean looked more closely at the group's matching clothing. "What kind of uniform is this, anyway?"

"We're Morris dancers," Ms. Red Braids piped up again. "It's a traditional English style, but we obviously put our own American brand on it. Your buddy Len's our newest acquisition."

I had diners needing attention. "Enjoy your meals," I said.

"Thank you," the older woman said.

"Join us for a few minutes, dude," Len said to Sean, and began introducing him to the group.

"I'll see you at the opening later, Sean." As I left, Sean pulled up a vacant chair next to Len's. He smiled and acknowledged the introductions. I glanced back after busing a four-top. Len and Sean were conferring and both looked serious. What was up with that?

CHAPTER 44

I'd taken over the grill a few minutes ago, and Sean swung by to talk with me before heading across the street.

"Len isn't sure he wants to work with Aunt Krystal," Sean said. "She's acting kind of crazy."

"What did he mean by crazy?"

"I'm not sure. Frantic, maybe, or paranoid."

"That's no good."

"I know."

"Can you tell me more?" I asked.

"He said he'll reevaluate after he works with her on Monday." The old school clock ticked over to ten. Sean muttered a mild obscenity. "Sorry, Robbie. I'm late. See you over there."

"What's with the frown?" Danna asked me.

I stared at the door though which Sean had left a moment earlier. "Sean told me something kind of disturbing."

"And?"

The door opened to admit a bunch of white-haired and dye-job seniors.

"Oh, boy," Danna groaned.

"Please go help them," I said. "I'll tell you later." We'd recently gotten on top of the rush. Everyone who had been waiting was seated. I had only three tickets yet to fill. The members of the still-cheerful Morris gang were standing and leaving money next to their plates. *Good*. We'd need those tables. One thing I knew—I was grateful people had returned to eat after the Board of Health closed us. That hadn't been guaranteed, not by any means.

I focused on the next order on the carousel. But even as I scrambled eggs and slid sausages onto a plate, as I popped bread into the toaster and dished out fruit cups, I thought of my soon-to-be-stepson's message and puzzled over what Len had told Sean.

The dancers were nearly at the door, jingling their way out. Len caught my eye and waved. I was dying to run over, to stop him and ask him what he'd meant. But I had breakfast orders urgently calling my name. I couldn't abandon my station, my livelihood, to do some possibly insignificant snooping. In a pinch, Lou would give me Len's cell and I could ask him later. I turned back to the job at hand.

I pushed around a pile of peppers and onions and loaded them onto a waiting omelet. I folded it over, added toast and sausages, and hit the ready bell.

"Robbie?"

I whirled. Len stood at my elbow. He hadn't left, after all.

"Len, you startled me. Was your breakfast all right?"

"It was delicious. Listen, I only have a second. I'm driving half those drunken dancers home." He grinned, but his pale green eyes—exactly like Lou's—held an intense look.

"I'm listening, but I have to keep cooking."

"I understand. How well do you know Krystal Krueger?"

My wish come true. "I don't know her at all." I wanted to stop and concentrate only on Len, but I couldn't. Instead, I poured out three pancakes and another future omelet. "I only met her a few days ago. Monday, I think. Why?"

"She seems kind of unstable. I'm not sure I should work with her, after all."

"Sean hinted at that. What did Krystal do to make you think she's unstable?"

"Perlman," one of the dancers called. "We need to go."

"Crap," Len said. "Can I call you later? My sister said you're super-good at, like, figuring stuff out."

I nodded slowly. "Lou has my number, or you can grab one of the store cards by the door. Hey, take care, okay?"

I watched him leave. He held the door open for none other than Adele. She gave me a warm wave, then hurried over to the eight-top Turner had finished wiping down a minute ago. As Adele swept one of the white-haired ladies into a big embrace, I smiled to myself. It was Adele's old friend, Vera Skinner. The big group must have come down from Zionsville, north of Indy, where Vera lived. I hadn't noticed her in the crowd.

When Danna brought over two tickets, I said, "Can you take over cooking?"

"Sure." She gave me a sideways grin. "So you can do some sleuthing?"

"You never know." I took a full coffeepot to the big table. "Good morning ladies. Coffee all around? It's so good to see you again, Vera." I held the pot out to the side and bent down to give her soft-as-new-flannel cheek a kiss.

Vera's brown eyes never stopped smiling. "It's been too long, Robbie."

She and Adele had fought off a couple of attackers at Adele's house one time almost two years ago.

"I know." I poured coffee. "Have you ladies come down for the day?"

"We're going to attend the antique store grand opening," Vera began. "But I told the girls they shouldn't miss your breakfast, so here we are."

The "girls"—all of whom were at least of Medicare age, with half of them clearly over eighty.

"I'm just tagging along, obviously, and I'm going to kidnap Vera here for a extra day," Adele said. "We ain't getting no younger."

"Lordy me, we certainly are not." Vera grinned at her childhood friend.

"I'll give you all a chance to make up your minds. The specials are up there." I pointed to the board. "I'll be back in a minute." I tended to the two other tables of sprightly older women, took orders from a two-top, and emptied the carafe into the mugs of a couple of gentlemen.

Turner was loading dishes in the kitchen area while Danna wielded the spatulas.

"Guys," I said. "I think I'm going to have to drop into the grand opening at around eleven. Can we manage?"

"Okay by me," Danna said. "Turn?"

"We usually have a lull by then, right?" he asked. "Go. It's not like we won't be able to find you."

I laughed. "True. I want to go out of respect, but also everything seems kind of precarious right now, you know?" I frowned as I started more coffee, and I lowered my voice. "Too many questions about those mushrooms are still hanging in the air. I don't like it, and everyone involved will be in one place. Seems like I might need to be there, too."

"No worries, boss," Danna said. "We got it."

"It's not for another hour yet," I said. "With these hungry ladies on board, we'll need every hand."

And we did. We were pretty much run ragged. They cleaned us out of muffins and we exhausted the biscuits. Danna whipped up a few more batches in double time.

Adele and Vera were finishing up their meals when my aunt beckoned me over.

"You're coming across the street with us, ain't you?" she asked. "They're cutting the ribbon pretty soon."

I glanced at the wall clock, which read ten minutes before eleven. "That hour sure flew by. Yes, I plan to attend."

"Vera here knows Hattie even better than I do," Adele murmured.

Vera nodded, raising her eyebrows at me in some kind of signal. "Yes, I do, and that's a fact." She wiped her mouth. "Can we get our check, please, hon? We don't want to be late now, do we, Addie?" She was the only person I'd ever heard use a nickname for Adele—and Adele never objected.

Adele pulled out her wallet.

"Forget it." I held up a hand. "Your two meals are on the house. I'll see you across the street."

Adele and Vera told the other women they were scooting across to the antique store. I wondered what Vera had been telegraphing to me, because I had not understood.

CHAPTER 45

I passed the closed KK's Sandos truck and a local news van parked in front of the antique store. I slid in the propped-open front door—and halted. A line of people ahead of me waited to sign some kind of book on a table. The entire building seemed chock-full of people. The room to my left, the hallway ahead, the big room to the right, all full, with more voices coming from upstairs. I glanced over my shoulder. I'd barely noticed the weather when I hurried across the street. The Sands were lucky it was a sunny Saturday, although it was cold and windy for May first. This would be an entirely different opening if it were pouring rain, which was entirely possible on the first of the month. I'd seen snow on peach blossoms before, too, and these days you never knew what the weather would bring.

In the big room, somebody tapped a microphone. Corrine's voice rang out from a speaker.

"Good morning!" She stretched it into her best Minnie Pearl imitation, swinging the pitch up at the end. Her voice imparted a smile even though I couldn't see her.

I didn't need to sign a book. I excused myself a few times, slipping through the crowd in the hall until I reached the interior door at the back. On the wall next to the door, coats and jackets hung from pegs. This must be the family's coatrack, because I recognized the jacket Hattie had been wearing at the fair last weekend.

My plan was to cut through the kitchen and ease into the back of the big room. Instead, I found Sean in oven mitts drawing a large pan of mini-quiches out of the oven. Jan arranged doilies on several round trays. A platter of mini–pigs in a blanket sat ready next to an assortment of tiny muffins. This was a working kitchen today, not a showroom.

Sean glanced up. "Robbie?" He wore a white shirt and black pants, as if dressed to be waitstaff.

Jan shot me a sharp look. "We're busy," she snapped.

"Can I help?"

Jan's nostrils flared.

"Mom." Sean spoke quietly. "Let her help."

"All right," Jan said. "You can take and carry the muffins and the pigs through to the food table. It'll be on your left."

I wasn't going to touch the food, so I didn't bother washing my hands. I picked up the platters and escaped Jan's ire. I hadn't done anything to deserve it, and the last thing I wanted was to engage with her.

But once through the swinging door, I found myself behind Corrine, Hattie, and Francis, with Corrine extracting a microphone from a stand. A woman in black was at the front of the crowd holding a video camera on her shoulder, and a young necktied man held a professional-looking mike. A wide blue ribbon stretched from the back of a dining room chair to the opposite wall in front of the owners.

"Welcome to the grand opening of Sand Timeless Antiques," Corrine said. "Are y'all ready for this?"

I did my best to move unobtrusively along the side to the food table as a few observers muttered, "Yep," and "Sure." I set down my trays and found a piece of wall to lean against. Surveying the crowded room, I spied a uniformed Buck along the opposite wall, with Adele and Vera a few rows back.

"I can't *hear* you." Corrine beamed her thousand-watt smile, still channeling Miss Pearl. "Are all y'all ready?"

A roar of "Yes!" went up, followed by a murmur of conversation.

"Well, now, that's better," Corrine continued. "Quiet down now, please." She waited until the room was nearly still. "Mr. Francis Sand here and his lovely wife Hattie are the owners of this fine new establishment. They're going say a couple few words before we get the show on the road."

Francis stepped forward, today clad in a nicely tailored gray suit and an open navy blue shirt. His beard looked freshly trimmed. Hattie wore a simple purple dress that matched her hair. Krystal and Orland stood to the side beyond the couple.

Francis cleared his throat. "My family and I welcome you to Sand Antiques. Opening this store has been a dream of my wife and me for some years. We hope you make it a regular stop when you're shopping for fine home furnishings, small or large. Every room in the house has items for sale, and you'll find lower-cost purchases out back in the barn."

Hattie stepped forward. "Please sign the guest book in the hall, if you haven't already, and help yourselves to food and drink."

Krystal handed each of them a half-full glass flute of bubbly.

"This is my daughter, Krystal Krueger." Francis slung his arm over her shoulders. "You're going to want to avail yourself of a meal from her very fine food truck out front." He turned and beamed proudly at her. "She'll be opening for lunch in a few minutes."

Krystal caught sight of me. The glare on her face shocked me. I glanced away from her vitriol. What did she have against me?

"Won't you, sweetie?" Francis pressed her.

"Yes, of course." She gave the audience a perfunctory smile, then stepped back to stand next to Orland.

After that, I avoided looking at either of the Kruegers.

Corrine regained the microphone. She handed an oversized pair of scissors to Francis. "As the mayor of South Lick, I wish this new business many years of profitability and service to the community. Let's open Sand Antiques!"

Francis and Hattie each held one of the handles and managed to cut through the ribbon. The crowd cheered and clapped. Sean carried in two platters of bite-sized quiches and set them next to me on the table. On my other side a woman was pouring sparkling wine into plastic cups as fast as she could, and a young man beyond her served sparkling cider.

"I'm sorry if I got on your mom's bad side," I murmured to Sean. "I didn't mean to."

"Robbie, don't worry. She's been in a rotten mood all morning. Seems like I'm always on her bad side." He let out a long exhale.

I squeezed his hand for a moment. Vera approached the table.

"Vera, this is Sean O'Neill. Sean, Adele's friend Vera Skinner."

"Pleased to meet you, ma'am." He smiled politely.

She gazed up at him. "I hear you'll be joining the family soon. I'm glad of it."

"Yes, ma'am. I'm glad, too." His cheeks pinked up.

"You'll be at the wedding, right?" I asked her. I'd told Adele she was welcome to invite Vera.

"Wouldn't miss it for anything." She spied the quiches. "What do we have here? I downed one of Robbie's breakfasts not long ago, but these look downright delectable."

Sean pointed. "Those are cheese and those are mushroom, ma'am."

I gave him a sharp look. "Who made them?"

He rolled his eyes. "They asked the restaurant who catered my uncle's wedding to cook for this opening, but the chefs refused."

Phat Cats. I didn't blame them for not wanting to deal with the family.

"The cheese quiches are from the market," Sean continued. "But Krystal made the mushroom ones."

"Vera, no!" I grabbed her hand when she went for one of the little mushroom pies. "I'm sorry. I wouldn't recommend those."

"All righty." She withdrew her hand, nodding slowly.

"I'm pretty full, anyway. I'm going to go give my old friend Hattie a big hug." She trundled over to where Adele was talking with Hattie.

Sean gave me a puzzled look. "Why did you do that?"

"Did your dad tell you what happened in my restaurant this week?" I didn't have to keep my voice too low. The buzz of conversation in the place had turned into a roar of talking, laughter, and exclamations over the furnishings.

"Not really."

"Let's just say I'm off mushrooms for the moment." Especially where Sean's aunt and uncle were involved. I looked up to see Orland glaring across the room at me. He averted his eyes. I shuddered and turned my back.

I gazed at the little mushroom pies. It could prove deadly for anyone to eat them. When Sean returned to the kitchen, I grabbed the platter and stuck it under the table, sliding it back along the floor so the tablecloth hid it. Maybe they were fine to eat—and maybe they weren't. Lots of people were milling around, but I didn't care if anyone thought I was crazy. That was better than a person possibly being poisoned. I straightened and glanced back to where the central characters stood. Francis was looking away from me, but I could swear he'd turned his head the instant before.

It was already noon, and my stomach reminded me I was hungry. A pig in a blanket should be safe to eat, and a cheese quiche. Those, plus a celebratory sip of bubbly, and I was so out of here.

CHAPTER 46

Getting away didn't turn out to be that easy. I was chewing a pig in a blanket, quite yummy despite its grocery store provenance, when Corrine handed me a plastic cup of bubbly.

"You're going to need something to wash that down with." She beamed and sipped her own celebratory drink.

I nodded and swallowed. "Thanks."

"They got some kind of turnout, didn't they?"

"They did. I wonder if it will translate into sales for them."

She shrugged. "An affair like this puts the place on the map in people's minds. Takes a while to build a business." She looked down at me. "Except for yours. Your place hit the road running. Seems like it gets more popular all the time."

"I've been lucky." And I'd worked hard at making the

business a success. "My luck started with having Danna as my right-hand woman from the very start. Do you still regret she didn't go to college?"

"Shoot, no, Robbie. She's a smart cookie and self-educated. When she gets the hankering to get more schooling, she will."

This September would mark the fourth anniversary of my store's own grand opening. If Danna had gone to college as Corrine had been pushing her to instead of working for me, she'd have a degree by now. I knew Danna would probably head to either culinary school or IU before long, or even to a higher-end restaurant kitchen. I'd earned a degree, and so had Turner. Danna deserved that, even though I'd miss her terribly if—when—she left.

"Here's the face of South Lick law enforcement, himself," Corrine said. "Howdy, Buck."

He ambled up. "Ladies." He selected a muffin and stuffed the whole thing in his mouth. One hundred percent Buck.

"So, what progress, Lieutenant?" Corrine folded her arms over her chest. "In the matter of the incident at Robbie's place this week, I mean. That needs solved, and fast."

He held up a hand, chewing. I glanced over at the Sands. Krystal was no longer with them. Off to open her food truck, I expected, as promised by her doting father. Orland had disappeared, too. A half-dozen of the women who had traveled from Zionsville clustered around Francis, lauding the store. Vera was chatting with Hattie. She grasped Hattie's hand, producing a look of panic below the purple hair. What was Vera up to?

"Anyhoo," Buck began. "As I mentioned to Robbie this morning, we're—"

Sean hurried up. "Have you seen my mom? I can't find her anywhere. She left stuff in the oven and it's nearly burned." He sounded panicked.

Buck went on high alert. "Is that like her, to abandon her station?"

"No," Sean said. "I mean, she's not much of a cook, but I've never known her to forget what she was baking."

"Did you rescue it?" I asked.

"Yeah, I took out the pans. They're too browned to serve, but they didn't catch on fire or anything."

"We'll find her, son," Buck said. "Maybe a customer asked her for help out back in the barn or something. Come on." He ushered Sean back toward the kitchen.

Shoot. Had he been about to give Corrine and me some news? Whatever. Helping Sean came first.

"Catch you later, Robbie." Corrine waved at someone across the room and turned away.

I drained the rest of my bubbly. My phone buzzed with a text from Turner.

Heating up over here. Come back when you can.

My return message was simple.

Soon.

First, though, I was obliged to congratulate the owners. Sweet, mild-mannered Vera still had Hattie cornered, with Adele's help. I smothered a giggle as I extended my hand to Francis, who had moved away from his wife with so many visitors greeting him.

"Congratulations," I said. "I wish you the best with your business."

"I appreciate that." He shook my hand briefly, then dropped it.

"You got a fabulous turnout for this event."

"Yes, we did." When he turned his head to look at Hattie, his nostrils flared, likely from seeing Adele with her.

"Sir, how much is that hutch?" One of the women who had come with Vera approached Francis.

"I'll leave you to it." I took a few steps away as he answered the woman. I touched Adele's arm and murmured, "You and Vera stop by the store before you leave, will you?"

She examined my face, then gave me a silent thumbs-up.

"Hattie, congratulations and best of luck," I said.

"Thank you." She didn't smile.

I exited into the kitchen, not wanting to wade through the crowds of shoppers and nibblers. No one was in here. The air smelled of burnt food, and the two pans on the stove top were full of way overcooked quiches. I peered at the middles. More of the mushroom kind, too. I wasn't touching those. Or . . . maybe I should. I rummaged until I found a box of sandwich bags. I put one over my hand and scooped up a quiche, then turned the bag inside out over it the way I'd seen dog owners do when they picked up their pet's poop.

Glad it wasn't excrement, I tucked the bag into my coat pocket. I spied a big mixing bowl in the sink and bent over to examine it. Bits of chopped mushrooms mixed with milk and eggs lined the bottom. I grabbed another bag and scraped up a little of the mixture, too. If these were made from the same mushrooms that went into my omelet, somebody needed to test the mixture.

I made my way into the hall, now unoccupied. I again spied the pegs holding the family's coats. Dare I poke around in their pockets? No. Any of their owners could step into the hall and catch me. I didn't know what I thought I would find, anyway.

I could, however, use a quick pit stop before I resumed work in my own kitchen. When I was here before, I'd spotted a half bath nestled under the stairs. I tested the doorknob. It was unlocked, so I pulled open the door.

Jan O'Neill bent over the sink, her shoulders heaving. My breath rushed in. Had she eaten poisonous mushrooms?

"Jan, are you all right?" I stepped closer.

She straightened slowly, turning toward me. Her face was tearstained, not marred by vomit.

"Everybody's part of a couple." She spoke slowly, in a low voice. "My brother and Krystal. You and my ex-husband. Even my little boy has a girlfriend. Everybody has someone but me."

"I . . ." What could I say? I cast about for jewels from the Effective Communication class I'd taken. "It seems like that's really hard for you right now."

She blinked. Grabbing the hand towel, she dragged it across her face and squared her shoulders, the grief seeming to evaporate in an instant.

"Ya think?" she snarled. "What are you doing, barging in on me like this?"

"I'm sorry." I started to back out.

Jan cried out and bent over the sink again. This time she did throw up, violently. Specks of undigested piecrust and brownish-gray bits came out amid the bile. Mixed with the putrid smell of vomit was the earthy aroma of fungi.

CHAPTER 47

"I'll go get help," I told Jan.

"No!" She swore at me. "Go away."

All righty, then. I stepped into the hall and mostly closed the door, then hurried out back, where Buck and Sean were emerging from the barn. The cold air and wind were refreshing after the overheated and crowded indoors, although the sunshine had disappeared. A male cardinal showed off his pretty scarlet coat along with his mating song of *bree* repeated a dozen quick times.

"Jan's not in the barn," Buck said.

I had my mouth open to speak when a group of women neared us on their stroll toward the barn.

"I love them cute chairs I bought. They'll go perfect in my den," the shortest one said.

Another rubbed her hands together. "I hope they have some vintage cookware out in that barn."

I didn't warn her that a few of the pieces of cookware actually belonged to me.

After they'd passed, Sean added, "We looked everywhere for Mom."

"I know. I found her," I told them. "She's in the house, in the bathroom under the stairs. She's . . . um, not feeling at all well."

Sean drew down the corners of his mouth. "I'll go see if I can help her."

"Good." She should take more kindly to him than she did to me. After he loped toward the house, I beckoned Buck closer. I murmured to Buck, "Jan was vomiting. And it looked and smelled like mushrooms."

"That's not good." He made an expression as if he'd tasted them himself, which he had earlier in the week.

"Krystal made all the mushroom quiches for the party. I think you should confiscate them. They might contain the panther mushrooms I texted you about."

Buck bobbed his head once. "*Amanita pantherina*. I looked it up. Them are bad."

"I'll say. After Sean told me Krystal made the quiches, I slid one tray under the table where the food is. It's still on the floor. You need to make sure nobody else gets sick."

"Right." He dragged the word into three syllables.

I pulled out my two baggies. "I snagged these from the kitchen."

He gave me a stern look. "You know you should oughta leave evidence in place."

"I do know. But I didn't want somebody to come in and start cleaning up!"

"All right. Calm yourself down, now."

"You'll get them analyzed, right?"

He grabbed an evidence bag out of a back pocket and held it open for me to drop the bags into. "I'm on it, Robbie. Thanks for the alert." He scribbled something on the bag.

"We should go see how Jan is. I hope she doesn't need an ambulance."

Buck nodded and I followed him in and along the hall. Sean hurried toward us, eyes wide.

"She needs help!" His voice cracked.

Buck activated the mike on his shirt and spoke into it. He disappeared into the bathroom.

"Sean, did you eat any of the mushroom quiches?" I asked, my tone urgent.

"No."

Whew. "Good."

"Do you think . . ." He hadn't finished his sentence when a *thud* came from the restroom. He whirled and dashed back there.

"I'll tell your dad," I called after him.

I didn't think I could help by hovering in the hall. After I stepped out the back door, I took a moment to text Abe that Jan was ill at the antique store, Sean was with her, and Buck was helping.

Steering myself around the side of the building, I started toward my restaurant. I didn't need to wade through the crowd inside, and I was overdue back at the store. I felt terrible for Jan. She'd opened up about her loneliness before reverting to type and telling me to get lost. I couldn't help her, but I felt bad.

Swearing to myself, I realized I'd had a chance to ask Buck what he'd learned and I blew it. I slowed to a stop.

A box truck was backed in next to the building, with *Sand Timeless Home Furnishings* newly painted in an ornate script on the side. The door, which looked like it rolled up and down, was closed with an impressive-looking thick metal hook that curled into a slot in the bumper. The truck looked new, with clean tires and a sleek design.

Next to the truck was a panel van with a magnetic *FH Foods* sign on the passenger door. I glanced at the building. The truck blocked the view of the van from the windows on this side of the house. Nobody was in the driveway.

I crossed the fingers of my left hand and tried the handle on the back with my right. *Shoot*. The double doors were locked. As with the coats, I wasn't sure what I expected to find inside, anyway. I snapped a picture of the license plate with my phone, then moved up to the passenger door. If I was caught, I had absolutely no excuse for snooping in what I assumed was Orland's vehicle. But my fingers—and my puzzle brain—itched to search the seat, the glove compartment, whatever presented itself. Fortunately for my as-yet-nonexistent criminal record, this door had been locked, too. I pressed my hands to the glass to shield it from the light and peered inside.

The whole front was messy. Coffee-stained paper cups filled the cup holders. Crumpled napkins and takeout sacks littered the foot wells. A sweater I recognized as one Krystal had been wearing on Monday was pressed into the seat as if someone had sat on it. A brochure lay on the dashboard. It faced the opposite direction, but I'd taught myself to read upside down a long time ago. The brochure was from Nashville Mental Health Services.

A man's voice sounded from around the corner of the house in the back. Orland? It didn't matter. I hurried toward the street.

Out front, a line of customers waited for lunch at KK's Sandos. I steered clear of that scene, too. I had my own sandwiches to prepare and serve. If we hadn't lost all our customers to Krystal, that is.

CHAPTER 48

As it turned out, Pans 'N Pancakes was plenty busy, although not as much as on a usual Saturday. I'd been back in the store for twenty minutes, taking orders and serving, when Abe strolled in. I delivered full plates to a table of hungry diners, then made my way to where he was frowning at his phone.

He glanced up at me. "You said Jan was sick."

"She was. I found her in a bathroom throwing up about half an hour ago." I gestured with my thumb across the street and kept my voice to a near-whisper. "They were serving little mushroom quiches. Sean told me Krystal made them." Was she mentally unstable? Was that the reason for the brochure in the vehicle? Or was the information for Orland's mother-in-law Hattie, to work on her compulsive stealing? I knew the two women weren't related, so any mental illness Krystal had wasn't inherited from Hattie. "Krystal might have used bad mushrooms in the appetizers. Maybe those panthercaps you told me about."

"Like what happened here with the omelets?" His eyebrows went up.

I nodded.

He blinked. "So, probably not fatal, but no fun."

"Unless Jan has an underlying health problem?"

"I don't really know. She didn't while we were married—other than depression—but that was a long time ago."

"Does Sean want your help with her?"

"I'm not sure. He's not answering my texts."

"Buck was there." I laid my hand on his arm. "And she has family with her, right? Her brother, and her sister-in-law's parents."

"Right. Let me tell Seanie I'll give him a ride home or to my place if he needs one." He turned away and bent over the phone again.

The same women who'd been heading to the Sands' barn a little while ago bustled in through the door, setting the bell to jangling.

"Welcome to Pans 'N Pancakes. I'm Robbie Jordan." I smiled at them, counting five in the group. "Are you here for lunch?"

"Yes, ma'am," the tallest in the bunch said.

"We didn't want to get no sandwich from a truck and have to stand up eating it." A silver-haired one shook her head. "We need to set our bones down after all that shopping."

"And we want to check out your pans and all whatnot." Tall grinned.

I checked the restaurant. I could combine a four-top

with a two-top for them. "We'll get a table ready for you ladies. You're welcome to browse the shelves while we do." I gestured toward the retail area.

"Goody," the chair buyer said. "They didn't have all that much acrost over there."

The women aimed for their shopping. My business plan was intact, despite the lunch competition. Some of my clientele would be happy to grab a breakfast or lunch on the go, but most people I served would rather sit down and enjoy a hot meal at their leisure.

Abe slid the phone into his pocket. "I'm starving."

I kissed his cheek. "Come with me, sir." I sat him at an empty two-top, the one Buck usually occupied. *Buck*. I still had no idea if he'd made progress with the poisoning in my restaurant, and now it appeared he had another one on his hands.

"I want a burger with the works," Abe said after glancing at the Specials board. "I'm sure it would be healthier to get quiche and salad, but I'm too hungry."

"No guilt, darling."

"And a glass of milk, please?"

"You got it. You weren't at work this morning, were you?"

"No." He beamed at me. "I was working on a special top-secret project at home, though."

"A top-secret project?" I tilted my head. "What's that about?"

"If I told you, it wouldn't be secret, would it?"

I laughed and ruffled his hair. "How did your show go last night?"

"Good. It was well attended, and we had a lot of fun playing. I hope you'll come next time."

"Maybe I will." I loved watching and hearing him play. "It'll have to be a Sunday night show, though, so I don't have to get up before dawn the next morning."

I gave Danna his order.

"Turner, give me a hand?" I asked. "We have a party of five waiting."

We pushed tables together and set them for the ladies. I hoped none of them had helped themselves to a mushroom mini-quiche before I'd hid them. As I worked, I kept watching the front door. I wanted to know what Adele and Vera had been up to with Hattie. I even more urgently needed to know what Buck knew—and how Jan was.

I seated the women. Brought Abe his lunch. Delivered checks to three tables. Took the women's orders. Conveyed them to Danna. And watched the door.

But the next person to set the bell jangling was none of the three I awaited. Instead Phil, arms full of desserts, pushed through. Just in time, as it turned out. We were down to our last half-dozen brownies.

"Thanks for bringing these." I helped him unload.

"What's going on across the way?" he asked, gazing back at the door. "There's an ambulance in the antique store driveway."

"There is?" I hurried to the door. I hadn't heard a siren. I stepped out onto the porch to see EMTs load a prone figure, swathed in white blankets and strapped to a wheeled stretcher, into the back of the ambulance, which had its lights flashing. The vehicle drove off with its sirens wailing into life. Was that Jan, being transported for observation? I brought my hand to my mouth. Sean's mom was alive, wasn't she? Or had it been someone else?

I hoped the person in the ambulance hadn't been one of Vera's elderly friends.

Behind me the ready bell dinged. Someone called out, "Ma'am?" I turned back and shut the door. I glanced at Abe, but he didn't look alarmed. I had a restaurant to run. I'd find out when I found out.

CHAPTER 49

I set coffee down in front of Adele and Vera fifteen minutes later. They'd snagged the last open table.

"Shooee, it smells good in here," Adele exclaimed.

I sniffed the air. Meat and onions frying did have that effect, unless you were a vegetarian, I supposed. But sometimes one had to come in from outside to realize the allure of the aromas. "Can you tell me what happened at the opening?" I asked. "Do you know who was in the ambulance?"

They exchanged a glance. "It was your sweetie's ex." Adele cast her gaze toward Abe. Phil had ordered lunch, too, and had joined Abe. "Jan."

I gasped. "Excuse me." I hurried to Abe's table. "Abe, Adele says Jan was just taken away in an ambulance."

Abe looked aghast. "No."

Phil folded his hands and closed his eyes, as if praying.

The bell on the door jangled. Abe's gaze whipped toward the front. I looked, too, to see Sean hurrying toward us.

"Dad!" Sean ended the word on a sob and a gasp.

Abe rose, taking his tall son into his arms. "I'm here, honey."

I choked up at his affection for Sean, who would always be his little boy.

"We have to go to the hospital right now. They said Mommy—" his voice broke off and he buried his face in Abe's shoulder.

Abe stroked Sean's hair, gazing at me with both concern and alarm written all over his face. I stepped closer and touched Sean's arm.

"What, Seanie?" Abe asked. "What did they say about your mom?"

"She might not make it," he mumbled through his tears. "Uncle Orland told me. The hospital called him."

My breath caught again, and I brought my other hand to my mouth. Poor Jan. And poor Sean.

"Let's go." Abe kept his arm around Sean's shoulders and steered him to the door.

Sean let himself be pulled along, his hand shielding his eyes. Abe glanced back before they went out. He made the thumb-and-pinkie phone gesture and mouthed, "I'll call you."

I blew them a kiss. I wasn't much of a praying person. But I mustered up an intention for healing and sent it out to Jan. Adele signaled to me.

"Are they off to follow the ambulance?" she asked.

I nodded.

"That tall policeman friend of yours shut down the food truck a couple minutes ago," Vera said.

"What?" I asked. "Buck shut down KK's?"

"It's true." Adele nodded. "And some lady showed up and posted a big old orange sign on the front, saying it's closed. County Board of Health."

"Wow," I said. "That's got to be awful for Krystal." Buck must have called Elizabeth Lake about the bags I'd given him. That was quick. No way a lab had time to analyze them already. Or maybe someone had lodged a prior complaint against the food truck.

My mind spun in furious circles. Was Krystal nuts? How could she not have known the mushrooms she'd used in the quiches were poisonous? Unless . . . someone else had substituted them. Orland? Hattie or Francis? Definitely not Jan, or she never would have eaten one.

"I hope neither of you tasted one of the mushroom quiches," I said.

"You warned me off 'em," Vera replied. "And I passed the word onto Addie here."

Whew. "Good. I found Jan ill in the bathroom in the store before I left. I'm glad neither of you ran that risk." I looked from Vera to Adele and back. "What were you two cornering Hattie about, anyway?"

"As a matter of fact," Adele began. "We ran us a small little intervention. I wanted to get your graters back."

"And we did." Vera beamed as she opened her voluminous bag. The green handle of the grater I'd bought last Saturday peeked out. "We twisted her arm just a tiny itsy bit."

"Literally?" I asked.

"Hon, you don't even want to know." Adele laughed.

"Actually, I do." I folded my arms. "Come on, out with it. How did you get them back?"

"Us and Hattie, we go way back," Vera began.

"You can believe we got us some dirt on her. All it took was a tiny reminder that she wouldn't want said dirt to go all public, like." Adele grinned.

I just shook my head. "Vera," I said. "Was that plan what you were trying to signal me about earlier?"

"Sure was, hon." Vera pointed as a dozen people surged into the store. "That looks about like the size of the line of folks who was waiting for their so-called sandos."

I checked the clock. It wasn't yet two o'clock. We should be able to accommodate the current diners as well as the new ones before we closed. And if we had to stay open a little longer to fill the food truck gap, so be it.

"Do you want to order quick before we get any busier?" I asked.

"You still got some of that quiche?" Adele asked.

"We do." At least I hoped so.

"I'll take a plate of that and a small salad."

"Make that two," Vera chimed in.

"Old Samuel's always harping on me to eat healthy." Adele shook her head but smiled. "I'll be able to give him a good report." She chuckled.

I gave Danna their order, then made my way to the newcomers.

"Welcome." I smiled at the crowd. A couple looked familiar, but most I'd never seen before. "It'll be a few minutes' wait, but we should be able to get you all seated pretty soon."

"I'll be glad to set myself down for my meal, anyway," an older man said. "Didn't much fancy getting a takeout lunch, but the wife here insisted."

The woman at his side elbowed him. "We was going to

have a picnic in the park, Eldridge. You know that." She gazed at me. "Having a food truck parked across the street must have been bad for your business, miss."

"We've been doing fine," I said. "There's room for both businesses." I didn't really mean it, but what could I say? I'd hoped Krystal would move her truck elsewhere, but I certainly hadn't been praying for her to be shut down. I knew exactly how tough that was.

The woman shook her head. "I can't imagine she's going to make much of a go of it, being shut down by the Board of Health and all such like that."

I felt how tight my smile was. These two were clearly not local, or they'd know I'd been shut down in exactly the same way only a few days earlier.

"Feel free to browse the antique cookware or take a seat here while you wait." I left them and the rest to it and turned away.

In the kitchen area, Turner was taking over the grill from Danna. Simply cooking and not schmoozing with customers sounded good to me right about now, but they'd already accomplished the switch. I never had gotten my bathroom break, so I pointed myself in that direction. I slowed at Phil's table.

"Do you think she's going to be okay?" he asked. "Sean's mom?"

"I don't know, Phil. I hope so." If Jan was that bad off, she must have some other health condition. High blood pressure, maybe? Heart? I had no idea. All I knew was that she didn't look like a fitness freak, which didn't necessarily mean anything.

It was hard to focus on work, but I had to. I'd been about to clear Phil and Abe's table when Sean had come in. Phil pulled out his wallet.

"Forget it, bro," I said. "Both lunches are on me."

"Thanks, Robbie. I hope Sean's mom is going to be okay."

"You and me, both. He's only fifteen." I blew out a breath. "Thanks for the desserts."

"Sure. I'll be praying for Jan. I'll tell Gramps, too. He's got a pretty powerful prayer group going."

"I can see Samuel being powerful that way." I spied a customer trying to get my attention, plus two more tables needed clearing, and Adele looked worried. "I gotta run, Phil." I extended my hands to gather up the plates.

Phil gave me a quick hug. "Let me get those."

"You're the best." I bustled over to the customer.

"Can I get my check, please, Miss Jordan?" He was a kindly regular who had lost his wife to early-onset Alzheimer's not long ago. He ate lunch here every day of the week and always ordered a grilled cheddar-and-ham on rye bread.

I handed him his ticket. "Have a good day, sir."

CHAPTER 50

"What up with Abe and Sean?" Turner asked from the grill a few minutes later.

"Yeah." Danna set a new pot of coffee to brew. "It looked like something bad went down."

I glanced around the restaurant. Things were quiet for the moment. "I didn't get a chance to tell you what happened across the street earlier. In a nutshell, Krystal had made mushroom mini-quiches for the event. The rest of the appetizers were ready-made. I . . . um . . . confiscated one platter of the mushroom apps before anybody could eat them and the rest burnt. But apparently Jan O'Neill ate some, because she got really sick. I found her in a bathroom."

"What?" Turner sounded astonished. "Krystal using bad mushrooms at her own parents' store celebration. That's crazy." He flipped a couple of burgers.

"I know," I said. "An ambulance took Jan away—at least I think it was her. Adele and Vera said the Department of Health shut down the food truck."

"Jeez," Danna said. "Maybe they were onto her even before today. She must have been the one to slide those panther mushrooms into our order."

"Maybe." I frowned, thinking.

"Getting back to Sean, what happened?" Turner asked.

"Apparently the hospital called Orland and said Jan was in bad shape. Abe drove Sean."

"Man." Danna shook her head. "That's tough for the kid."

Turner set down his spatulas and brought his palms in front of his chest, closing his eyes. His lips moved almost imperceptibly in silence. He bent his head and touched his fingertips to his forehead. He opened his eyes to see Danna and me giving him our full attention.

"My version of a Hindu prayer." His grin was sheepish. "And—uh-oh! Now we need a prayer for the buns." He rescued two hamburger buns from a smoking toaster.

"Compost, my friend," Danna said.

"No worries, Turner," I said. "Just start over."

Adele had her hand in the air, trying to get my attention.

"Let me go see what my aunt wants," I said. Outside, the sky had turned dark. Another storm must be blowing in.

"Robbie, hon, did you hear anything yet?" Adele asked.

I checked my phone. "Not yet."

Vera closed her eyes and folded her hands. Another prayerful person. *Good.*

"Did they go to Bloomington?" Adele wasn't the sort who prayed, but her heart was big enough to hold the world.

"Huh," I said softly so as to not disturb Vera. "I don't actually know." Sean hadn't said which hospital. I knew Abe would let me know.

"Hope they upped and took her to IU." Adele slapped the table.

Vera's eyes jerked open. "Addie, I was praying."

"Sorry, girl." Adele patted her hand. "It's just that there ain't no better health facility in all the Midwest."

I smiled at my aunt. Chicago had world-class hospitals, as did several other Midwestern cities. I let it go. The IU hospital was certainly the best within ambulance range. "Can I get either of you a brownie or a cookie for dessert? Baked by Baker Phil."

"He's a good boy." Adele beamed. "I had such a healthy lunch, I'll take one of each."

"A brownie for me, please, Robbie," Vera said. "And a touch more coffee, if you have any."

"You got it."

By two-forty-five we'd delivered the last order, and all the newcomers seemed happy with their meals. I pointed myself toward the door to turn the sign to *Closed*. Buck stood inside the entrance, searching the premises with his gaze. How had I missed him coming in? He saw me and beckoned me toward him.

The silver-haired antique shopper stopped me as I passed their table. "What does that cop want?" she asked.

The rest of the group stared at me with alarmed expressions.

"He's a regular here, and a friend." I mustered a smile

I didn't feel and prepared to lie. "There's nothing to worry about."

"All righty," she said. "Thanks."

The tall one chimed in. "This food is so good, hon. Mark my words, we'll be back."

"I'm glad. If you'll excuse me?" I continued my trajectory.

"You saw Ms. Lake took and shut down the food truck?" Buck asked.

"Yes. She couldn't have analyzed those mushroom samples so quickly, though."

"Nope. She found some other issues." He cleared his throat. "Listen, I know it's past closing time. But I've got a hunger that's about to bring me to my bony knees. Can I get me some lunch?"

Despite the bad news, despite all the unanswered questions, despite the worry about Jan, I had to laugh. "Sure, Buck. You can get some lunch."

CHAPTER 51

All our customers had left by three-thirty. The table where my crew and I sat with Buck, Adele, and Vera didn't count. Danna, Turner, and I had worked steadily cleaning up, table by table, the grill, the floor. Buck had inhaled both a cheeseburger and a grilled cheese sandwich with tomato for his lunch. He'd stayed on talking with the older ladies, with my blessing.

Now the six of us were gathered, my team and I downing our much-delayed lunches. It had gotten even darker outside and we'd turned on the lights in here.

"We got some talking to do, sugar," Adele said. "Okay if we break out the good stuff?"

I nodded as I swallowed a bite of turkey burger. "You know where it is." I headed to my apartment for beers and to let Birdy join us.

The cat found a patch of floor near our table and proceeded to bathe. I poured IPAs for Danna, Vera, and my-self. Turner surprised Adele by holding out his coffee mug for a splash of Four Roses. I kept checking my phone. Nothing yet from Abe.

"Buck, what about you?" Adele asked.

"Welp, I shouldn't. But I'll take a peerie dram."

Five pairs of eyes went wide.

"What?" Buck asked in mock surprise. "You don't know what that means?"

"It ain't that so much as you saying them words for wanting a splash of whiskey," Adele said.

"My pop's mama hailed from them Shetland Islands. You know, up there way at the top of Scotland. When I was a small little thing, Gran McNally always talked about me as a peerie boy, and shoo, did she ever love her dram after dinner." Buck grinned and extended his mug.

"Cheers, then." I held up my glass. "Or whatever they say in Scotland."

"I think it's time all us put our heads together." Adele sipped and set her mug down. "We can't have no more people getting sick and dying around here."

"Right. We can't," I agreed.

"No kidding," Danna said. "My mom is getting worried about the town's reputation."

"Let's talk about what we know," I went on.

"And what we don't," Buck added.

"Right." I extended my thumb. "One, we know Jan and Orland Krueger are kind of experts about mush-rooms. They founded that society, that mushroom club, and Abe said Jan taught him."

Adele nodded.

"And Orland has been acting angry, at least toward me." A shiver ran through me, remembering.

"Two," Turner jumped in. "He owns the company that delivered the box here."

"The outfit Francis and Hattie used to own," Adele said. "Three, Francis holds a stupid old grudge against me. He mighta been hoping I'd eat all them bad mushrooms in one omelet and croak right in front of him."

Vera gave a knowing nod. "Four, Hattie's so jealous of Robbie's business she stole a bunch of her cookware."

"Wait a chicken-pickin' minute here," Buck said. "She did what, now?"

"Hattie's a known klepto," Adele said. "She mighta stole 'em even if she didn't have no reason for it."

"True," Buck said. "You didn't report the theft, Robbie."

I lifted a shoulder and dropped it. The graters hadn't seemed like a big enough offense to report.

"But we got them back for Robbie." Vera beamed.

"Glad to hear it," Buck said. "Five, Krystal made them little mushroom pies for the shindig today. The ones what apparently have Jan O'Neill seriously ill."

I glanced at my phone. Still nothing from Abe, which I hoped meant good news. I raised a finger. "Six, Len was going to work with Krystal, but even before this afternoon he was questioning the wisdom of that. He said Krystal was acting kind of unstable. He didn't get a chance to tell me in what way." I checked my phone. He'd said he would call me, but he hadn't. I rued not getting his number. When we were done talking, I'd call Lou and get it.

"Weren't you wondering if maybe Jan was responsible for the first batch of bad shrooms, Robbie?" Danna asked. "Because even though she and Abe split up a long time ago, she didn't want you to have him?"

"I was." I wrinkled my nose. "But I think that idea's out the window now. I mean, why would she have eaten the quiches today if she knew the mushrooms were bad?"

"Maybe her knowledge of mushrooms is rusty," Buck offered.

"She would know what to look for," I said.

"Or Jan hadn't arrived yet when Krystal was making them," Danna said. "Jan might not have seen exactly what went into them."

"That seems more likely," I agreed.

Quiet fell over us. I popped in the last bite of my burger. Turner frowned at his mug and tapped the side of it with his finger. Danna sipped her beer.

Vera shifted uncomfortably in her chair. "My old bones are telling me it's going to rain soon."

"And this girl's bones don't never lie." Adele grinned and pointed at Vera.

With these dark clouds, rain had to be close behind, bones or no bones.

I faced Buck. "What have you learned about FH Foods, Buck? Alibis? Did you talk to Pat, the woman who works at the company?"

"Welp, I don't know a heck of a lot." He shifted uncomfortably, too, but it seemed more as a result of our attention than from the weather. "I wasn't able to get ahold of that Pat lady. Nobody else claims to know a dang thing. One or more of thems is definitely lying, but I ain't figured out which one. Leastwise, not so far."

"Really?" Adele sounded incredulous. "Nobody saw nothing?"

He lifted a shoulder and dropped it.

"Did you talk to Krystal this afternoon, Buck?" I asked.

"I tried, after Ms. Lake shut her down," he said. "Krystal claimed she wasn't feeling too hot, herself, and said she had to get home and go to bed."

Danna narrowed her eyes. "If she served bad mushrooms, either she's clueless and stupid, or she was faking being ill. Why would she eat them?" She bent over her phone.

"Do the Kruegers live here in town?" I asked.

Adele nodded. "Got a cute cottage over by South Lick Creek. On the Beanblossom border. You know, where the covered bridge is."

The bridge where a woman had been murdered during a bluegrass festival two years ago. I knew it too well.

"I just got a text from my mom. She's going to go pay Krystal a visit," Danna announced. "She says Orland went to the hospital where they took Jan, so she's going to bring Krystal one of her little Mayor Cares packages." She rolled her eyes. "That is, she's going to be a politician and also see what she can find out."

"That's Corrine, all the way." Maybe I'd pay Krystal a visit later, too. Or not. The mayor stopping by was one thing. Me doing it to snoop would be a classic too-stupid-to-live move, and I'd been getting better at avoiding those lately. I looked toward the street, even though I wasn't positioned to see a thing outside. "Did they close the antique store when Jan was taken away?"

"Francis said it was the grand opening and they were staying open." Buck shook his head. "Not sure how wise that was. At leastwise they put all the food away."

"I guess that's all we know." I surveyed the group.

A jagged flash of light illuminated the dark windows. I

was about to ask what it was when a huge crack split the air. Vera yelled. I jumped in my seat. The interior lights went out as a bedlam of rain hit the western windows and crashed down on the porch's metal roof.

"Wow," Danna said. "I did not know that was forecast."

It wasn't too dark in here to see, but I hurried over to the walk-in and flipped the auxiliary power switch. After our last major power outage, I'd invested in a generator and gotten it wired to my various cooling units—the walk-in, the freezer, the drinks cooler, and the under-counter fridge in the cooking area. I couldn't afford to lose food I'd already paid good money for. When I got back to the table, Buck was reading something on his phone.

He looked up and wagged his head with a mournful air. "Jan didn't make it."

No. I brought my hands to my forehead and stared at the floor. Poor, dear Sean. I knew on the deepest of levels what it was like to lose your mother, but I'd been ten years older than him when mine had died. He was a kid. Jan might have been difficult. She was still his mommy. I felt guilty for not staying with her when I found her sick, despite her telling me to leave. I took a deep breath and gazed around the table. Everybody looked sad in different ways.

I ended with Buck. "Thank you for telling us. Is she, are they, at the IU hospital?"

"Yep. Abe and Sean made it there."

I stood. "I have to go be with them. Rain or no rain."

"Go on, hon, but drive careful," Adele said.

"I will."

"We'll close up, Robbie," Danna said. "Don't worry."

"Thanks."

Adele rose and wrapped me in a tight embrace. "Your menfolk need you. Send them both my love."

CHAPTER 52

I texted Abe before I left South Lick that I was on my way. He wrote back right away, in as few words as possible.

Jan's heart failed.

He added directions for where to find them within the large facility. The hospital complex on West Second Street had undergone a major building project since the last time I was here, and it still wasn't finished. I got caught up in a couple of detours and closed parking lots. Despite the heavy rain, and despite making it to Bloomington from South Lick in under forty minutes—record time—I didn't reach my guys as quickly as I'd hoped.

I spotted Abe and Sean in the small waiting room before they saw me. I hurried toward them, but I slowed my step. I wanted to enter the room holding them in a calm love. Neither of them needed more angst. Abe gave me a sad smile, but Sean didn't look up from where he slumped on an orange couch, head on his forearms. I sat on the other side of the boy and put my arms around him.

"I'm so sorry, Sean."

His slender shoulders shook. I held on. Abe reached his arm across Sean's back and connected with me. We were a unit, these two and me. Even though Abe and I weren't yet officially married, I knew sticking with him—and his son—through sickness and in health was a promise I would easily and happily make.

After what seemed like a long time, but was probably only a minute or two, Sean straightened, sniffling.

"Thanks for coming, Robbie," he whispered.

"Of course, honey." The endearment fell lightly off my tongue. I looked at Abe. "Are you . . . did you . . ." I didn't know how to ask what was happening right now.

Abe opened his mouth, but Sean spoke first.

"Mom wanted to be an organ donor. We're waiting—" A sob choked off his voice.

His dad took over. "They're taking her organs now, the ones they can use. We'll be able to say goodbye to her when they are finished."

Oh. I'd read about organ donation, but I'd never been close to it. I'd signed a commitment to be an organ donor when I renewed my license. What I remembered from the information was that the hospital left the person tidy and covered after they were done so the family could make their farewells.

I nodded. "Is Orland here?" Not that I wanted to run into him, but he was Jan's brother.

"He was. I'm not sure where he went."

I squeezed Sean's shoulder. "You guys could be here a while. I'm going to get you something to eat and drink." I held up a hand when Abe looked about to protest. "Trust me." I kissed Abe's forehead and made my way out. Sean would totally collapse if he didn't eat and get some sugar into him. It wouldn't hurt Abe, either.

I wandered around, asking questions a couple of times, until I found a café. Equipped with a tall Coke, a coffee laced with sugar and cream, and a sack holding two ham-and-cheese sandwiches and two big peanut butter cookies, I made my way toward the elevators. Hospital staff in scrubs, some also wearing white coats, bustled by in both directions. A tired-looking man leaning on a walker shuffled past, and an orderly pushed a woman about my age in a wheelchair. A beaming guy carrying a newborn in a carrier walked next to her. The life of a big hospital.

Turning a corner, I nearly ran into Orland. As in physically. I barely hung onto the drinks, I had to put the brakes on so fast. Was I in for another angry confrontation? I took a second look at him. Probably not.

He took a step back. His arms hung at his sides as if they barely belonged to him, and his shoulders bent forward.

"Hello, Robbie." His voice was gravelly, his eyes anguished.

"Orland, I'm so very sorry about your sister."

He gazed at me. "Thank you." He skirted me and wandered away, mumbling to himself.

All I caught was, "I can't believe . . ." He couldn't believe what? It was hard to believe that Jan was gone? Or maybe he was trying to get his brain around the fact that his own wife might be responsible for her death.

CHAPTER 53

I waited with Abe and Sean until they were summoned to say goodbye to Jan at around five o'clock. Orland hadn't reappeared. Abe tried to call him, but he didn't answer. Abe, his arm around a grieving Sean, asked if I wanted to come in with them.

"No. You guys go." It felt like a polite invitation, but I didn't think either of these dear men needed me along. I hugged them. "I love you both. We'll talk when you get back."

"They said we could take as long as we needed," Abe murmured. "We'll probably head to my parents' place when we're done."

Sadness for them slowed my steps as I returned to my car. It had to be doubly hard for Abe. He needed to hold up his boy, and he himself had loved Jan once.

I sat in the little Prius, feeling in need of a good friend. I texted Lou.

Am in B'ton. Meet at Phat Cats bar?

Tonight was to have been my date night dinner with Abe, I remembered, as I waited for her reply. I couldn't imagine a better reason for a rain check, but I didn't feel like being alone right now. I perked up to see Lou's answer.

Be there in ten.

K. Thx.

I put the restaurant's address into my map app. It didn't take me more than ten minutes, either. The hour was early enough to get parking as well as tall bar seats. The bistro was intimate, seating maybe four dozen at regular tables and another dozen and a half along the L-shaped bar.

I greeted Lou. "Do they have a coatrack?" I shed my hooded jacket, but it was too wet to hang over the back of the stool.

She pointed to a row of hooks in a hallway beyond the bar. I hung up the garment and fluffed the water out of my hair, then slid onto the stool next to her. It looked like the place had just opened for the evening. A ponytailed man was setting tables, and a pass-through window into the kitchen emitted the most wonderful of smells. Only a two-top was occupied so far, by a couple both working their phones instead of talking with each other.

Chris stood behind the bar. "Hey, Lou. And Robbie from South Lick, right?" Her curly hair was a little fly-away, and she wore an Indian-print gauzy top.

"Yes. Good memory." I smiled.

"What can I get you ladies?" Chris slid menus toward

both of us. "Bar offerings are on the back, but I can fix pretty near anything."

Lou checked with me. "Are we doing real drinks?"

"Maybe one. I have to drive home in this rain." I hadn't gotten myself a sandwich at the hospital, and I was suddenly ravenous. Maybe not quite as hungry as Buck often proclaimed to be, but I needed food in me, and soon. "As long as I eat."

"I'll have a peach Hoagy," Lou said, looking up from the menu.

I tilted my head. "What's that?"

"Hoagy Carmichael was born here in Bloomington and wrote some of his famous songs right down the street." Chris smiled. "He wrote 'Georgia on My Mind,' so we invented a peach cocktail in his honor."

"I guess I'll try that, too," I said. "What's in it?"

"Peach nectar, peach moonshine, bourbon, and a squeeze of lime."

"Moonshine?" Lou asked.

"Yep. We get it from a little distillery across the border in Kentucky."

My stomach growled. "And can we get an order of the sweet potato empanadas to start, please?"

"You got it." Chris turned to the pass-through. "Paul, Lou is here, and she brought Robbie Jordan. They'll start with the empanadas."

Paul, in a black chef's tunic, leaned his head out and waved. "Welcome to Phat Cats, Lou and Robbie. One appetizer, coming right up."

"I'm glad to be here," I said. "Oh, Chris. You might have a reservation for two a little later tonight for Abe O'Neill? He's my fiancé, and he had a death in the family today. I'm afraid we'll need to cancel that."

Lou gave me a sharp look. I held up a finger to signal I'd tell her in a minute.

"No worries," Chris said. "I'm sorry for his loss, and yours, I expect."

"Thank you."

"We always have a wait-list for reservations." She tapped into a tablet in a stand behind the bar.

"Who died?" Lou whispered with saucer eyes.

As Chris busied herself making the drinks, I filled in my friend on the day's events.

"I'm really sorry for Sean. But how could a mushroom quiche cause a heart attack?" Lou asked.

"The older man who ate the mushroom omelet in my restaurant was already ill, and the toxins did him in. But . . ." I stared at her. "I don't actually know if the same thing happened with Jan. Or if she had a bad heart and it was her time." Or if somebody poisoned her on purpose. My mind raced along this path of reasoning. Who would want Jan dead? Did she have enemies? There had to be a poison that either caused or mimicked a heart attack. I didn't know what it might be, but I had no doubt one existed.

"I can tell your detective brain is on overdrive," Lou said.

"Kind of." I wrestled my thoughts back to having drinks and dinner with my friend. "Anyway, I left the hospital when they came to tell Abe and Sean they could go say goodbye to her."

"That's so sad."

Chris set two brimming martini glasses in front of us. She grabbed a square plate filled with puffy, tasty morsels from the window and slid that onto the counter, too.

"Enjoy, and let me know what else you'd like to order."
She smiled and turned away.

Steam rose up from golden brown pillows. My fingers
itched to pick one up.

Lou raised her glass. "Here's to no more deaths,
right?"

I frowned, nodding, and carefully clinked my glass
with hers. "Zero more." I sipped the concoction. I'd had a
kind of peach daiquiri years ago, and it had been too
sweet by half. But this was a much more refined cocktail,
served in an elegant stemmed glass instead of a tumbler.
A ripe peach slice was stuck on the rim. The peach nectar
was smooth, and it mellowed out the moonshine, which
cut the fruity sweetness. The bourbon and the lime finished it off.

"I like it." Still needing food, I set down the glass, bit
into an empanada, and savored the flavors. "This tastes
like California to me," I said to Chris. The smooth sweet
potato had been mixed with black beans, bits of red sweet
pepper, and cheese. I picked up the tastes of lime and
fresh cilantro. The puff pastry crust was perfectly crisp
and flaky, too.

"Thanks," Chris said. "We got inspired by a trip to
Santa Barbara last January. We always close up shop and
take a real vacation during the two weeks after New
Year's."

"Santa Barbara is Robbie's hometown," Lou offered.

"Lucky you," Chris said.

I agreed, but I was still thinking. How would we get to
no more deaths if we didn't figure out this week's? I
glanced around. No new diners had arrived. The ponytailed dude was attending to the two-top.

"Chris," I began in a low voice. "I don't know if you

heard that a man unfortunately passed away after eating in my restaurant earlier this week."

"Sure, we heard," she said. "Word gets around in the business."

I nodded. "And you and Paul had a similar experience a few years ago, I understand." I watched her, but she didn't seem to turn defensive. "I'm only trying to understand a few things."

"Okay. Like what?"

"Is it true that FH Foods was your supplier at the time?"

Lou observed our back-and-forth with an interested expression, but she didn't chime in.

"Yes, but they aren't any more." Chris gave a glance toward the kitchen, then focused on me. "I still think something was up with the delivery they made to us. Krystal Sand was both packer and driver for her parents' business at the time." She set her forearms on the bar and leaned toward us. "Paul doesn't agree with me."

"It was bad oysters, wasn't it?" Lou asked.

"Yes, and anyone can get an off oyster. But we served them with a mushroom appetizer."

Lou and I exchanged a look.

"Do you think there was anything malicious about the delivery?" I asked the petite chef.

"I don't know, Robbie." She folded her arms, thinking. "We didn't know the family personally. I can't think of a reason why somebody would deliver bad food here on purpose."

"You went ahead and catered their wedding in Story last year," I said.

"Kind of against my better judgment. And believe me, we used mushrooms from a reliable vendor. I wasn't about to risk my entire career on a bunch of fungi picked by amateurs." She gazed beyond us at the entrance. "There's the five-forty-five group, right on time."

In the mirror behind the bar I saw a good-sized crowd of people enter, laughing and shaking off raindrops.

My phone's buzzing got my attention. Abe texted me:

All done. Taking Sean to my parents. Love you. Call later if you want.

Good. Abe's parents, Freddy and Howard, would take care of both of them in South Lick.

"Will you be ordering dinner?" Chris asked us.

"Please," Lou said. "Right, Robbie?"

I nodded my agreement. I could join them later, or have a quiet night alone with my breakfast prep and my thoughts.

"I'll be back to take your order whenever you're ready. Excuse me, ladies." Chris bustled off.

I perused the menu. I read descriptions of dishes like Cajun Seafood Stew and house-made Gnocchi with Prosciutto and Roasted Tomato Sauce, but I didn't absorb the meanings. As far as I knew, Jan was the only person to fall ill at the antique store opening. Was that because I'd hidden all the appetizers? Or because something else had caused her to get sick?

CHAPTER 54

The rain was much lighter on my drive home. I was delightfully full of a Fallen Caesar salad, the gnocchi dish, and a slice of one of the best triple dark chocolate cakes I'd ever tasted, baked by Chris. I'd switched to seltzer after my one drink, so I was fine to drive, and Lou and I hadn't spoken of death again.

Now, at seven-thirty, with my car pointed homeward, it all came back. My mushroom delivery. Jan getting sick at the opening. Orland's previous threatening behavior. Hattie's thieving. Francis's comments and glares at Adele, and at me. Krystal's food truck being shut down and her acting strange toward Len. I felt like I was tiptoeing toward the edge of some imaginary ridge in twilight. I couldn't quite see my way clear to figuring out what was happening. Couldn't quite summit the top and have all the facts in view.

I pictured how sad Orland had seemed about Jan at the hospital. They were twins, and they'd stayed close as adults. Georgia had commented on it. I'd seen them taking joy in each other outside the store that day Krystal opened her food truck. Of course he was devastated.

My car's Bluetooth signaled an incoming text from Abe. I found a place to pull over and read the message.

Sean says Krystal urged Jan to sample the mushroom quiche. He didn't eat any.

Krystal could have added poison to the ones she pushed at Jan. I tapped back a reply.

Pls let Buck know. Am driving back to SL. Love you both.

His reply came immediately.

K. Love you too.

I resumed driving. I'd given Buck samples of the quiches and the filling. My breath rushed in as I thought of something. If Jan had been purposely poisoned, could that affect her donated organs? And would they still do an autopsy? This was getting a lot more complicated. Why would Krystal want to kill Jan, anyway? Maybe she was jealous of Jan's relationship with her twin, Krystal's husband. She'd really have to be crazy to kill over that.

I gave my head a shake. I couldn't do anything while I was in the car unless I stopped again, and I wanted to be home. I passed the sign for Greasy Hollow Road. I'd be back in my apartment in twenty minutes. At least the rain had stopped. The sky, still an hour before sundown, was dark and gray from the clouds. Maybe we'd be getting more precipitation later. I flipped the radio over to Aux and smiled as one of my mom's favorite albums began to play, one I kept in the CD slot ready to go. Mary Chapin Carpenter singing "A Road Is Just a Road" had become one of my own favorite driving songs. I sang along with abandon.

I slowed on Main Street as I neared my store. The back of the Sand Timeless Antiques truck was open. The front door to the store was ajar, too. Francis stared into the back of the truck, hands on his hips. He turned as my car approached. When he beckoned to me, I groaned. This was pretty much the last person I wanted to interact with right now.

No cars approached behind me, so I pulled up in front of Pans 'N Pancakes and opened my window.

"Can you give me a hand for a minute?" he called from across the road. "Got a table I need to move out of the truck and into the building. It's not heavy, but it's awkward for one person, and Hattie is indisposed."

I didn't think I'd ever heard someone actually say that word. I considered his request. He was a neighbor, after all, and would be one for the foreseeable future. Maybe doing him a good deed would help him feel more positive about Adele. In some kind of warped way.

"Sure. One second." I parked in one of the diagonal spots in front of the restaurant. Should I bring my bag? *Nah*. It could get caught up in the table transfer. I'd have to move the car to the back when the favor was completed, anyway. I dropped the keys into my jacket pocket, then waited for two cars to pass before crossing.

"If you get in and push, I'll lower the table to the ground." He pointed inside. "It's on a quilt, so it'll move easily."

Sure enough, a sleek modern table in the Shaker style sat on a quilted moving cloth inside. It looked more like a desk, about five feet by two feet, and was the only piece in the truck. But did I want to climb in there? This man might have caused my customer's death. I supposed he might even have poisoned Jan, although I couldn't think of why. Would he try to harm me?

I swallowed. "How about I receive it out here, and you get in?" I asked.

"I'm a lot taller than you." He was calm, all business. "It'll work better if you push. Believe me, I know the best way to move furniture."

"All right." We were on a main thoroughfare, after all. I set my foot on a kind of step that hung down, grabbed a handle at the side of the door, and swung up into the truck. I could easily stand inside. I moved to the back of the table. A grinding, sliding noise began, and I whirled.

Slam. The door shut. My world turned dark.

CHAPTER 55

"Francis!" I yelled. "Open the door." I let out a string of words that would have earned me a heap of scolding from Adele. "Francis!"

No response. I felt my way around the table to the door. Would it even have a handle on the inside? I felt all around the edges. I knelt and moved my hands along the bottom. No handle.

A rumble came from the front. *No!* The truck jolted as it moved. It knocked me against the metal door, making me whack my head and my left elbow. Where was he taking me?

Wait. He was driving forward. If he'd backed up, I would have been thrown toward the front. Maybe he wasn't taking me to some isolated gulley or hillside, some deserted locale. We eased over a bump, then the rumbling ceased. I pounded on the door with my fists.

"Let me out of here!"

Silence was the reply. And then a *thunk*. What? I thought hard. He must have driven into the barn. The bump would have been the threshold. And now he'd closed the barn door. Even if I yelled, I didn't have a chance of anyone in public hearing me. Why did Francis do this? He couldn't have planned it. He didn't know when I was going to drive up. I might have been out all night if my evening had gone as planned. He'd seemed calm, not nervous about abducting me. Curse him a thousand times over.

The "why" for his actions dawned on me. Francis was protecting his mentally ill daughter. She was his only remaining child. He must have suspected what she was up to. He might have seen me talking to Buck after Jan took ill. Francis might even have spied my peering into the FH Foods van. And I knew he'd noticed me hiding the platter of mushroom quiches. Plus, it wasn't exactly a secret that I had been involved in homicide investigations before. He must have seized the moment when he saw me drive up.

But the more immediate question was why I had climbed in here. Maybe I wasn't getting better at avoiding too-stupid-to-live moves. When would I ever learn to listen to my gut? How long would I be stuck in—? I figuratively slapped my forehead. I had my phone. I wasn't stuck. I could call for help.

I patted my jacket pockets. Keys and multi-tool. No phone. My back pocket, where I usually stuck the device, was flat, too. I pressed my eyes closed. I'd taken the cell out for dinner and the drive home so I didn't sit on it. My phone was safely in my cute turquoise cross bag. Which sat safely on the front seat of the Prius. *Brilliant*. I blew out a breath, drawing up my knees and leaning my arms and head on them. I could die in here. Who would ever look? Francis could wait until I passed out and then drive me somewhere to expire alone.

A sob slipped out. I didn't want to die. I wanted to run my business. Ride my bike. See Adele through to the end of her natural life, which I hoped was many years in the future. And, most important of all, marry my lovely, dear Abe. I wanted to help him care for now-motherless Sean and maybe produce a baby or two of our own to round out the family.

"No, dammit." I sat up straight and swiped my eyes. "I'm not going to die. I'm going to get myself out of here." I would not become a victim. I wouldn't. I sniffed, smelling old wood and dust. Air from the barn was coming in. That was good. I wasn't thirsty, but I wouldn't mind using a bathroom. That need was going have to take a number.

I climbed to my feet. I didn't think I'd seen a pry bar or a tool kit in here, but felt my way around the periphery, just in case. All I found was a stack of folded quilts in the front corner and a coil of rope hanging from the left-side wall.

"So be it." I had a tool, I had keys, I had a reasonably strong body. And I had a brain. I pushed the table farther toward the front so I had room to work. I drew out my multi-tool and felt for the biggest, strongest blade. Remembering the heavy hook closure I'd seen on the back of the truck earlier in the day made me hesitate for a moment. I squinted my eyes, thinking. The door had made the sliding noise of closing, but I hadn't heard the clunk of a hook being levered into place. I'd guess Francis had been slightly panicked and hadn't thought about securing the door, because he knew he wasn't going to drive far. *Good.*

I knelt. All I needed was to raise the door an inch so I could slide my fingers under it and start it sliding upward. I gently maneuvered the blade into the intersection between the floor and the door. Or I tried. The floor had a half-inch lip, exactly enough to mess with my leverage. I tried down a little farther. The blade had to slide far enough in to lift with it, but the lip prevented me from getting it flat enough to get underneath the door.

Realizing it wasn't going to work resulted in more swearing. I sat back on my heels and closed the blade. I felt the door. Because it rolled up into the top of the truck, it was made of horizontal sections of metal. I pulled out the corkscrew. I pressed it between two sections and pushed hard as I turned. But it wasn't a metal drill bit. Instead of inserting into the metal so I could use the multitool as a lifting handle, the corkscrew slid sideways and snapped back into the tool, which in turn slid out of my hand.

"No!" I refused to be trapped in here. I felt around until I found the tool. What else could I try? I pushed up to standing and pressed both palms against the door, bending my knees, pressing upward. It didn't budge.

Stepping back, I crossed my arms. I thought back to when I'd seen the truck earlier. It had looked new. Surely the vehicle would include an emergency button to raise the door in case someone got stuck inside by accident. I doubted the designers would have envisioned a malicious act like the one that trapped me. But everything was electronic these days, wasn't it? Maybe I needed to rethink my brute-force approach.

I stashed the tool again and felt my way to the left side of the door. I reached as high on the frame as I could and ran my hand slowly down, not missing a centimeter. Nada. The edge of the door was close to where the truck's side met the back. I did three more sweeps, one next to the door, one on the side next to the corner, and one more next to that. I did not encounter a button or a lever, only smooth metal walls.

I couldn't give up yet. I felt my way back to the right side. On my very last pass, flooded with desperation, my hand encountered an obstacle. I felt a rectangle the size of a playing card. In the middle was a flat, round shape. An emergency release button? Oh, let it be so. And let it not need the truck to be running to operate.

About to press it, I froze. What if Francis was outside the truck waiting for me? Or his deranged daughter, or Orland? Or even Hattie. I shook my head, hard. I didn't have an alternative, but I did have a multi-tool. I pulled out the knife blade and held it ready. My heart thudded as I jabbed my thumb onto the button and leaned into it.

The grinding sound of the door sliding up sounded better than angels singing Hallelujah.

CHAPTER 56

Even better, nobody awaited as I cautiously climbed down. I pressed my back to the truck and gazed all around. Maybe Francis—or someone else in his family— hid behind that chipped red tiller or lurked in the shadows behind a rack of dusty, dry horse tack. I waited. No one emerged.

My legs wobbled from relief and adrenaline. I stayed in place another moment to take a deep breath. All I could hear in my head was that politician's slogan from a few years earlier: "Nevertheless, she persisted." If I hadn't persisted, I'd still be locked in that stupid truck.

But I wasn't home yet, which meant I wasn't safe yet. I headed around to the truck's cab, just in case Francis had left the keys in the ignition. I could drive it across the street, but no such luck.

I hurried through the dimming light to the barn door. When I'd been here before, the door had been wide open. Now the door was slid shut over the eight-foot space. I grabbed the rusty handle and yanked to the right. My shoulders drooped when it didn't budge. Not again. Francis must have locked it from the outside. I glanced up to see the wheels that ran along a track above the door. Also rusty.

Unlike the newer model truck, this barn had to be at least a hundred years old. But similarly unlike the truck, this place was full of useful stuff. The Sands apparently collected more than fine furniture and purloined kitchen implements. Either that, or the barn had come complete with items dating back to its construction. On a wall behind a table full of assorted glassware hung a burglar's dream full of old shovels, rakes, pitchforks—and pry bars. If I couldn't pry the door open, I could probably pry the handle off the old wood.

But I had to make this speedy. It was getting darker by the minute. A long, hooked iron bar in hand, I turned back to the door. And froze at a noise from outside the door.

Was Francis back? Crap. I had to get out of sight. The barn had lots of places to hide. I cast my gaze about wildly. Maybe I could get up to the loft or sequester myself in a corner of one of the old stalls in the back. But then I'd be trapped. Better to stay close to the front.

The door began to move. I didn't have time to go anywhere. I crouched and crept forward so the nearest table would shield me enough to avoid his scrutiny. I hoped. The door slid all the way open, affording slightly more illumination.

"Robbie," Hattie called.

Hattie? No way was I answering. She was married to Francis. She had her own dysfunctions. She might be here to lure me out, to shut me in the truck again, or worse.

"I'm glad you got out of the truck," Hattie went on. "I had to wait until Francis left. I'm really sorry."

Jeez. Now what did I do? Believe her? Make a mad dash past her? Right into Francis's clutches, maybe. But I had to get out of here. She might be telling the truth. And I was younger, stronger, and taller than her.

"Wherever you are, please come out," she pleaded. "He's gone. I saw him trap you in the truck. I'm so sorry he did that."

I slid my keys into my hand so they stuck out between my knuckles for insurance as I strode toward her. "And you didn't call the police?" I kept my arms loose at my sides, in case I needed to use them, and I still gripped the crowbar.

"There you are." Hattie, empty-handed and wearing an embarrassed smile, shook her head. "He's my husband. I couldn't. He was simply worried about Krystal."

"What about Krystal?" I glanced nervously at the door, but she seemed to be telling the truth. Unless she wasn't.

Hattie fluttered her hands. "She's not quite right, you know. But she's his baby girl. That's where he went, to her house."

I dashed past her. "Thanks for opening the door. You have a good night now."

I dropped the tool and jogged across the street, beeping my car open as I did.

"Wait," she called after me.

Nope. Not waiting for anything. I'd never driven around to the back faster, nor been more relieved to be in my apartment a minute later with a locked door between me and the outside—and a phone in my hand.

Birdy didn't seem to care. He ran to his treat dish and gazed up at me with that "Where have you been?" look. My laugh came out half sob.

"Hang on, Birdman." I jabbed 911. I could have called Buck, but this seemed more urgent than that. Plus, he'd been off duty as of this afternoon. He deserved an evening with family, not tracking down poisoners.

After the preliminaries of giving my name and address to the dispatcher, I said, "I am fine and not in danger. But an hour ago I was shut into a furniture trunk on purpose by Francis Sand. He drove it into his barn and locked the outer door. He apparently now is at the home of Orland and Krystal Krueger in South Lick. I don't know the address, but it's near the Beanblossom covered bridge. Buck Bird has been covering the case."

"Are you still locked in the barn, ma'am?"

"No. His wife, Hattie Sand, let me out a couple minutes ago. I'm in my apartment behind my store, Pans 'N Pancakes, at the address I gave you. With the doors locked."

"Please hold the line, ma'am. Lieutenant Bird is right here."

A moment later Buck came on. "Robbie, say what, now? Are you all right?"

"I'm fine." Barely. "I'm home and safe. Francis tricked me into the back of his truck. He closed me in and locked the truck in the barn. I managed to get out of the truck. After he went over to Krystal and Orland's, Hattie let me out of the barn. I am pretty sure Krystal poisoned Jan, as well as my customers, and Francis is trying to protect her."

"Shooee. Glad you're okay. O'Neill called me about what his son saw. We got the hospital onto it all, and I have me a plainclothes officer watching the Krueger home. I got word about Sand showing up there."

"Good. Thanks for telling me."

"I'll get a team over to that barn, too, and to interview Ms. Sand," he said. "Why she didn't call and tell us what happened is beyond me. Sometimes I think she's as lost as last year's Easter egg."

"She must have seen him—us—from the upstairs window. She told me she couldn't rat on her husband."

He made a scoffing sound. "Some husband. Anyhoo, we'll need a statement from you, but tomorrow'll be fine as far as that goes."

"Thanks. I appreciate that."

"You stay safe, now. I have to say, Robbie Jordan, you're one brave cookie."

I thanked him and hung up. I didn't feel particularly brave. A person did what she had to do. Did I feel relieved? Abso-effing-lutely.

CHAPTER 57

"Call the man," Adele insisted.

I had my phone on speaker half an hour later as I mixed biscuit dough in the restaurant, with the day's laundry churning away in my apartment. I'd filled Adele in on what had happened. "But I don't want to bother him, Adele. Sean just lost his mother." I did want to talk to Abe, tell him what happened, hear his voice.

"Roberta, you're about to be married to him, for corn sake! Don't you think he wants to know what you been through?"

I slowed my hands in the dough. He absolutely would. "You're right. Thank you. I'll call him."

"I'm awful glad all's well that ends well, hon. You sure do know how to get yourself into a spot of trouble, don't you?"

I laughed. "Apparently. I love you, Adele."

"Love you, too, sweetheart." She disconnected the call.

I waited to call Abe until I finished cutting in the butter and had the disks stowed in the walk-in. "How's Sean?"

"He's devastated and exhausted. He went to sleep a little while ago, thank goodness."

"The poor kid. And how are you doing?"

"I hate that my kid has to go through this, and I'm sad for Jan. My parents are rocks, though."

"Good. You're lucky to have them."

"I know. Hey, remember when you asked me about Jan's health? Sean told me she took a lot of prescriptions and was supposed to cut down on salt but never did."

"That sounds like high blood pressure," I said. "Maybe she already had an underlying condition."

"I expect so. Now tell me how you're doing."

"I had a kind of run-in this evening." I blurted out a high-speed summary of what happened to me. "I thought you would want to know, but I'm fine."

"Oh, Robbie." His voice thickened. "I'm so glad you're safe. I need to come see you and make sure. Is that all right?"

My eyes welled up. "It's more than all right. I didn't want to ask, because of Sean, but I'd love to have you here."

"I'm good leaving him with my folks."

"I'll be in the store doing prep."

"Gotcha. See you in ten." He disconnected.

I sent out a mental thanks to Adele for nudging me in the right direction. I hadn't let myself realize how much I wanted to see Abe. I looked down at my long-sleeved store T-shirt, which I'd had on since five-thirty this morning. I'd raced off to the hospital in my work clothes and hadn't brushed my hair since the morning, either. Ten minutes was plenty of time to freshen up a little.

I felt better clad in a magenta tunic and leggings, with a clean face and my hair brushed out and loosely clipped in back, although the blue Pans 'N Pancakes apron spoiled the look a little. When Birdy came back into the store with me, I crumpled a small ball of tinfoil and tossed it in the air for him to play with. I stared at him as an image of Cocoa, Sean's black Lab, flashed in my mind. The dog would now be moving to Abe's, too. How would the two beasts get along? I'd kept Cocoa for a night in my apartment when he was a puppy as an emergency favor. He'd slept in his crate overnight and, after Birdy hissed at him, I'd kept them apart. I blew out a breath. We'd just have to figure it out, and really, that was the least of our worries after all we'd just been through, my new family and me.

I was measuring out flour for pancakes when Abe sent me a text he'd arrived. He simultaneously knocked at the store door. His long, tight embrace was exactly what I needed.

"Let me help with prep so the work goes faster," Abe said. "Give me a job and tell me everything, if you're willing."

I pointed to the basket of clean napkins, towels, and aprons. "Fold and then roll silverware? Please?"

"I'm your man," he said with a wicked grin.

"And for that I am seriously blessed. Want a bit of Four Roses?"

"Thought you'd never ask."

I glugged bourbon into two mugs and left the bottle on the table. We clinked, although it was more like thudding, and sipped. My pancake mix wasn't going to assemble itself, so I resumed what I'd been doing as I talked. I related leaving the hospital, eating with Lou, driving home, being hailed by Francis. "My first mistake was agreeing to help him at all."

"You were being neighborly."

"I guess. The second and bigger mistake was leaving my phone in the car."

"That thing is like part of your skin or something. You always have it."

"I know. Nuts, right? The third misstep was agreeing to get into the truck to push the stupid table out. I thought it might be a bad idea, but I ignored my gut. Never ignore the gut." My phone buzzed on the counter. "It's Buck, and he's here."

"Maybe he has news."

I hurried to the door to let him in. "Come on in."

"Evenin' Robbie, O'Neill." He ambled over to Abe's table, hat in hand. "Got a small little bit of info for y'all, if you want."

"Sit down, Buck," I said. "We want to hear what you know, but I thought you were off duty this afternoon."

"Me, too. Got called back in. But now I am, for sure. Let me say in person, O'Neill, that I am sorry for the loss of your boy's mother."

Abe inclined his head. "Thanks, I appreciate that."

"I lost my mama at about the same age," Buck added.

Another thing I didn't know about Buck.

"I'm sorry to hear that, man," Abe said.

"No kid should have to go through such an experience." Buck wagged his head. "My mama was up and murdered, too. Main reason I pursued a career in criminal justice."

Murdered? I wasn't going to ask him now, but I would in the future. I brought Buck a mug. "Bourbon's on the table." I gazed at both men. "Wait. Are you guys hungry?"

Both shook their heads.

"Got me a sandwich a little bit ago," Buck said.

"Okay, but how does one of Phil's cookies sound?" I grabbed the big Tupperware box from under the counter and set it on the table. "Help yourselves."

"Thanks, sugar." Abe gave me one of those tender smiles that melted my heart, over and over.

"So what do you know, Buck?" I asked. "What happened at the Krueger house?"

"We picked up the whole lot of 'em. Orland claims he's innocent. Maybe he is, and maybe he isn't."

I wasn't sure how Orland couldn't know what his own wife had been up to, but that determination wasn't up to me.

"I think Krystal might not be totally right in the head," Buck continued. "Said she put a little something extra-special in them pies for Jan."

"Like poison?" I asked. "Or like bad mushrooms?"

"She didn't confess to what all it was. They'll look for toxins in them samples when they git to it, including that there *Amanita pantherina*."

I'd never been gladder that Sean didn't like mushrooms. I exchanged a glance with Abe, who looked like he'd had the same thought. And that was why Buck had added "too" when he said his mother had been murdered.

"But why would Krystal do that?" Abe asked.

"She thought her husband's twin was getting too cozy." Buck lifted an eyebrow. "Leastwise, that's what she said. Go figure. She knew the man had a twin when she up and married him."

"Was Krystal also responsible for the bad mushrooms delivered here?" I asked.

"Yep. The logic is faulty, but she wanted her truck to be the only breakfast and lunch option around here."

"I'm not sure that's so illogical," I began. "Isn't it called sabotaging the competition?"

"Yup," Buck said.

"I wonder where she got them," Abe said. "Orland is the mushroom expert, not her."

"Right. Buck, a minute ago you said maybe Orland isn't innocent," I said. "What else do you know?"

"We put us a team to work checking into both of their movements, especially heading into the woods. Got some intel this afternoon of a witness seeing them Kruegers digging last week in a area known to sprout pretty dang dangerous mushrooms. Also just got us a warrant, so a couple fellas are sweeping down their house right now." His phone buzzed. He read a text and looked up. "Bingo. They found a paper sack with a skull and crossbones on it. Setting out on their kitchen counter, of all places."

"With panthercaps in it?" I asked.

Buck nodded as he popped in the rest of his cookie and swiped at the crumbs near his mouth, which only brushed them down onto his shirt.

"Wait," I said. "Corrine went over to the house this afternoon. I wonder if she saw the bag."

"Madam Mayor called me, told me she talked to Krystal at the door but didn't get let inside. Leastwise you don't have to worry about Krystal," Buck continued. "She's getting herself a free ride to a psychiatric hospital for evaluation. Under guard, 'course."

"I guess that's the right place for her," I said. "But you don't have to be insane to commit murder." I knew that from experience. Shoot, I'd never gotten back in touch with Len to find out what he'd meant by *unstable*. I could have asked Lou for his number. Oh, well. He wouldn't be working with Krystal now. "Is Krystal ranting, acting out of touch with reality?"

"She wasn't making too much sense when we was over there, no. Nuts or not, she won't be harming no one else for the time being."

"Even if she's crazy, her husband isn't," Abe said. "If Orland knew what Krystal was doing, he's as guilty of Jan's death as she is."

"It's possible she acted alone in that one," Buck said.

"But with poisonous mushrooms in plain sight in their kitchen, he had to be with her all the way in sabotaging my store and in causing Mr. Ward's death." I shook my head, remembering him continually telling me his family wasn't involved. "What about Francis?"

"He says all's he was doing was protecting Krystal."

"Did he admit he locked Robbie in the truck in the barn?" Abe asked.

"He did." Buck stretched his legs halfway to Bloomington and sipped from his mug. "He's looking at a charge of assault and battery at the very least, and kidnapping too."

"And Hattie?" I stored the pancake mix, washed my hands, and grabbed the silverware caddy. Abe had folded all the napkins, so I joined the men at the table and started rolling.

"Not sure. Yes, she didn't call the authorities when she saw what Francis done. But she did let you outta that there barn before too long. For now, anyhoo, she's home because she promised to cooperate."

I wondered how Hattie would manage the store if Francis went to prison. He'd wanted to protect his daughter. But the better protection might have been getting help for Krystal, keeping her from harming others. Still, Sand Antiques wasn't my problem. I was here in my favorite place, safe, with two men I trusted. That was enough for tonight.

CHAPTER 58

A be left early the next morning so he could be with Sean. His presence last night had been a huge comfort to me, but he had to get back to his boy. And even with everything that had happened, I still had a restaurant to open and run. It hit me that it had been a full week since last Sunday's mushroom omelets had thrown life as we knew it into a blender. I crossed my fingers. May it be smooth from here on out.

Adele and Vera were at the door when I opened it at our Sunday normal time of eight.

"Hey, hon." Adele kissed my cheek. "I want the full scoop."

"Good morning, you two. Adele, you have a line of people behind you." I gazed beyond my aunt, her friend, and the dozen hungry diners, to the antique store. I shivered involuntarily, remembering my scary time inside the truck. "I'll fill you in when I can, okay?"

Vera smiled.

"Sure, that's fine," Adele said.

"No Samuel today?" I asked.

"He's doing his church thing." She lowered her voice. "Special men's prayer circle for poor old Jeremiah Ward."

"May God rest his soul," Vera added.

Poor old Mr. Ward, indeed. And poor Jan O'Neill, thanks to Krystal Sand Krueger.

Adele bustled in. "We're going to grab us a four-top, in case some other folks show up."

And did folks ever show up. By eight-thirty the place was full and hopping. News—good or bad—tended to produce that effect in a community watering hole like this one. The Specials board was blank, and nobody seemed to care. Danna and I, as often happened in the hour before Turner arrived, were wishing we had extra sets of arms and legs like one of the Hindu goddesses you see in paintings.

But when Corrine appeared with a nervous-looking Hattie in tow, my eyes bugged out. Adele half stood and waved them over. I swore under my breath. I wished I could swap jobs with Danna, so I didn't have to interact with Hattie. The more I'd thought about it, the angrier I was that Hattie hadn't called in Francis kidnapping me. Because that was what it had been. She'd abetted his crime, husband or no husband. From what Buck had said, though, at least she was going to cooperate with the police.

My assistant was operating at high efficiency, and I didn't want to stop the flow. Instead, I delivered three meals, poured four coffees, and assured five diners that their breakfasts were on their way. Nine o'clock couldn't arrive soon enough.

I ended up at Adele's table, full coffeepot in hand. "Good morning," I said to Corrine. "Coffee for you both?" I avoided Hattie's gaze. I also avoided asking Corrine if she knew what Hattie had done. Like Adele, she loved her scanner, and she was the mayor. She would definitely have heard.

"We'd love some, Robbie, thanks." Corrine beamed. "Y'all are full up this fine morning."

"I'm getting full up, myself," Vera said, setting her fork down on her now half-empty plate of pancakes. "These surely are tasty, Robbie."

"Thank you, Vera."

Corrine pulled me close and cupped her hand around her mouth. "Ain't it great our little town's safe again?" she whispered.

All I could do was nod. The reason it was safe was because the husband and stepdaughter of the woman next to Corrine were behind bars, so to speak. After I poured the newcomers each a cup of Joe, I drew out an order pad. "Can I get you some breakfast?"

"I'm so hungry, I could eat a dozen horses." Corrine held up a hand. "Not that I'd want to. Gimme two sunny sides, ham, hash browns, biscuits and gravy, and wheat toast, darlin'. You, Hattie?"

"Only a small bowl of oatmeal, please." Hattie spoke so softly I could barely hear her.

"Sure."

She rose abruptly, straightening her shoulders as if it would give her courage. "Robbie, I need to apologize."

My eyes whapped open wide. "Okaay." I stretched out the word.

"I never should have let Francis do that to you. I should have called the police. I'm sorry. I don't need your forgiveness, but I needed to tell you." She plopped back down with a *thud.*

Jeez. Adele and Corrine exchanged a glance. Had they conspired to make Hattie say that?

"Um, thank you." I couldn't muster any more words than, "I'll put your orders in."

I stuck the order slip on the carousel for Danna. I'd filled her in on the news as we'd gotten ready to open.

"Isn't that the shoplifter lady with my mom?" she asked.

"It is. She just apologized to me for last night. But not for stealing my graters." I stared at their table. "People are confusing sometimes, you know?"

"Yes, I do." Danna laughed. "Okay, these four are ready." She pointed a spatula at the full plates under the warming light. "And that couple wants their check."

I spied the couple she meant. "Is it nine yet?" Turner couldn't get here a minute too soon. I loaded my arms with the plates. I was going to have to ask him to start coming in when we opened.

But when the bell jangled five minutes later, it wasn't Turner. Lou and Len blew in, both clad in cycling clothes. I'd finished clearing the two-top and nobody else waited, so I waved them over.

"How I wish I were out riding with you guys," I said in greeting. "It's nuts in here."

"Looks like it," Lou said. She sat and beckoned me closer. "I heard some news that Krystal was arrested?"

"She was." I kept my voice low. "Looks like your instincts were right, Len. She's not mentally well. She apparently poisoned her sister-in-law's food yesterday. On purpose."

Len nodded slowly. "I'm glad I didn't start working with her."

I had a flash of a brainstorm. "What's your early-morning schedule?"

"I don't have classes until late morning." He tilted his head. "Why?"

"Our early mornings are nuts, because my second assistant doesn't come in until an hour after we open. If you can commit to, like, six-thirty to nine-thirty on weekdays, I'd be happy to show you the ropes." We'd figure out how to work around and with him. My prior hesitation now seemed silly.

"You'd learn from the best, bro," Lou said.

A smile broke on Len's face. "Seriously? I'd love to."

"I can't pay much, but I don't expect you to work for free."

"Thank you," he said.

"Can you start Tuesday?" I asked.

"I'd love to."

A man waved his hand at me. Danna rang the ready bell three times. Corrine cast a smile in my direction even as she threw her hands in the air in a "Where's our breakfast?" gesture. And a woman holding two antique beaters and a cake pan waited to pay at the retail counter.

"See what I mean? It's nuts." I hurried off to tend to my darling—and even the not-so darling—diners. They were my livelihood, my vocation, and my dream. An extra pair of competent and willing hands and legs in the person of Len Perlman would make us all happier to serve. If the arrangement worked out, maybe he could come on as a regular employee. It would mean a lot for me to have more time to spend with family, whatever shape that took. I doubted any of us could prevent further crimes in South Lick, but keeping trouble out of the restaurant? That was worth paying for.

CHAPTER 59

I tried to breathe deeply as I waited with Adele, Roberto, and my two best friends in Adele's kitchen minutes before the ceremony was to begin. But, on this Memorial Day weekend, I was nervous. Happy—and nervous.

The wedding was finally today. In a few minutes, in fact, at four o'clock on the last Saturday of May. I was about to be married. The month had flown by, peacefully as it happened. I touched the delicate filigreed silver locket nestling in the hollow of my neck. Adele, always full of surprises, had given it to me.

"This was your great-granny Rose's," she'd said last week. "You're supposed to have something old to wear. She left this to me for my daughter to have. Seeing as how I didn't have me any children, I saved it for my sis Jeanine's little girl. You."

I had teared up, but let her fasten it around my neck. Now, on my wedding day, I had the requisite old, new, borrowed, and blue. My wedge espadrilles were blue, my dress was new, and Alana had lent me a silver bracelet I'd always admired, set with a lapis lazuli stone. In my ears were my favorite silver earrings, worked by a Hopi craftswoman in New Mexico. And on my right hand I'd slipped on Mom's favorite ring, of a heavy silver with a sizeable piece of turquoise set into it. When I fingered it with my thumb, I felt her presence.

I ran my hands down the white embroidery on the scoop-necked bodice of the dress, which fit snugly but wasn't too tight. The cap sleeves were embroidered, too, with tiny flowers and bells. The fine cotton of the skirt was gathered at the waist and fell to the floor, giving it a delightful swish when I moved, and it even had pockets.

Alana and Lou hovered in their deep-blue outfits. Alana, in an elegant sleeveless silk jumpsuit that complemented her short auburn hair, kept patting the pocket that held the ring box. Lou, wearing a square-necked simple dress that flattered her athletic figure, fussed with the flower wreath in my hair. I'd left my hair loose and naturally curled on my shoulders. Georgia would come and give us the signal when all were seated and it was time for the ceremony to begin. I'd hired her at the last minute to help with day-of logistics, and I was glad I had.

"You look a little nervous, too." I gazed at my handsome father, his silver-shot dark hair curling over the collar of a gray suit complemented by the rose-pink silk tie the other men in the wedding party were also wearing.

"*Sono*. I am," he admitted. "My daughter was married—my second daughter, I mean—but that was in Pisa. Here I do not know the customs."

"You'll be fine, Roberto." Adele turned to look at Sloopy. "Sit," Adele told him. The collie wore a pale gray silk kerchief that matched Roberto's suit.

Lou and I had come up with the color scheme of gray, deep blue, and dusty rose. It was easy for everyone to find garments in those colors, clothes they were comfortable in and could wear later, and it wasn't flashy. Lou and Alana both wore dusty rose heels. Adele was making a rare appearance in a dress, a muted pink with a lace bodice and sleeves, which she wore with blue flats.

"For example, I have never seen a dog in a wedding," Roberto added.

I was surprised when Adele wanted to have Sloopy participate, but I was fond of both of them, and so was Abe. We'd agreed without hesitation.

Adele nudged Roberto. "All's he's going to do is help us walk Roberta down the proverbial aisle."

"Come here." Alana beckoned to me. She laid her hands on my cheeks. "You got this thing, Robbie. You look gorgeous and you're marrying the man of your heart."

I swallowed down a suddenly thick throat. "What if I forget my vows?" I'd practiced a zillion times. Right now I had no idea what they were.

She held up a slip of paper. "That's what I'm for, remember?"

"Okay." I nodded. "Okay."

"Nobody's out there who doesn't love you." She fixed her gaze on me. "Right?"

"Right." This was true. We'd ended up with about seventy people who had said they could come, and none of them were obligation invites. I gazed down at my perfectly fitting dress, at our three bouquets on the table, at this kitchen where I was always welcome.

Georgia popped her head into the room. "Everybody ready?"

Alana hugged me and whispered, "Hey, I got through getting married. You can, too." To Georgia, she announced, "Ready."

CHAPTER 60

I peeked around the corner of the tent as Abe's older brother Don escorted Alana down the aisle between the rows of chairs set up facing the sheep pastures. Following them, Lou walked on Sean's arm, with Cat Stevens's "Peace Train" playing over the speakers. Adele used to play an album of his when Mom and I would come to visit, and I'd always loved the song.

Abe and his father had constructed an arch of saplings at the front. It was now decorated with greenery interwoven with daisies, pink hydrangeas, and blue ribbons. Corrine, holding a leather folder, beamed from the middle of the arch, wearing the most subdued dark dress I'd ever seen her in. We'd asked her to officiate, neither of us being churchgoers. Abe, in his new gray suit, stood near her. Even from here I could tell he was also nervous, tugging on his pink silk tie.

We had a rented tent set up for dining, and the barn was cleaned up for dancing, but we'd wanted the ceremony outdoors. Mama Nature had cooperated beautifully. After all the spring rains we'd had, it had been dry for a week. The fields that rolled down to woods were a bright green, with swallows swooping and clouds scudding. An extra audience of sheep gathered on the other side of the fence to watch.

The air was redolent with the alluring scent of roast pig. I snorted when my stomach growled. I'd triple-checked with the caterer that the food they used didn't come from FH Foods, even though I'd heard the company was closed for the time being, what with Orland's involvement in the deathcaps harvest. We'd kept the reception buffet menu simple, with baked mac and cheese, coleslaw, and chewy rolls to go with the pork. Phil's cake was a work of art, and during the predinner cocktails after the ceremony—Manhattans made with Four Roses—we were serving bite-sized *taquitos* in a nod to my birthplace.

When clipboard-carrying Georgia gave us the *go* signal, I tucked a hand through Roberto's proffered elbow on one side and Adele's on the other. And swallowed. We'd rehearsed last night, but it didn't make this any easier. I clutched my bouquet of pink roses, blue cornflowers, and white baby carnations a little too tightly.

"I am proud, Roberta, and grateful you invited me," my father said.

"She's something, ain't she?" Adele said. "And Robbie, hon, you know Jeanine's watching."

Thanks a lot. When my eyes threatened to overflow, I blinked away the tears. At least Lou had brought waterproof mascara for all of us.

Georgia cleared her throat and gave me two thumbs-up. We headed out, Adele keeping Sloopy on a short leash at her far side.

Abe's face when he saw me made all the nerves worth it. We weren't doing much according to tradition, but Lou and Alana had insisted he not see my dress before this moment. Abe's smile split his face as he watched us approach. He tilted his head and blew me a kiss. Sean stood to Abe's left, with Don next to him. Alana and Lou waited for me on the other side.

I had a pang, seeing Sean standing there, so handsome in his first suit—but also motherless. Abe had convinced him to see a therapist, who turned out to be a fairly hip young guy. Those visits seemed to be helping.

As we made our way slowly forward to the beat of the song, everyone twisted in their seats to watch, smile, and in some cases, pat their eyes with a tissue. Danna and Turner were there, with their own sweeties, as was Phil. Buck and his wife sat with Wanda and her Oscar. Vera gave a little wave, and my California friends who ran the Nacho Average Café beamed. I spied Len, too. Abe's parents smiled from the front row, with his father being one of the tissue users.

At the front, Adele kissed my cheek before sitting with Samuel in the front row, and Roberto patted my hand and then sank into a chair next to his wife, Maria.

When Abe took my hands and squeezed them gently, I didn't want to ever let go. Corrine said some things I barely heard as I gazed into Abe's face.

We held a moment of silence for our grandparents on both sides and for my mom. This time I didn't tear up. I knew somehow, somewhere, she was blessing us. Don, who usually looked a bit worried, stepped forward and read "All I Know About Love," a Neil Gaiman poem we'd asked him to offer. Georgia's love must be good for Abe's brother. He didn't wear his normal anxious face.

And I didn't forget my vows, nor did Abe. With rings also successfully accomplished, Corrine drew herself up.

In her best mayoral voice, she announced, "With the authority vested in me by the state of Indiana, I hereby pronounce you married!"

I pulled Abe's face to mine and enjoyed the best kiss of my life. We held hands and turned to face our cherished families and friends. Abe raised our clasped hands high. The cheer that went up made our sheep audience "baa" as if they were cheering, too. Sloopy broke loose, yipped, and dashed at the animals, running left and right, trying to herd them from the wrong side of the fence. Adele let out a guffaw, but didn't try to stop him.

Music started up again from the back, but this time it was live from Abe's bluegrass group playing, "It's Grand to Have Someone to Love You."

Corrine spoke into the handheld mike. "Congratulations to Mr. and Ms. O'Neill-Jordan! Please join them for cocktails outside the tent."

As my heart overflowed, Abe and I made our way down the aisle to applause and called-out greetings. Most of these people I'd met only after moving to Indiana. Others I wouldn't have known if we hadn't come into contact during a homicide investigation. I hoped not to run into any more of those.

I squeezed Abe's hand and lifted it to my mouth for a kiss. The adoring look he gave me in return was all I needed to go forward in this life, whatever it brought us.

RECIPES

Oven-Fried Catfish

Robbie loves the fried catfish sandwich she eats in a Scottsburg restaurant. She re-creates this oven-fried version to serve in her restaurant.

Ingredients:
olive oil spray
⅔ cup yellow cornmeal
¼ cup all-purpose flour
1½–2 teaspoons seasoned salt
½ teaspoon black pepper
¼ teaspoon cayenne pepper
½ teaspoon lemon pepper
¼ teaspoon paprika
2 large eggs
½ teaspoon hot sauce
1 pound catfish fillets
1 lemon
¼ cup chopped parsley

Directions:
Preheat oven to 425 degrees F and line a baking sheet with parchment paper liberally sprayed with nonstick olive oil spray.

In a paper bag, add cornmeal, flour, salt, pepper, cayenne, lemon pepper, and paprika and shake together.

In a deep pie plate or large shallow bowl, whisk together eggs and hot sauce.

Add each fillet to the bag of cornmeal breading to coat, then dip into beaten eggs on both sides, then lastly add back into the cornmeal breading and shake liberally to coat well. Place the fillet on the coated baking sheet. Repeat with each fillet.

Spray the tops of each fillet with olive oil spray coating the fish well until completely covered in spray. Bake for 25–30 minutes depending on thickness of fillets until golden brown, but still juicy inside.

Remove fish and cool for 5 minutes, then serve drizzled with lemon juice and chopped parsley in a crusty roll smeared with mayonnaise.

Lemon Rosemary Scones

Danna makes these yummy scones for a breakfast special.

Ingredients:
2 cups unbleached white flour, sifted
1 tablespoon baking powder
3 tablespoons sugar, plus more for sprinkling
½ teaspoon salt
4 tablespoons, cold butter, cut into 1 small cube
1 tablespoon rosemary, finely minced
zest of one lemon
¾ cup buttermilk
1 egg, lightly beaten
¼ cup milk

Directions:
Preheat the oven to 410°F. Line a large cookie sheet with parchment paper.

In a food processor, add the flour, baking powder, sugar and salt. Pulse until combined.

Spread the butter on top of the dry ingredients. Pulse until the mixture resembles fine crumbs.

Add the rosemary and lemon zest and pulse until combined. Transfer to a large bowl.

Add the buttermilk and egg over the flour mixture and stir, using a rubber spatula, until just combined.

Flour a work surface and transfer the dough on it. Knead for 1 minute.

Using your hands, pat the dough into a circle and cut

into wedges. Arrange scones in a single layer on the prepared cookie sheet.

Brush tops with milk, then sprinkle with sugar.

Bake until tops are golden brown, for 12–15 minutes. Let scones cool completely before glazing.

Grated Everything Fritters

Turner devises these yummy fritters for a Sunday lunch special, but it can also be a delicious breakfast dish or even dinner. You can fry them in hot oil, as they do on the grill in the restaurant, but the baking method in this recipe is easier and less messy.

Serves two.

Ingredients:
2 medium potatoes
½ cup broccoli florets
1 small onion
1 medium carrot
½ cup cheddar cheese
¼ cup ham, cut into inch-long slivers (omit for
    vegetarian version)
2 eggs, beaten
⅓ cup flour
½ teaspoon salt
¼ teaspoon black pepper
1 teaspoon curry powder

Directions:
Preheat oven to 400 F. Cover a large baking sheet with parchment paper.

Grate potatoes (a food processor makes quick work of the grating). Roll in a clean dishcloth and wring dry. Steam broccoli in microwave for two minutes and chop finely.

Grate onion, carrot, and cheese. In a medium bowl, mix together vegetables, cheese, ham, and eggs. Stir together flour, salt, pepper, and curry powder, then stir into other mixture.

Scoop out a half cup of the mixture and flatten into four-inch disks on the parchment paper. Leave a quarter inch between disks; they will not spread.

Bake for twenty minutes. Turn and bake ten more minutes or until browned and crispy. Enjoy plain or top with salsa, sour cream, or ketchup.

Serve hot for breakfast, on a toasted sandwich roll for lunch, or with a green salad for dinner.

Variations: add fresh chopped herbs, sliced green onions, grated and squeeze-dried zucchini; substitute sweet potato instead of regular; use a different kind of cheese.

Peanut Butter Chocolate Chip Cookie Bars

Phil bakes these easy desserts for Pans 'N Pancakes.

Ingredients:
2¼ cup unbleached white flour
1 teaspoon baking soda
½ teaspoon salt
½ cup softened butter
½ cup natural peanut butter
¾ cup brown sugar
¾ cup white sugar
2 eggs
2 teaspoon vanilla
1 package semisweet chocolate chips

Directions:
Preheat oven to 375 degrees F.

Add baking powder and salt to flour in measuring cup and mix in. Set aside.

Cream butter and peanut butter. Add sugar and beat until creamy. Add eggs one at a time.

Add flour mixture and chocolate chips and beat on low until mixed.

Spoon out dough onto a rimmed baking sheet. Flatten with your hand or a spatula until all is pretty much the same thickness. Tip: Dip your hand or spatula in a cup of water so it doesn't stick.

Bake for fifteen minutes or until edges are lightly browned.

Let cool in the pan on a wire rack. Cut into squares while still warm. Enjoy with a glass of milk, a cup of coffee, or on the run.

Mulligatawny Soup

Robbie learned this hearty soup from Abe and often serves it in the restaurant.

Ingredients:
2 cloves garlic, smashed and peeled
1 inch fresh ginger, peeled and roughly chopped
2 tablespoons water
2 tablespoons butter
2 tablespoon extra-virgin olive oil
1 large onion, chopped (about 2 cups)
2 ribs celery, chopped (about 1 cup)
12 ounces mushrooms, cleaned and sliced
2 carrots, chopped (about 1 cup)
4 teaspoons yellow curry powder
1 teaspoon kosher salt.
4 boneless, skinless chicken thighs, trimmed of visible
   fat and cut into bite-sized pieces
4 cups chicken stock
½ cup uncooked basmati or brown rice
2 tart apples, cored, peeled, and chopped (about 2 cups)
¼ cup heavy cream

Directions:
Grind garlic, ginger, and water in a small food processor or a mortar and pestle.

Heat butter and olive oil on medium-high heat in a large (4 to 5 quart), thick-bottomed pot. Add the onions and sauté for 5 minutes until just starting to soften the celery and mushrooms and sauté until tender. Add the carrots and garlic-ginger paste and cook, stirring, for 2 minutes. Add the curry powder and salt and mix to coat.

Add the chicken thighs and stir to coat with the vegetable-curry mixture. Add the stock, bring to a simmer, and reduce the heat to maintain a simmer. Cover and cook for 20 minutes.

Add the rice and the chopped apples to the soup. Return to a simmer on high heat, then lower the heat to maintain a low simmer. Cover and cook for 30 minutes, or until the rice is cooked through.

Stir in the cream and heat for 5 minutes more. Serve hot.

Adele's Blueberry Pound Cake

Adele serves this rich, delicious cake to Robbie and Lou after a hard bike ride.

Ingredients:
2 tablespoons butter
¼ cup white sugar
2¾ cups all-purpose flour
1 teaspoon baking powder
½ teaspoon salt
1 cup butter
2 cups white sugar
4 eggs
1 teaspoon vanilla extract
2 cups fresh or frozen blueberries
¼ cup all-purpose flour

Directions:
Preheat oven to 325 degrees F (165 degrees C). Grease a 10-inch Bundt pan with 2 tablespoons butter.

Mix together 2¾ cups flour, baking powder, and salt. Set aside.

In a large bowl, cream together 1 cup butter and 2 cups sugar until light and fluffy. Beat in the eggs one at a time, then stir in the vanilla. Gradually beat in the flour mixture. Dredge blueberries with remaining ¼ cup flour, then fold in.

Pour batter into the prepared pan.

Bake in the preheated oven for 70 to 80 minutes, or until a toothpick inserted into the center of the cake comes out clean. Let cool in pan for 10 minutes, then turn out onto a wire rack and cool completely.

Serve with coffee or tea (added bourbon optional).

Peach Hoagy

Phat Cats Bistro created this peach cocktail to honor Bloomington native Hoagy Carmichael and his song, "Georgia on My Mind," written in 1930.

Ingredients for one drink:
2 ounces chilled peach nectar
1 ounce peach moonshine (use peach brandy if you can't find moonshine)
1 ounce Four Roses bourbon
Juice of 1 lime quarter
1 slice ripe peach

Directions:
Combine the first five ingredients in a shaker with ice. Shake until chilled and pour into a martini glass. Garnish with peach slice.

Option: If it's too sweet for you, make in a Manhattan glass on ice and add lime seltzer, and/or increase the bourbon.